DANCI

DIFFERI

BE CAREFUL WHAT YOU WISH FOR

BILL CORSAR

This is a work of creative nonfiction. Some parts have been fictionalized in varying degrees, for various purposes. Any reference to historical events, real people, or real places are used fictitiously.

Copyright © 2021 Bill Corsar

ISBN: 9798783545894

Independently Published

Cover by: Ken Dawson, Creative Covers

The best laid schemes o' Mice an Men
Gang aft agley
An' lea'e us nought but grief an' pain
For promis'd joy

(Robert Burns – 1759 – 1796

TWO

The following Friday evening, Rob left work and walked to the local barracks of the Black Watch. His plan was simple. He wanted to go to their summer ball but could not afford the entry fee for civilians. He knew that members of the regiment got in, free of charge. Rob was going to join up. He would go to the summer ball as a new territorial recruit of the 5th Battalion of the Black Watch Regiment.

He entered the office and met Captain Lawson, who ushered him to sit down. Lawson sat at the table come desk opposite Rob. On the table lay a folder of papers. There was also a bible, an inkwell and a pen stand.

"We'll start with the paperwork first, and then the medical."

"Thank you, sir."

"Full name."

"Robert Spence Corsar."

"You're British, of course. Where were your parents born? Are they Scottish?"

"They are, sir. Born near here."

"Date of birth?"

"Fifteenth of June eighteen ninety-seven."

"That makes you seventeen then."

"Yes, sir."

The best laid schemes o' Mice an Men
Gang aft agley
An' lea'e us nought but grief an' pain
For promis'd joy

(Robert Burns – 1759 – 1796

ONE

It was Monday, 15 June 1914, in Montrose in the North East of Scotland. Mid summer's day was only three days away, but you would never have known. A glance out of the window might have convinced you that the calendar was wrong.

The dark early morning sky was full of dirty white and dark grey/black clouds. There was a fresh wind pushing the clouds eastwards towards the North Sea. The leaf-laden trees were bending and swaying in the gusting wind. The calendar was not wrong. It was mid-summer in Montrose. The bad weather was the edge of a storm due later that day. Montrose would only get exposed to the edge of the storm. Towns further north would not be so lucky as they suffered extensive damage.

Combining an early Monday morning and dirty black weather did not make for a happy start to the week. The sun had been up for two hours, but no one under the dark foreboding sky had seen it rise.

It was six-thirty in the morning, and there was a hive of activity in the three bedroomed terraced house in Market Street. The twelve members of the Corsar household were all up and about. First up, as always,

1

was Jean, the mother of the brood. She got up and lit a fire to get hot water for washing. It would also be needed to mix into the porridge she had made the previous night. Her porridge recipe was one cup of oats per person in the pan covered with water. The brew is brought to the boil before it is left to simmer. It soon becomes a hot gloopy mud bath consistency. Left overnight, it had set solid. Small animals could walk on it and leave no footprints. Lumps of the cold nutritious porridge get spooned into bowls for breakfast. Some added cold water to make the meal seem more palatable. Sandy, the patriarch, often ate it without any liquid. He had been used to eating oats like that during his time as an itinerant farm servant.

First in line for the toilet and a warm wash was Sandy. After him, there was always a scrum to use the bathroom or for any hot water left. It was a morning ritual. Those who were unlucky enough to miss out, and were desperate, used a potty in their bedroom. The four other working members of the family are Will, Jean, Rob and Annie. Next in line were the four schoolchildren, Emma, Mary, Frank and Jessie. Sandy and Mabel were below school age.

There was only one bed in each room. The six female children slept in the largest room. It also had the biggest bed. The four male children had the medium room, leaving Sandy and Jean with the smallest bedroom. The children's sleeping arrangements were very cramped. When any one of them got out of bed, all were disturbed.

Neither of the children's beds was big enough for the occupants to sleep shoulder to shoulder. In the girl's room, Jean, the eldest, was the boss. It was she who dictated the sleeping arrangements. Will, the oldest boy, had the same seniority in the boy's room. Sleeping was usually a head to tail arrangement to fit everyone into a bed. During cold winter nights, cuddling for warmth was more frequent.

The shortage of running hot water meant bathing was an infrequent activity. There were frequent arguments in both bedrooms.

"Emmy, your feet smell."

"No, they don't, Jean. Your nose smells, my feet stink. Aaah. What'd you do that for?"

"Get your stinking feet away from where my nose can smell them."

There was a clamour of people preparing for work and school in the two children's bedrooms. Three males in a small bedroom looking for clothes and boots was noisy enough. The noise from the five females could top that. It was the start of a new working week. It was very early in the morning, and everyone had only woken up. They were still tired and grumpy. Twelve people were all trying to use the toilet, get washed, find clothes and dress. This very cramped space did not make for a happy atmosphere any day of the week. There was bound to be irritation and minor conflicts between them.

At the first sign of trouble, Jean Corsar soon put it down. The children had learned not to argue with either of their parents. They were dour, harsh, disciplinarians. Attitudes forged through years of uncertainty and hard work. Emotions, if they had them, were kept well hidden.

Only one member of the Corsar tribe was happy this morning. Robert was celebrating his seventeenth birthday. Celebrating is hardly an appropriate word for what he experienced this year. It would be no different from every other anniversary of his birth. The Corsars were poor, and money was tight. It always had been. Five people were working and earning a wage. Even so, there was hardly enough to pay the rent, feed and clothe the twelve people. Like the other workers in the house, Robert deposited his weekly wage on the kitchen table at the end of the week. His mother sorted out what she needed for the household budget. What little remained, if any, was shared out to the others, father first and the rest by age. The young non-workers got no pocket money. There would be no birthday presents for Rob unless made by the donor.

It was why Robert, seventeen today, got a perfunctory, Happy Birthday from both his parents. No kiss from his mother and no handshake from his father. It was routine, so not unexpected. A couple of the younger children gave Rob cards made from scraps of paper. Twelve-year-old Mary and seven-year-old Jessie kissed Rob on the cheek and hugged him.

Rob always thought he should get more money to spend. He worked hard and thought he deserved more. Rob had once asked his mother for more, but the flea in his ear turned out to be a stinging wasp. He had learned his lesson. Still, today Rob turned seventeen. As a young man, he thought he deserved some entertainment and fun in his life. Rob saw others of his age dancing and having fun, so why not me, he thought?

Rob had been hatching a plan for some time now. To succeed, he had enlisted the help of his eldest sister, Jean. He did not tell her what he planned, just that he needed her help. His parents neither knew nor suspected anything.

It was Monday. On Friday evening, he would enact the second part of his plan. Despite the meagre celebrations and terrible weather, Rob went to work happy.

He put on his bonnet and jacket and went off to work in the docks on the banks of the River South Esk. The job was hard and dirty. He did not like it, but he earned a wage. On Friday evening, he would put his plan into action. He smiled as he walked to work.

He walked down Market Street before crossing the bridge across the South Esk River. The walk would take him about twenty minutes. As he went, he mulled over his plan for Friday. He had made the appointment, and he was determined to be on time.

That evening, the family had a piece of homemade cake and a cup of tea or lemonade to toast the birthday boy. Sandy was teetotal, so no alcohol was allowed in the house. What was done outside and out of view was frowned upon but tolerated. Given the lack of funds, there could be no great carousing. The odd glass of beer was all that they could afford. Sandy knew what was going on but turned a blind eye. As long as they did not have drink in the house or come home drunk, he accepted their peccadillos.

TWO

The following Friday evening, Rob left work and walked to the local barracks of the Black Watch. His plan was simple. He wanted to go to their summer ball but could not afford the entry fee for civilians. He knew that members of the regiment got in, free of charge. Rob was going to join up. He would go to the summer ball as a new territorial recruit of the 5th Battalion of the Black Watch Regiment.

He entered the office and met Captain Lawson, who ushered him to sit down. Lawson sat at the table come desk opposite Rob. On the table lay a folder of papers. There was also a bible, an inkwell and a pen stand.

"We'll start with the paperwork first, and then the medical."

"Thank you, sir."

"Full name."

"Robert Spence Corsar."

"You're British, of course. Where were your parents born? Are they Scottish?"

"They are, sir. Born near here."

"Date of birth?"

"Fifteenth of June eighteen ninety-seven."

"That makes you seventeen then."

"Yes, sir."

"What's your job?"

"Labourer in the docks."

"Married?"

"No, sir."

There followed a series of questions about any previous service. Given Robs' age, this was improbable. However, this was the army. Everything needed completing correctly. Questions would be asked and answers recorded on the forms.

"That's all for the moment. We will do the oath and signatures after the doctor has passed you fit to serve. Go into that office. Doctor Badger will complete the medical. Back here after that." Lawson's arm pointed to a second door in the office. He handed Rob the folder.

Rob walked over and knocked.

"Come in," called a voice from behind the door. Rob entered with his paperwork in his hand.

It looked like a basic consulting room. There was a desk. Behind it sat an older man.

Looking around, Rob saw a couch, a trolley and some instruments.

There were scales, a chair and some anatomical drawings on the wall. The doctor was sitting at a wooden desk. He was a man in his sixties, Rob guessed.

"Robert Corsar, isn't it?"

"Yes, sir."

"I'm Doctor Badger. Put the papers down on the table, then pop over there and strip down to your underpants, please?"

Rob moved to the chair indicated and did as requested.

"Stand up, please, and get on the scales."

Rob stood up and stepped onto the platform. The doctor fiddled about with weights and a slide on the arm. He recorded the weight when the balance was stationary.

"Just over eight stones. One hundred and fourteen pounds. Stand with you back against the tape measure on the wall over there."

Rob had not noticed the tape on the wall. It was a metal bar with figures, and it had a wooden arm sticking out. Rob shuffled into place.

"Stand with your back straight with your chin level." The doctor lowered the wooden arm until it reached Rob's head. "Five feet seven inches." It also got noted on the form.

"Stand where you are and put your hand over your left eye. What line can you read on the chart on the opposite wall?"

"The bottom line, sir." With that, Rob read the letters and repeated the exercise with his left eye.

"Right. Stand up, arms out." The doctor wrapped a tape measure around his chest. "Arms loosely by your sides, please. "Thirty-three inches. Now take a deep breath and hold it. Two inches. Exhale."

"Sorry, sir. What're two inches?"

"That's the range of expansion of your chest."

"Is that good?"

"It's not bad. Any scars, tattoos or birthmarks?'

"None that I know off."

The doctor walked around Rob, examining his body for any peculiarities that might help identify him in the event of death. He said nothing about that to Rob. The doctor picked up his stethoscope from the trolley and stuck the earpieces into his ears.

"Right. I am going to listen to your chest. Deep breath in. Exhale." The doctor listened to several other parts on the front and back of his torso. Rob breathed in and out as ordered.

"Right, march up to the door and back again." Rob did as told. "Now hop to the door on your right foot and back again on your left."

"Just a couple more things before we are finished. Complexion. Fair. Hair. Brown. Colour of eyes. Brown." The information got noted on the form

"Get dressed and go back to Captain Lawson."

Rob went back to where he had deposited his clothes and dressed. The doctor went into the other office with the paperwork in his hand.

"Robert Spence Corsar fit for service, James. He's all yours."

Rob finished dressing and went back to the office.

"Right, Robert, we need you to swear the oath of allegiance to the King. What's your religion then?"

"I have no religion. I'm an atheist."

"Don't often hear that. Still, even if you don't believe in Him, I'm sure He believes in you, Robert."

"Maybe so, Sir."

"Put your right hand on the bible and repeat the words on this form."

"I suppose I have to."

"Yes. It's what the King expects. You need to swear by his God that you will be his loyal soldier."

Rob went through the oath with his hand on the bible as proscribed in army regulations. He read his attestation document for accuracy and signed on the bottom line.

"Now that is complete, we will make arrangements for you to collect your uniform."

With that one signature, Mr Robert Spence Corsar became 1798 Private Corsar R.S. in the 5th Battalion of the Black Watch, Royal Highlanders. He is allocated to C Company, made up of men from Montrose and Arbroath.

His plan had worked. The following month, Rob was going to the Black Watch summer ball. There he would find lassies, cheap drinks, and dancing.

Rob went home in his new uniform and got met at the door by his dad. Sandy was a committed pacifist. Sandy was livid and unleashed a tirade. Rob tried to explain his reasons for joining the territorials.

"I want to go to the dance. I want some fun just like other lads my age are having. You keep all the money, and I get no chance for a bit of fun. This way I get in for free."

"Your mum gets all the money to pay for food, rent and clothes. I assume you like to eat, have clothes to wear and somewhere to live?"

"Yes, but. . ."

"But nothing, boy. All our lives, we've struggled to do these things. Don't you think that your mum and me might have liked a bit of fun ourselves instead of slaving away to house, clothe and feed ten children?"

"It's not my fault you had ten of us." As soon as the words were out of his mouth, Rob could see how they hurt his dad. He couldn't take them back now.

Sandy drew his hand back as if to smack his face for his cheek. He stopped, and Rob could see a wave of anger in his father that he had never seen before.

Rob was in the Territorial Army. There was nothing Sandy could do to alter that. At seventeen

Rob, was a man and had the right to choose his path, even if it was the wrong one, in Sandy's opinion.

"You have no idea, boy. You're old enough to make your own decisions, even wrong ones. I can't stop you if you've signed your forms. If it's dancing you want, you'll soon be dancing to a different tune," and with that, he turned and walked away.

Rob was shaken by what he had seen in his father. If looks could kill, then the glare he got from his mother would have ended his life there and then.

Rob shrugged off his father's anger. He was going to the Summer Ball on Saturday 25 July 1914.

THREE

Listening to his sisters' talk, Rob could hear that lassies looked for three things in a man. First was stunning good looks. Examining himself in the mirror, Rob thought that he was not ugly. However much he looked, he could see that he did not have the smouldering looks described by his sisters. He concluded that his looks would not make women swoon. That avenue was closed.

The second attribute was money, lots of it. As a poor dock labourer, it was another attribute that he did not have.

Last, there was the ability to dance and sweep a woman off her feet with his skill. Rob had been to a ceilidh when he was much younger. He danced with other children, each doing their own thing. It was not a proper dance, but enjoyable all the same. Rob could not dance. Going to a Ball meant dancing with the opposite sex. It was what Rob wanted. Dancing was his way to a woman's heart. It was a skill that could be learned, even by an average-looking poor man.

It is where he enlisted the help of his eldest sister, Jean. He persuaded her to teach him to dance. She seemed to know how to dance, as she often talked about doing it. Jean was hesitant at first, partly because there was no music in the house. It was part one of Rob's plan.

"Why do you need to know how to dance, Robert Corsar?" Jean's tone was very sharp.

"I'd like to go to a dance at some time and meet a nice lassie. I need to know how to dance to do that."

"So, you're old enough to be interested in lassies then? What makes you think any lassie would be interested in you?"

"I don't know, and I won't know unless I'm able to meet one. Will you teach me dances and the steps?"

"How can I teach you to dance without music?"

"Can you not just teach me the steps and hum the music?"

"The only thing that hums around here, Robert Corsar, are your feet. Maybe they could supply the music."

"Very funny, Jean. Come on. If I'm ever going to impress a lassie, I need to know how to dance. You and my other sisters talk about it often enough. Help me, will you?"

"All right. We'll start tonight in the back green."

That evening, Rob's dancing instruction began in the back green of the house. There were just the two of them present. Their clandestine efforts would not stay secret long.

"We'll start with the waltz, the easiest to learn. You only have to count to three. Let's see how you hold your partner?"

Rob stepped forward and grabbed Jean around the waist. Jean broke free.

"Dancing with a lassie is refined and elegant. She's not a sack of turnips to be mauled." With that, Rob got a cuff on his ear.

"Ouch."

"We'll start again, and this time we'll do it right, or you get more of that."

Any secrecy that Rob hoped for did not last long. The back green was not a particularly secluded space. Soon, his younger sisters became spectators. They clapped in time to the rhythm when he got it right. They laughed and squealed when he got it wrong. Stepping on Jean's toes got him the promised cuff on the ear. That made the youngsters squeal with delight.

"The man leads. That means you guide the lassie around the floor in time to the music."

Rob smirked.

"Does that mean I get to put a bridle on you?" It was a light-hearted comment, but he still got his ear boxed.

"Now, take your partner. Remember, she's a lady."

After some repositioning of his arms by Jean, he was ready.

"You start by moving your left foot forward as I put my right one back. Now step sideways with your right foot. Not that far. Now put your left foot next to your right one. Step back with your right foot. Step back and sideways with your left foot and bring your right foot next to your left one."

Jean was leading, and Rob was trying to follow. His steps were awkward.

"Not such big steps. Just count one, two, three and repeat as you move your feet. It's easy."

After many attempts, Rob could follow the steps to a waltz. Over the next few weeks, Rob would learn the quick-step, foxtrot, strip the willow, and the dashing white sergeant. All this without the benefit of music. Rob learned the dances and became more adept quite quickly. He was not a natural dancer, but he was a quick learner. Rob did not know whether his sore ears made him a swift learner, but his increasing proficiency had a pleasing outcome for his ears.

By the time of his secret enlistment, Rob was still an awkward dancer. His sister suddenly realised why he had enticed her into teaching him to dance.

"You'll need to do better than this if you're going to a proper ball," said Jean at their next lesson in the back green.

"You'd better get on wi it, then."

"You're as stiff as a plank of wood when you dance. You need to be more relaxed."

"I can't relax. I need to keep the time and the steps in my head. I need to count."

"One dance wi Rob the stiff plank, and that'll be enough for any lassie."

"I need more practice. Come on, Jean, help me. . . please."

"Since you ask so nicely. Ready?"

On the Friday night before the ball, Jean gave Rob his final lesson and instructions on treating his partner.

"Your grip should be firm but not tight. You're dancing, not doing hand to hand combat. Relax while you lead. Keep your steps in time to the beat of the music and stay off her toes. You don't want to be crushing her toes with your muckle great army boots. Now, one last dance, and we're off to bed."

FOUR

The evening of the Ball, Rob was wondering what to wear. Will had offered him his suit, but it did not fit. Will was broader than Rob, so it hung on him, making him look like a scarecrow. Rob had a fleeting thought about asking his dad if he could borrow his suit. The idea passed quickly. The opposition of his father to his enlistment in the army, and he was even more broad-shouldered than Will. The only option was his uniform. Many of his battalion pals had told him that was all they had to wear so he would not stand out.

As Rob approached the hall, his anxiety started to grow. He had been here several times since enlisting, so he knew it well. Those visits were for army drills and exercises. It was different, and he had no idea of what to expect. He could see town worthies in suits and bow ties arriving with their female companions resplendent in their gowns. He felt out of place. Rob faltered and wondered if he should continue. He thought about turning around and going home.

"Come on, Rob." There was a slap on his back, and he turned to see Drew McMillan. Drew was dressed just like Rob, which made him feel better. There was no turning back now. Recognised, so he had to go on.

"Aye. OK, Drew."

The two walked towards the door. Rob felt comforted by having someone with him as the pair stepped into the hall. There was music from the band that was on a stage to the left. The band consisted of two violinists, a drummer, a piano player and an accordionist. Food and drink were on tables along one side of the hall. On the two remaining outside walls were a series of tables and chairs. In the centre of the floor, a few couples were dancing. Rob watched their feet to see if he could work out what dance they were doing. It was a foxtrot, he thought.

Looking around, he saw some officers in full dress uniform and some in suits and ties. Many others like himself and Drew were in standard Khaki uniform tops and kilts. Rob was a small slim man typical of an underfed seventeen-year-old. While he was strong, as befits a labourer, his thirty-three-inch chest did little to fill out his tunic. His slim hips meant that the kilt he wore did not swing as those of men with broader buttocks. It did not matter to him. His plan had been a success, and he was here at last.

The ladies were all dressed in their finery. There was music from the band and guests talking in a room, slowly filling with the smoke of cigarettes and the occasional pipe.

"Get yersel a drink," said the soldier at the door. He was pointing to a table down the hall. "Try the punch from that bowl there. It's free, but beware, if you get drunk and unruly, you'll be on a charge in the morning."

"Thanks," said Rob to the man he did not know. He also did not know if a charge would result should he be found drunk. It seemed reasonable, given army discipline, so he decided not to drink too much. The punch contained whiskey, not a drink Rob could afford. It caught the back of his throat as he drank. The burning sensation caused him to gasp. He tried to look nonchalant and hoped that no one had noticed.

Rob had sneaked a drop of whiskey at a ceilidh when he was young. It made him feel sick. He had also supped a dram last New Year, and the burning sensation in his throat reminded him of both events. He knew that many glens in the area had their illegal stills for making whiskey. He also knew that some could tell what Glen the whiskey came from by the taste. Rob only knew it was whiskey he was drinking by the burn in the back of his throat. He could feel the strength of the drink, and that reminded him to take it easy.

Standing with his glass of red-orange whiskey punch in his hand, Rob looked around for young single lassies. Looking at and identifying likely women was the easy part. If he wanted a dance with a female company, he would have to pluck up the courage and ask one to dance. That was the hard part. Jean had suggested ways of introducing himself to young women. For the life of him, Rob had forgotten most of what Jean advised. He was very nervous. It was a proper Ball, not a ceilidh where almost anything went.

Rob was unsure around women he did not know. He was awkward with them, even though he had six sisters at home. Sisters were sisters, not real women in the sense that Rob wanted to meet. Sisters were always quarrelling or getting in the way. When they kissed him, it was a peck on the cheek. It was to wish him a happy birthday, Christmas or New Year. They did cuddle him a lot, but that was during the cold winter nights when all the children slept in the same bed if they could. These were keeping warm so as not to freeze cuddles, not what Rob was hoping for tonight.

He wished for a cuddle and lip to lip kiss that would make his heart race and feel warm. Not a brother-sister thing, but a man-woman thing. He was grateful to his eldest sister, Jean, who had taught him how to dance. Doing the waltz, foxtrot, or quickstep with a sister was one thing. Doing it with an unknown woman was quite another. He was anxious but determined.

He stood back and watched men and women dancing, chatting, laughing, and having fun. If he was going to have fun, he needed to ask a girl to dance. What girl and how were the questions that occupied his mind?

Looking around, he saw that many of the women that were not dancing were sitting with men. There were only a few who seemed to be sitting on their own. He spied a woman on her own across the hall. She looked nice, so he girded his loins and strode towards her. He was very nervous. He stood close to her, looking down at her brunette hair and smooth complexion. She looked up, and her bright blue eyes transfixed him. He was speechless.

"Yes?" She stared straight at him.

"Em. Would you like to dance?"

"Aye, thanks."

Rob put his hand out to help her up and lead her onto the floor. He placed his drink on the table. She was tall for a woman, he thought. She had a very engaging smile. He had got his first proper dance with a lassie who was not related to him.

The woman who stood in front of him was about five feet four inches tall. Her brunette hair was in the latest chignon style. She had a lacy white linen shirtwaist top with a long, narrow skirt in blue, ending at her instep. She looked elegant.

Lucky for him this dance was a waltz. It was an easy one to start. The two adopted the correct posture for the dance, and remembering some of his sister's advice, Rob led. He said nothing at first because he was concentrating hard on getting the steps right and not standing on her toes. Rob was counting, one, two, three, one, two, three in his head in time to the music. He was also trying not to be too stiff and hoping he did not step on her toes. Still, trying to remember the steps, the grip, relaxing and leading had him anxious. She did not yelp, so he thought he was doing OK and relaxed a bit. As he became more comfortable with the music and his dancing ability, he spoke.

"I'm Rob Corsar."

"I'm Elizabeth Ross. Everyone calls me Lizzie.

There followed another awkward silence.

"You look awful young to be a soldier, Rob."

"I'm seventeen," said Rob, quickly trying to sound older and more experienced. "I only joined up last month to get to this dance." Suddenly, Rob became embarrassed by what he had blurted out. "I'm sorry."

"What for?"

"I didn't mean to say that. I'm nervous."

"That's no bother. Not been to many dances then?"

"No. This is my first proper dance."

A few more bars of music and the dance was over.

"Will we sit down?" Lizzie asked.

"Yes, please." Rob was a little too quick with his answer. Lizzie just smiled and walked with him back to her table.

"Would you like to sit with me?"

"Yes, please." Rob sat down. Lizzie looked around as if looking for someone.

"Are you here with somebody?"

"Yes. I came with my brother, Willie. I'm his guest."

"No boyfriend then?"

"No."

Struggling to make conversation, Rob saw that her glass was nearly empty.

"Would you like a drink?"

"Yes, please. I'll have another punch."

Rob got up and walked to the table to get two more drinks. He was wondering what to say to Lizzie as he walked. She was pretty. He wanted to make an impression. The last thing he wanted was to appear to be a young country teuchter. "A punch, please and a beer."

"No violence at these affairs," said the server with a huge grin.

"Sorry." There was a pause before Rob realised the joke. "Very funny." Rob's face broke into a grin.

"Here you go then. One beer and one punch and no violence. That'll be tuppence, please."

He fished the coins out of his breast pocket. "Thanks." He picked up the drinks and strode back across the floor to the table where he laid them down.

"The barman said something funny. You have a big grin."

Rob explained the joke. "You're here with your brother. No boyfriend then?" Rob realised he had just repeated himself and felt self-conscious again.

"No. My folks are very strict with me. They object to me leaving the house without a chaperone."

"I'm sorry."

"Why, are you sorry? It's, not your rule it's my parents."

"It just seems a bit harsh, and I suppose I'm sorry for you."

"It's, Willie, my brother, you should be sorry for. He has to do it although he doesn't like it. He's a good son and does what he's told. He's in the army too, so he would come anyway. I get to come because he does."

"So, if your brother wasn't in the army, you wouldn't be allowed to come?"

"That's right."

"Oh. That's a bit strict. I'm sure you can take care of yourself."

"I'm sure that I can, but that's my folks rule. My mum is very religious and makes me go to church every Sunday."

"Don't you want to go to church then?"

"I don't mind church, but I don't like being forced to go. Are you a churchgoer?"

"No. My folks never had much time for all that. My dad always thought that God was too busy taking care of the gentry to have time to worry about the likes of us Corsars."

"I'm sure He has time for everybody."

"Perhaps so."

"What do you do when you're not training to fight?"

The ice broken, at least for Rob, the conversation took a turn to things slightly more personal. Rob learned about Lizzie and the fact that Willie was a corporal in the battalion. It made his anxiety return. He had not learned much in the army so far, but he had learned not to cross a non-commissioned officer such as Willie. He knew that crossing a corporal could spell trouble of the worst kind. He began to wonder if he should leave, but Lizzie was a bonnie lassie and seemed to like his company. There were a few more dances together. Rob stuck to the dances Jean had taught him. If he stood on her feet, she was too polite to say.

Lizzie learned about the Corsar clan. The fact that Rob had nine siblings did not faze her. Large families were a common feature of the time. Still, ten children were a lot, and Lizzie had genuine sympathy for any woman who gave birth to so many.

"Ten is a lot of children for one woman to bear."

"Is it? I never gave it any thought."

"Are you the oldest?"

"No. I'm third in line. I have an older brother and sister. The rest are all younger than me. You have a brother here. Are there any more in your family?"

"No, just Willie and me."

After a couple more dances, Lizzie noticed Willie heading to the toilet. She took her chance.

"I could do with a bit of fresh air. Will you come outside for a couple of minutes with me?"

"Aye." With that, they both rose and headed outside.

They stood chatting awkwardly for a couple of seconds. Suddenly Lizzie leaned over and kissed Rob full on the lips. Rob was both surprised and delighted. He had not gathered his thoughts before Lizzie broke the kiss. His cheeks reddened, and he tried to mumble something but failed.

"I'm sorry. Did I upset you?"

"Not at all. I was surprised."

"You're a nice lad. I wondered what it would be like to kiss you."

"I see. I don't know what to say."

"What about, can I kiss you?"

"Yes, a good idea. So, can I?"

"Best be quick. We need to get back, or Willie might come looking for me."

Rob leaned in and kissed Lizzie as best he could. He was a novice at this and had no idea whether he performed adequately. His efforts showed just what a beginner he was at these things, but if Lizzie noticed, she said nothing.

"That was nice. We should go back in now?"

Going back in now was not what Rob wanted to do, but he followed her anyway. They could not see Willie, so both he and Lizzie were relieved. Had he seen them returning, the situation might have been awkward.

At the end of the evening, Willie came to the table and collected his sister.

"You're a new lad? What's your name?"

"Rob Corsar. I only joined a few weeks ago."

"He's been looking after me, Willie. He's been very nice."

"That's OK then. Thanks. Come on, Lizzie, time to get you hame."

"Thanks, Rob. I had a nice time."

"Thanks, Lizzie. So, did I."

Rob had a great time. He stood and watched Lizzie disappear into the gathering night gloom. He watched her hips sway and caught the glance over her shoulder as she walked. His heart leapt with joy.

The following day, at about 10:45 on the 28 June, Rob walked along Traille Drive by the seashore. He looked at the families sitting on the sand, drinking coffee and squash, and having a good time. He smiled to himself, remembering last and the kiss. Rob was a happy young man. A few hardy souls were swimming in the sea. Rob shook his head as he watched them. It's is the North Sea, and that should tell you all you need to know about how cold it will be, he thought. Still, it was their choice. Rob had no idea that two thousand miles away, an event was unfolding. that would change the rest of his life forever, and not in a good way.

FIVE

In a city called Sarajevo in Bosnia, Franz Ferdinand of Austria and his wife Sophie were in a motorcade through the city. He was the heir to the Austrian Empire and was there to inspect imperial armed forces. Bosnia was part of the Austrian Empire, but it was also a hotspot of revolutionaries wanting freedom.

The Archduke was advised that it was a dangerous visit, but he ignored the advice. He travelled, as always, in an open-topped car. Ferdinand and Sophie were enjoying their day when a grenade exploded, injuring several people in the car behind the couple. Ferdinand ordered the motorcade to continue.

Their car took a wrong turn into the main highway, and the driver stopped to check where he was. A young Serb stepped out of the crowd. He shot the Archduke in the head and his wife in the abdomen. The couple died later that day.

The news of the assassination of the heir to the Austrian throne generated a few headlines in the British press the following day. Rob read the headlines and wondered who these people were. He had never heard of Sarajevo or the Archduke. The story had no significance for him, so he scanned it moving quickly on as he did. Rob noticed a by-line in the paper that made him smile. It reported that the Hapsburgs, the Archduke's family, had produced many lunatics and only one great statesman. No great loss to the world, it would seem, thought Rob. All that interbreeding in royal families was bound to produce plenty of lunatics. Rob laughed.

"What's the joke, Rob?" asked Davey Johnston, who was sitting beside Rob drinking tea in the shed where they worked.

"This story in the paper. Says the Austrian Royal family produced a lot of lunatics."

"Is the one that got shot one of them lunatics?"

"Doesn't say."

"Don't look now, but the foreman is giving us the hurry-up. Best get back to work, lad."

Rob and Davey rinsed their cups and trudged back to their benches.

There was no hysteria in the UK, and the story quickly faded away. The Guardian newspaper report indicates the feeling of the nation of the event.

"It is not to be supposed that the death of Archduke Francis Ferdinand will have any immediate or salient effect on the politics of Europe."

At home later that day, Rob met his father, who was reading a paper.

"The Austrians might want revenge for this," said Sandy pointing to the headline. "Could start a war unless Germany puts a stop to it."

"Why would Germany bother? None of their high up yins got killed."

"Germany and Austria are big friends. They have treaties to help each other in the event of trouble."

"The papers don't seem to think that it will amount to anything."

"So, I see, but it's no guarantee. We're dealing with powerful forces here. Countries all over Europe have treaties with each other, and what might seem like a small fight could turn very nasty."

"How'd you know this stuff?"

"Through the Labour party meetings that I attend."

"Well, it's not happened yet, so I'll wait and see if it does."

Rob was correct insofar as this was not yet a world-shattering event. Unfortunately, Sandy was also accurate. A minor conflict in some far corner of Europe escalated just as Sandy had intimated.

His membership of the Independent Scottish Labour party and his friendship with Keir Hardy had given him an inkling of what might happen. Rob's plan to get free admission to the pre-eminent event in Montrose was also to get him a free entrance to an even weightier event. He had underestimated his fathers repeated warnings of how easily war might come to Europe.

Left alone by the politicians, the assassination would have passed into history as a footnote of no great significance. Politicians picked at this small pimple until it became a running sore. The resultant Machiavellian machinations led Europe sleepwalking into war.

A few days later, Sandy talked to Rob about the situation in Europe. Rob had paid no heed to much in the newspapers since the initial report.

"Looks like we might have some trouble in Europe, boy."

"How so?"

"The Austrians want revenge like I said."

"Didn't you say that Germany might stop it?"

"Seems they might if they want to, but no sign of that yet. You'll be regretting joining up to go to that dance if war comes. You'll be sent. Then you best hope you have enough dance steps to dodge bullets."

"Surely the politicians and the King won't let that happen?"

"We all might get dragged into this family feud."

"What family feud?"

"The Royal families of Europe feud."

"What do you mean by that?"

"The Royals of Europe are part of the one big family."

"How's that?"

"Our King, the Kaiser, and the Tsar are all related. Every royal family in Europe is related to the children of Queen Victoria. She bred like a rabbit, and her kids are everywhere." Sandy missed the irony of what he had just said.

"Surely that's a good thing. They won't want to be fighting each other?"

"They might be heads of government, but they are not in charge. Politicians run countries, and they are not related. Most of them are motivated by money and power. The two go hand in hand wi that lot. None of them would want to lose their Empire. They would much rather expand them, even if it means war. They won't be doing the fighting."

"Oh. I see."

"Nothing's fixed yet, lad, but it is not looking promising."

"Bugger."

"Mind your language, lad, but you're right."

SIX

It was a warm summer night on the Mains of Ardovie farm. Jean Corsar was lying on her bed, sweating. It was not the normal perspiration you might associate with a warm summer night. It was the sweat of hard labour. Jean was trying to produce her third child.

Some said that after the first pregnancy, those that follow are easier. The huffing, puffing and shouts from Jean Corsar would suggest that these people lied. Jean also told her husband, Sandy, that she would withdraw his conjugal rights after this birth. The oath was loud and somewhat rustic as in, "I'm no letting you near me wi that thing o' yours ever again."

Jessie Reid, who was attending to the labour, just smiled. She had heard similar oaths many times before and knew most to be worthless. Her continued attendance at such events was a testament to this. In the other room, Sandy Corsar heard the oath. He had heard it from Jean twice before, and he was sitting on a bed with the cause of both promises - his eldest son William, always called Will, aged four and his daughter Jane, aged two and always called Jean. He was not unconcerned by her pain, for he knew that natural home births were dangerous.

He also knew that pain-free births were now common but cost money. These were funds he did not have. Only those with money could afford such luxury because Chloroform and a doctor were required to administer it. It was a privilege reserved for those that had the where with all to pay. Living in the countryside in remote rural areas means that physical access to doctors was difficult.

The best maternity attention that the Corsars can afford came in the shape of their neighbour Jessie Reid. Jessie was not a qualified midwife, but she was the nearest thing to a one in these remote parts. She had attended an unspecified number of human births and many more in cows, horses and sheep.

When pain-free birth was introduced to the UK in 1847 by James Simpson in Edinburgh, it caused anger in the clergy. They held the view that the pain was:

the natural and physiological forces that the Divinity has ordained us to enjoy or to suffer.

Jean was not a church-going woman, but she knew what ministers thought. If she could have got hold of a minister at this moment, she would happily have wrung his neck. While she was panting and shouting, Jessie spoke.

"Will you be getting the bairn christened, Jean?"

"I'll get my kids christened when ministers have laboured like us. Until then the church. . .Aaah."

"Not long now, Jean. It's nearly here."

"About time."

"One more heave Jean."

This third child makes his presence known at five minutes to midnight on Tuesday 15 June 1897. Jessie Reid washed down the child, wrapped it in a blanket and handed it to Jean. She then cleared up the mess associated with birth before returning to her cottage next door.

In the bedroom, young Jean was anxious to see the new baby. Her brother is less enthused. He remembered her birth and its consequences for him. The new baby became the centre of attention for the parents, and Will moved one step away from their affections. He also became an unpaid part-time nanny.

"Will. Just mind the bairn for a bit while I make the denner," his mother would call. At first, Will did not mind. The bairn was a sort of substitute for toys that he did not have. However, there were times when Will did not want to take care of the bairn. There were frogs spawn and tadpoles in the pools nearby that needed his urgent attention. Local burns had small fish in them that he could catch. Then there were also bird nests he could watch as the parent birds worked furiously to feed their young. Sometimes the request to mind the bairn set Will in a dilemma. If he did not mind the bairn, his denner would be late. There was not much food to be had, so mealtimes were important. Will's stomach always had the better of the argument.

This new baby was unable to see or understand what was going on. He was busy suckling on his mother's milk. He could not see or appreciate his surroundings. Had the baby been able to see and understand his surrounding, he might not have been in such a rush to leave the wet warmth of his mother's womb. It was too late as there was no going back.

His home was called a farm cottage. It was no thatched roof house with all mod cons and a picket fence around a rose garden. It was a single storey granite stone building divided into three homes for the servants of the Mains of Ardovie farmer. Each of the three cottages has two identical rooms. The baby was in the multi-function main room of the home. He was too preoccupied with milk to notice the dark grey granite walls. Flickering candles, a paraffin lamp and the dull glow of the fire in the open grate lit the room.

The bed his mother rests on was in a curtained alcove giving her and her husband some semblance of privacy. It was in the main square room. There was a large open fireplace, a sink with cold running water and a wooden cupboard.

Furnishings consisted of a wooden table, two wooden benches and two wooden chairs. The only carpet was a small rug beside the main bed.

The second room was the only bedroom. It was where the children slept. The bedroom contained one bed, a small wooden cupboard and an open fireplace. The outside shared toilet of this house will forever be a mystery to this baby who will have moved before becoming big enough to use it. He will suffer many worse indignities in his lifetime than a shared outside toilet.

There had been some discussion between mother and father as to the name of the boy or girl. Robert was her preference for a boy. That was the name of her younger brother and Grandfather. Spence was her family name, so Robert Spence Corsar it would be. Sandy did not argue. He knew better.

It took Sandy three weeks to register the birth at the county offices in Brechin, only four miles away. He needed time off work to attend the registration, but June and July were busy on farms getting ready to harvest a few weeks away.

Most children have their names shortened, and Robert was always to be called Rob. If the full name is not going to be used, it's a mystery why they don't register the short version. Perhaps the full name was used for those occasions when the child was in trouble.

"Robert Spence Corsar, come here." The words and volume of the call would tell the child all that he needed to know. He was in trouble.

SEVEN

Farm servants work was hard and unrelenting. Sandy and Jean had both been born into the life, so it was routine for them.

By the time he was fifteen, Sandy had already left home and lived in a bothy with three older men. He was doing a man's work for little reward.

Every six or twelve months, servants attend a feeing market in their nearest local town. They are inspected and questioned by the farmers who might offer a contract for six or twelve months. Wages were usually half cash and half goods in kind. Single Servants usually slept in bothies on the farmland. If there were no servants cottages on the farm, even married men slept here. The farmer had no interest in any of the servant families. They had to fend for themselves.

Sitting in the bothy eating his meagre evening meal, Sandy had listened to the men grumbling about the job, their reward and the landowners hold over them. As an illegitimate child born to a farm servant, Sandy was only too aware of their grievances. While they talked and grumbled, Sandy noted that they seemed to have no answer to their problems. He wondered if there was something that he could do. He had heard stories of workers in towns banding together to force employers to provide better wages and conditions. Some said that there were similar moves among farm servants. He wanted to find out.

At the next feeing market, Sandy came across another servant who talked about doing something. While he was waiting, Sandy chatted with the man. Jimmy Prentice was older than Sandy, probably mid-thirties. He was a hard-looking man, worn down by his life of hard toil in all weathers. He was not happy with his lot and had plenty to say about what he might do.

"What do you think could be done, Mr Prentice?"

"I'm just Jimmy lad. None o' that Mister stuff. There are workers in towns setting up combination movements to force owners to pay better."

"I've heard about them. Do they work?"

"You can imagine, lad, that bosses don't want to improve anything but their profits. They happily keep us workers on starvation money so they can live in big houses, eat the best food and drink the best wine. All the while, we workers can starve and die for all they care. They don't want change, but some of these movements have brought some change."

"That sounds grand. Are there any such movements on the land around here?"

"There is one lad, but it is a secret."

"How do I get into it?"

"I'd have to introduce you, and we need to be sure that you are not a farmers spy. If you are, then you're dead, and nobody will find your body. If you get a contract today, tell me where you are. I'll make contact as soon as I can. We can use all the help we can get."

Sandy got his contract, and he informed Jimmy.

"I'm on the next farm over from there. I'll be in touch. Good luck, lad."

A month passed before Jimmy turned up on Sandy's farm while he was in the fields. Sandy saw him waving to him from behind a tree. Looking around to make sure no one was watching, Sandy strode over.

"Hi, Jimmy. How are you?"

"I'm fine, Sandy. What about you?"

"OK, thanks. Have you come to talk about a meeting?"

"I have, lad. It's on for Sunday night at ten. It's in that little wood over there between our two farms. Don't let anyone know you're coming, and be sure that they don't see you leave your bothy."

"I'll do that. Thanks, Jimmy. See you Sunday."

Sandy crept out of his bothy on Sunday night. The only other resident was out with a girl, so he had no cause to care about Sandy.

Sandy crept into the wood and started looking for the others who might be there. He found three men sitting on the ground, whispering.

"Jimmy?" Sandy asked in a loud whisper.

"Aye, lad. Come and sit down."

With Jimmy were Archie Gemmell and Doug Harrison.

"Are you expecting anyone else?"

"We hope others might come, but they might have trouble getting away. They don't want the farmers finding out."

"What if the farmer learns of their meeting? What'll happen to them?"

"The farmer will bully them. Two of them have families who will be bullied. They play rough these wealthy shites."

At the meeting, Sandy heard about their altruistic philosophy. Help others even if it results in a disadvantage to yourself. It took Sandy a little time to fully understand this, but he was a willing participant. Getting farm servants together for meetings was a problem due to the spread-out nature of their employment. The meetings were not well attended. They needed to reach more people. Doug came up with the idea to pin notices on kirk doors. Many people attended church on a Sunday, so that was agreed.

"I don't go to church," said Sandy. "Never thought this God thing existed."

"You don't need to go in. Pin the notice on the door. You can sneak out on a Saturday night and do the deed. Are you prepared to do that?"

"Aye. I'll do that."

"The more people we get to join us, the easier it should be to convince the farmers. Don't get found out."

"There's a story about a servant who took his farmer to court. It shows us why we must fight and beat these greedy bastards," said Archie. "The man was ordered out of bed after a hard day's work. He had to harness his horse to a cart and take a sideboard to the owners' friend."

"Aye. I heard that one," said Jimmy. "It was the middle of the night, and he had to be up at five the next morning as usual."

"What happened?" asked Sandy.

"The magistrates said that the servant was in the wrong. He had to do what his master wanted whenever he ordered. He could only get free time if his master let him have it. He had no rights. The servant lost, and I think he had to pay costs, something he could not afford. The farmer kept him on past his contract date for free until he had paid off the owners' costs. All legal in their eyes."

"Hasn't slavery been abolished?" said Sandy.

"Not for us, lad," said Jimmy. "It's why we have to fight. We need to get proper wages and working conditions. Our families get thrown in the street or the poor house, starve or die young. We can't let this go on."

"It's not going to be easy, and we might get bullied. They might even stop us from working on the land anywhere in the area. Nothing out in the open but no contract offered even if you are the best for the job," said Archie. "They keep an eye out for trouble makers, get rid of them and tell other farmers not to hire them. It's why we keep meetings secret. Are you ready for that lad?"

"Aye, I am that. How do we get farmers to change their minds? They can ignore us and do us dirty at the end of our contracts. I'm sure plenty others will do the work for the wages."

"That's why we need lots of people at meetings. If we get enough then we can ask for more money and better conditions at the feeing market. If enough of us stick together, they'll either not have enough workers to do the job or pay us our fair due. All we're asking for is a fair days pay for a fair days work."

Over the next few years, Sandy became more active. He heard what unions did in mining communities in the West of Scotland. He also saw what their owners did in retaliation to strikes. Police and soldiers helped to put down resistance.

In 1885, Sandy attended a meeting convened by the Land Restoration League in Brechin. There he met a prominent activist called Keir Hardie. His philosophy chimed with Sandy's.

"Mr Hardie, nice to meet you. I'm, Sandy Corsar."

"I'm pleased to meet you, Sandy. What brought you to my meeting today?"

"I'm a farm servant. Farmers have kept us under their heel for years. We get paid poor money, work all hours, our families starve and die. If we fight back, they bully us. All we are asking for is a fair deal. That seems to be your message."

"Indeed, it is. Is there somewhere we can sit and talk?"

Sandy found a suitable spot, and the two compared their experiences. Hardie could see that Sandy Corsar supported his ideas in this part of Scotland.

"I'll need to go," said Hardie. "I want to keep in touch if it's OK with you?"

"It is."

Hardie visited Sandy a couple of times in the next three years when he was in the area. In early 1888, during one visit, he gave Sandy some news.

"Some of us are setting up a new political party. It's going to be the Scottish Labour Party. We'll be working for better pay and conditions for the working folk of Scotland. I'll take your name if you'd like to join?"

"Aye. It's one thing to have unions in trades fighting for better conditions, but we need parliament to change the laws. Without that, we'll struggle."

"I'm going to stand for parliament if I can find a suitable seat."

"I wish you luck. Sitting on the benches in parliament will be a lot better than sitting in our run-down bothy."

"I was born and brought up in worse. I was down the mines when I was just seven. Sitting out in the country in the company of friends is considerably nicer."

Sandy gave his name and became an activist for the cause. His friend, Hardie, did quite well. He found a seat became and MP for a constituency in Essex called South West Ham in 1892.

By this time, Sandy had become entwined with another farm servant called Jane Spence. Like him, Jean, as she wanted to be called, was keen on helping working people. She had attended meetings and voiced her views. She and Sandy had much in common. Both were dour, hard-working and socially conscious. In early December 1892, they had their first sexual encounter. It was not entirely an act of love or passion. It was more one of respect and mutual admiration. After the encounter, Sandy spoke.

"Jean."

"Yes, Sandy."

"I think we should get married. Will we?"

"Yes, we will."

Bans were posted in the church in Duns, and the marriage was performed there on Friday, 6th January 1893. Witnesses to the marriage were Jean's sister-in-law, Jessie and Sandy's friend and Labour Party member, Archie Christie.

There was no traditional scattering of coins on the church path for the local children who were otherwise at school or working. The couple had no money to throw around.

The church was a plain simple building with minimal fussy adornments. The only decoration of note was the ornately carved pulpit on the west wall opposite the main door. The minister had given the couple a stern lecture on their non-attendance at his church before the wedding. Sandy's repost was simple and effective.

"It needs to be legal, and that means a church wedding. You don't want us living in sin, do you?'

"You would not be the first in this parish to do that, but no, I don't. I will marry you."

By this time, his activities were a thorn in the side of farmers. They were not slow to retaliate. Sandy was in danger of losing his ability to work on the land anywhere in the area. Word was getting around about this troublemaker.

The couple had both become members of the new Independent Scottish Labour as soon as they married. Both supported the aims of the party and knew the possible consequences of their action. Despite this, they both became wholehearted members. It would not be long before their fears became a reality.

Work contracts became harder to acquire. Life was to become progressively more difficult for the couple and their growing family.

EIGHT

By his second birthday in 1899, Rob and his family had made his first move. It was to a farm in Blacklawburn some eight miles north of where he had been born. Ten days before this birthday, Rob got a new sister called Annie. There were now six mouths to feed and clothe. The annual salary for a farm servant would be about £40 to £50, half of which was goods in kind.

The family cottage here had a very unusual feature. There was a burn running through the house.

"It's all they'll offer us, Jean."

"I know, Sandy. We'll just have to make the best of it. At least we're not out on the street or in the Poor House."

During one particularly trying day of work and crying kids, Jean had an idea. She had a big waterproof tub for bathing in. If water did not leak, then it could not get in. She popped the youngest two, Rob and Annie, into the tub and then put the tub into the burn. It could not escape the building and just bobbed about in the slow running water.

"You can be the captain Rob, with Annie as your crew."

It seemed to please Rob, who played away happily for an hour or so. The gentle rocking of the tub kept Annie asleep most of the time. It was a perfect solution and one used frequently.

His third birthday, in 1900, was also celebrated on the farm in Blacklawburn. His birthday present was another sister called Emma, born on his birthday. Now there were seven mouths to feed. It was an unusual situation that two of the Corsar children were born in the same house. Sandys position here was more than a single twelve-month contract.

During this period, children who were resident with their families in farm cottages had to work in some small capacity on the farm. The low wages paid to their father meant that money was scarce. At age three, Rob is a boy labourer.

"You need to come with me today, Rob."

"Why?"

"The farmer wants you and your friend George to chase the birds from the fields. You can also keep an eye on the cattle to make sure they don't stray."

"I don't want to go. It's raining, and I'll get wet."

"We'll all get wet, but you might also get your backside skelped if you don't come now."

"Mum. Do I have to?"

"Yes, you do. Do what your dad tells you."

"It's not fair."

"I'll tell you what's not fair, boy. I have to scrimp and work my fingers to the bone so that you children can eat and get clothed. Any money we get from your work helps pay for that. Do you want to go hungry and cold, or would you like to eat and be warm?"

"Alright. I'll go."

Rob did not mind going into the fields when it was warm and sunny. Chasing birds waving a stick was good fun. He could also get vegetables from the ground when they were ready, and he was hungry. The work did have its rewards for his family, even if he knew nothing about money.

Surprisingly, Sandy got a second contract at the farm in Blacklawburn. Rob was only three years old, but he had to work on the farm and look after his two younger sisters when he did not work as his mother did some work at the big farmhouse. Looking after his sisters during the warm summer months did not please Rob at all. Still, he thought, better than clearing stones or planting potatoes or turnips in the fields. On miserable wet days, Rob preferred to be indoors looking after his sisters. He became quite a dab hand at bottle feeding Emma with milk. It made him feel grown-up. He even got quite used to wiping her bum and changing her nappy.

Living in the countryside did have advantages as well as disadvantages. There were wide-open spaces for a child to play if they were not working. When the weather got warmer in the spring, there were bird nests to watch and frogs in ponds to collect. Sticklebacks could be caught and kept in jars, old basins or buckets. Despite putting green river weed into the receptacle, the fish always died. Small boys, even those born and bred in the countryside, had no idea why this happened. In the summer and autumn, crops ripened. Potatoes or turnips straight from the field fed hungry children. There were also a few fields of strawberries and raspberries close by and the occasional apple orchard. Fruit and vegetables, plus porridge oats, were a very healthy diet, even if Rob did not know it.

In early 1902, Rob and the family up sticks and move for the second time in his so far short life. They are now some eight miles further north on a farm in Balfield, Glen Lethnot.

By now, Rob was five years old. He was legally obliged to attend school. He needed to earn some money if he was resident with his father in a farm cottage. He does both. He is a boy worker who works when he is not at school. Long light summer days, weekends and school holidays mean little respite for Rob and his siblings. Play was taken anywhere it could be found, however short.

Will, the eldest at nearly nine, was classed as a lad labourer. Lads expected to do more manual work. Will might have to lift heavy boulders when clearing ground for new fields. Then there was the lifting of heavy bales of hay during harvest season and even, on occasion, small animals. All this while still attending school. Rob worked alongside his brother in the fields and sheds but was still a boy labourer. He could see his future life in his brother.

"I don't want to go out in the field today," wailed Rob one day. "It's cold and wet. I don't like it."

"You'll just have to lump it then as we need your money."

"What for?"

"You like to eat, don't you, boy? We need to buy food for you, your brother and your sisters. You don't see Will whining, do you?"

"He's older and bigger than me."

"He is, but he does harder work than you so, stop your whining or I'll skelp your arse."

In the summer fruits, and vegetables were growing all around. Supplementing his diet, Rob picked and ate turnips, peas and carrots in the fields. Local orchards were also a source of ripe fruit. The usual punishment for being caught was a clip round the ear or a boot in the behind. There was another lesson Rob learned from getting caught. Rushing home and crying to his parents to say that the farmer or orchard owner hit him for no reason. A smack on the other ear was his reward for telling a lie.

"People don't smack you for no reason," would be her retort. "You must have done something wrong. Here's another for lying." Smack. Double jeopardy.

It was a valuable lesson to Rob, who learned to take his punishment and keep his mouth shut.

In July 1902, after his fifth birthday, Rob had yet another sister. This one was named Mary Ann.

One evening, while working in the fields, Rob saw his dad collect the horse's urine in a bucket.

"Why are you doing that, dad. I thought they could pee anywhere?"

"It's for medicine, lad."

"Yuck. Are you going to make him drink it?"

"No. It's not for the inside, I put it on the outside."

"What for?"

"Horses, like us folks, get chilblains. Washing their feet in their pee stops that."

"If I get chilblains, will I get the same treatment?"

"No, lad. It only works for horses."

"Good."

There was a local school in Glen Lethnot where Rob attended as proscribed by law. On his first day, Rob sat at a desk near the front of the class. He looked down at his brown wooden desk that had some scratches on it. He knew it was writing but didn't know what it said.

Mrs Sims, his teacher, started by explaining her rules. "Each morning, I will read the register. When I call your name, you will raise your hand and answer here."

She proceeded to call the register. Not all of the names called answered. Rob saw the anger in her face when she got no answer after a second call.

"Lift the flap of your desk and find your writing slate." There was a cacophony of noise.

"Do it quietly," she shouted. "There is chalk and a duster in there. Take them out." It generated more noise.

"Quietly," she bellowed.

"On the blackboard behind me, you will see letters. Do any of you know what these letters are?"

There were a few yeses heard.

"If you have an answer to give, you will raise your hand. I will then select one of the raised hands and permit you to speak. Do you understand?" There was no sound from the pupils. "Well, do you?" she shouted.

"Yes, Mrs Sims."

"You." Mrs Sims pointed to one girl. "You put your hand up. What's your name?"

"Agnes Peters."

"Right, Agnes, stand up. What are these letters?"

"They're the alphabet, Mrs Sims."

"Correct. Sit. These twenty-six letters make up all of the words that we speak. You are going to learn them. I will point to a letter, say its name, and you will all repeat what I say."

She had a long wooden pointer in her hand. She tapped on the first letter.

"This is the letter a. It sounds like the a in apple."

She looked around at the class. "Now you."

There was a loud chorus repeating her words. Regimented learning by rote had begun.

"Copy the letter on your slates."

There was a scratching of chalk on slate all-round the class.

"Hold your slates up with the writing facing me. I want to see what you have done."

She walked up and down the rows of desks, commenting as she went.

"What is your name, boy?"

"Robert Corsar."

"That is quite good, Robert. Stand up and show the class."

Rob did. He had pride in what he had done. He did not mention that his older siblings had helped. Others in the class were less fortunate. Badly formed letters were met by shouting. There might also be a slap on the back of the head.

Pupils spent the whole day doing this. In between times, Mrs Sims would get the class to recite the letters as she tapped each with her pointer. Before she dismissed the class, she dropped a bombshell.

"Tomorrow morning, I will ask one of you to come up here and recite the letters that I point to on the blackboard."

Rob, like everyone else, was horrified at the thought that they might be the one chosen. Fear of being asked to stand in front of the class would pale later on in the week when Mrs Sims introduced the children to the tawse, the teacher's pet. It was a two-foot piece of leather, about a quarter-inch thick, cut halfway up the middle to produce tails. The belt would be applied forcefully to an outstretched hand as punishment. A wide range of misdemeanours received abuse.

Talking in class, getting letters or numbers wrong or poor writing were just a few of the many minor crimes that introduced a pupil to the tawse.

After a couple of sessions learning the alphabet and numbers, the class moved on to times tables. The same strict rules applied. Miss Sims conducted the recital using her blackboard pointer like a conductors baton. As she smacked the stick down, her eyes scanned the class to make sure everyone was taking part.

She would occasionally stop, point to one child and asks what does so and so times so and so make. It was her way of checking that each child had learned their tables. After she was satisfied that the class knew the two times table, she moved on to the three times, and so on. Fear of the tawse was a powerful motivator for every child to learn.

There was little paper in schools to write on as it was an expensive commodity. Rob and his fellow pupils used a slate and chalk at first. A slate was easy to clean when the exercise was complete. There was usually a rag to clean the chalk, but the sleeve of a jumper often substituted.

After a while, Rob and his fellow pupils got to use paper. They also got ink and a pen. The pen was a round piece of wood with a metal nib. A slight improvement on a quill, but not much. This presented problems for the pupil and an opportunity for the teachers to punish them. Loading the nib with excess ink from the inkwell could lead to blobs on the paper. Smudging the ink as you wrote was another peril. It was particularly difficult for left-handed pupils. Still, teachers had an answer to the left-handed problem. They forced children to use their right hands and beat them if they did not.

Children walked around, blowing on their stinging hot hands after strapping. Rob often had hot hands.

In 1902 the family increased by one more child. Sandy was now a ploughman. A ploughman was also known as a Hind. He might expect to have the keep of a cow as part of his fee. Sandy had a cow behind his cottage on Bellfield farm. Now, the family had as much milk for their own use as the cow produced. What the family did not use could be sold to pay for feed for the cow. Until they had their cow, the family had to buy milk from the farmer at cost. Popping out for milk meant sitting on a stool and milking the cow. Rob learned to milk the cow, an activity he enjoyed. He also had to muck it out, a task he did not. Manure from the cow got piled into a dung heap. It was used as fertiliser in the little vegetable garden that the family cultivated behind the cottage. It always struck Rob as strange that what came out of the rear end of a cow went in to the ground to help the vegetables grow. He and the rest of the family ate the vegetables grown with the aid of cow shit.

Sandy, like most of his kind, ate lots of porridge oats. They were cheap and plentiful, being the main crop in the area. Jean would add one cup of oats per person to water in a pot and boil it the night before. Cold porridge for breakfast could be eaten with a fork and knife, as it would be solid. Children who were working got up at the same time as their father. They would sit around the small wooden table eating their porridge. Jean had stirred the solid porridge breaking up the solid lump, making it look more digestible. Spooned into bowls, hot water or milk would be added. It was a regular breakfast meal for the family. Porridge and water were a more regular combination. Milk was for the coffee that they all drank. Milk was not part of the goods in kind remuneration. Tea was an expensive commodity, so coffee was the drink of choice or necessity.

Sandy and the boys who worked in the fields had leather sporrans that hung from their belts. They contained porridge oats. At lunchtime, the horses got at least an hour rest. Servants did not get such leniency. The worker would take a handful of oats, dip them in a burn and pat them dry. They then ate them as oatcakes as they worked. It was lunch.

In 1904, Rob and the family were now living in Brechin. It was becoming harder for Sandy to get contracts on the land. He was an experienced farm labourer and ploughman. He was also an agitator. Farmers wanted one but not the other. Frequent warnings made no difference to his activities. Sandys skills as a ploughman or farmhand outweighed his political activities in the eyes of farmers, at least in the short term. Because of his and others activities, wages were on the rise at the feeing markets. It did not go down well with the landowners. All the farmers in the area eventually refused him employment. He had to find alternative means of supporting his family.

Losing his position on the land meant the workers in the family had to find jobs in towns and rent accommodation. They were a large family, so had to take any housing on offer.

Sandy had now become a general labourer, and Jean was pregnant yet again. Frank was born in August of that year. The nine of them are living in an alms-house attached to Brechin Cathedral.

Rob attended a new school in Brechin, but he needed to work to help the large family. Even Annie, at five, is expected to help out after school. All, put their wages on the table at the end of the week. Jean takes what she needs for the house and clothing. Any that is left is given to Sandy and the elder children as pocket money. Pockets are most often empty.

In 1907, Sandy's loses his job, and the family are on the move yet again. This move takes the family to Montrose. Another house brings another child. This girl is called Jessie. Sandy is registered as a carter, working for a brewery Montrose, delivering drinks. Sandy is teetotal, so will not carry ale. He will only deliver soft drinks. He is a man of principle despite its drawbacks. Rob is now a lad labourer. He does more manual

work, on the long summer nights or at weekends. He is an occasional worker in one of the Montrose linen factories. He earns a few pence a week for his efforts after school hours. It is dangerous, dirty work.

It's Friday night, and the family ritual is about to be enacted. Jean calls them all into the main room of the house.

"Let's have your wages then." One by one, the working members of the family put their money on the table. They each leave all that they have made. Jean knows what they make, and she knows if they are short. She counts out what she needs for household bills and pushes the rest to one side. This money is then divided among the family, starting with Sandy, then the rest by age. When the money runs out, the younger ones get nothing. There is never enough to go around. Rob is ten and works hard. He wants more money.

"I work hard so; can I have some money?"

"Why would you want more, boy? You're only ten years old."

"I work for it. I think I deserve more."

"What you deserve is this." The comment comes with a stinging smack on his ear. Rob has learned not to mess with mum.

In 1910, Rob has another move, his fifth. He remains in Montrose in Ramsey Street. This year things are different. He now has a new brother, Alexander, born in the spring. All previous Corsar children have been born in the summer or early autumn. The long cold dark winter nights in North East Scotland have a lot to answer. The cuddling of his mother and father during cold winter nights was for more than warmth. Sandy is still a carter working for a different company. Rob is looking forward to his birthday the following year. Aged fourteen, he will be allowed to leave school. What follows means he will leave much earlier.

NINE

The census of 1911 did not record the Corsar family anywhere in Scotland. They had not gone to England or migrated abroad.

Sandy was out of work and without a house. The family were camping out in a disused bothy in the Angus countryside.

It was dirty and rundown with a rusted tin roof. The dark grey granite walls had the odd weed growing out of cracks. There was muck everywhere. Along one wall were several broken wooden bunks. They required repair. There was an old open fireplace. It was black with soot and full of ashes of long-dead fires. The chimney was blocked and needed sweeping. Outside the house, there was a toilet that drained into a cesspit. The door was broken and needed mending. There was no running water inside the house. The only water came from an outside pump that they also had to fix.

It was the bleakest time for the family. They had few belongings, such as blankets. Old sacking would have to do for some beds. The bothy had been unused for some time. Sandy knew about the bothy from his time in this area in the past. All the family muck in to get the place reasonably clean to make the best of a very desperate situation.

The family dug a small patch of ground behind the bothy to make a small garden. The kids found and planted seed potatoes and turnips. There was hope that they wouldn't be here long enough to see them grow. They were wrong.

The seven who were old enough spent their time looking for any work. They would work for food rather than money. Raiding employer's bins and larders for any morsel was humiliating but necessary.

Winter was the hardest as there was little to do on farms. They took hard, back-breaking labour on the roads or railway if offered. They also poached rabbits, hares, pheasant, fish or the odd deer. They hunted anything that could be caught and cooked. Potatoes and turnips were filtched from farm stores. Even the odd hen's egg found its way into the pot. It could have had dire consequences if caught. Poaching was such a serious offence that it could result in a prison sentence if caught.

Rob learned a whole lot of new skills. He learned to set traps for rabbits and caught fish in the local rivers. He learned to sneak onto properties to steal food, sacking or old clothes. He spent much of his time covered in muck, unable to wash himself or his clothes. There was a burn running near the bothy. The family occasionally was used it for the odd washing session, even in the cold winter snow.

Rob did get some day work during the harsh winter. It was usually heavy work, but he could not be choosey. The cramped accommodation pushed people closer and made for more disagreement and arguments. Jean and Sandy put a swift end to any such altercations.

There was more day work on farms, especially during planting and the harvest. Crops needed reaping and sent to market. Daily pay rates were higher. Life in the bothy was a little less arduous. It was a blessing for Rob to move from this to his sixth house in 1912.

Sandy got a new job as a carter in Montrose in April of this year. It was Rob's seventh home and was in Market Street, Montrose. The winter nights of 1911 were cold in the bothy. Sandy and Jean did a lot of cuddling to keep warm. So, in keeping with the Corsar tradition, Rob got a new sister in the Summer of 1912. She was named Mabel. The family now numbered a football team.

Rob was working a dirty job in the Montrose docks. He was only fifteen, but he was tired of a life constantly on the move, from one dump to the next. The miserable winter in the bothy made him yearn for anything better. He also wanted to stay in one place. He got his wish. This house in Market Street would become his home for the next three years.

Starvation had gnawed at his bones and those of his family in that dreadful winter of 1911. His parents had done the best they could for him and his siblings in desperate circumstances. He felt duty-bound to do his bit towards getting the family back on their feet. That didn't mean to say he liked it. He did not. He got a labouring job at the docks.

At work, Rob listened to some of the older men talk. The conversations that catch his imagination are about the Black Watch. During breaks, he hears stories about the Summer Ball. They wax lyrical about it. He wants some of that. Entertainment, amusement, and enjoyment are activities that Rob could only partake in if they are almost free of cost.

"What's it like then, Archie?" Rob is inserting himself into a conversation.

"It's braw, lad. Lassies, beer and food in the drill hall. It's all decorated, and the band plays dance music."

"Sounds great."

"It is, lad. You want to go, do you?"

"Aye. I'd like that. What do I need to do to get in.?"

"Sixpence entrance fee for you as a civilian, but for us territorials, we get in for free."

"Are there lots o' lassies then."

"Aye. They are all dressed up in their finery, just itching to dance with a good-looking lad like me."

"What about a drink? Is it expensive?"

"It's cheaper than in the pubs. The punch is usually free, but it can be lethal."

"Do you mean that the punch can kill you?"

"No, lad. It can be quite strong if you're not used to whiskey."

"Sixpence to get in is expensive. I don't think I could afford that and any drink."

"That's the rate, lad. Unless you join up."

"Would they take me?

"I expect so. They took me."

With that, Rob hatched his plan. He would be going to the Ball.

TEN

After the Summer Ball, Rob wanted to meet Lizzie again. To do this, he needed to attend training sessions at the battalion drill hall in Wellington Street. It would enable him to meet her brother. He thought that routine army drilling would be worth the trouble. It was not until his second session that Rob saw Willie. He went over and spoke to him after the session had ended.

"Corporal Ross." Rob was standing to attention as was expected of a private when he spoke to a non-commissioned officer.

"Yes, Corsar."

"Corporal Ross. I'd like to meet your sister again...if that's OK?" Rob was stumbling over his words.

"Would you now?"

"Yes, please."

"You'd like to walk out with her, is that what you're asking?"

"Yes, if she'll have me."

"Well, I'll need to ask her what she thinks about that. Can't see why she might want to see you. Still, if she agrees, you'll need to put up with me as her chaperone. Our folks won't allow anything else."

"That's OK."

"I'll ask her and let you know next week."

"Thank you very much."

"Don't thank me yet. She may not want to meet you again. I think my sister has better taste." He said that with a smile on his face.

With that, he did a smart about turn and marched away with a wide grin on his face.

The following week Rob was eager to get to the barracks. Willie was there. By now, the army was on alert for war. The death in Sarajevo would affect the politics of Europe after all.

"Hello, Willie."

"Hello, Corsar."

"What about Lizzie? Will she see me again.?"

"The girls no right in the heid, but she will."

"When?" The eagerness in his voice was painful for Willie to hear. The lad's smitten, he thought to himself. I'll need to watch him with my sister.

"You can meet us both at the pavilion on the Trail Drive at seven on Tuesday evening."

"That's great."

"Now, get into line as we might be at war soon."

"Thanks, Willie." Rob turned and marched smartly back to his position in his company formation. The comment about the possibility of war had not fully sunk in.

There was a series of drills, without and with rifles. The men fell in and stood to attention. They received instructions on the correct method of basic military moves. The men then practised these moves.

"Pick up your rifles." The order came from the Sergeant.

The men walked over to the wall where there were many broom handles. These were their rifles.

"Maybe we get a brush head at some point so we can brush the enemy away." It was said by a man some way from Rob.

"Any more of your cheek Robson and you'll be sweeping up the hall after we're finished."

"Are we ever going to get any rifles, Sergeant?" asked a chastened Robson.

"When the army sees fit private, and not before. Now get fell in."

On Tuesday evening, Rob arrived early at the recently opened Traill Pavilion on Traill Drive. He hurried around the building to see if she was inside. The weather was not particularly good with clouds, a breeze and occasional drizzle. Rob was wearing his bonnet. It was partly to protect himself from the rain. It was considered appropriate for men to wear hats and women to wear bonnets inside the Pavilion.

The Traill brothers who had donated the money to build the new sea-front road and Pavilion had not made this stipulation. It was a local council decree.

Just about seven, Rob saw Lizzie and Willie walking along the road towards him. He was both excited and disappointed. A chaperone was not what Rob wanted. He had the warning, but he hoped that Willie would not attend. Unknown to him at this moment, it was not what Lizzie wanted either, but her parents insisted. Still, it was better than sitting at home with his parents and squabbling siblings.

"Hello, Lizzie. It's nice to see you again."

"Hello, Rob. I'm pleased to see you too."

"We'll sit inside out of the rain." Willie's voice was full of authority. "I'll sit over there away from you, but close enough to see if anything is going on. OK?"

"OK." Her voice had a clear note of disappointment in it.

"Do you want to go up the stairs to the upper deck?"

"No. It's wet, and I don't want my best hat to get damaged or blown away. If it is fine with you, we'll sit here for a while? I'm used to having Willie close. I hope it doesn't bother you too much."

"It's fine. I'm used to a house full of people watching everything I do. "

There was a short awkward silence when neither knew what to say next. Lizzie spoke first. She was awkward. She was only rarely able to go out with a young man. Like Rob, she was not sure how to act.

"You're in the territorials then, with Willie?" The question showed her discomfort. Of course, Rob was in the territorials. She had seen him in his uniform at the dance.

"Aye. I only joined a couple of weeks ago so that I could get into the summer ball for free."

"What is it you do for a job?" This was getting onto firmer ground.

"I work in the Docks on the South Esk. It's a dirty hard job. The pay is not so good, but it's a job. What about you? Do you work?"

"Yes. I work in a draper shop in the high street."

"Why does Willie have to come with us?"

"It's our parents. My mum is a strict Catholic. She's always going on about wicked men and young women. They insist on church every week for me and Willie and confession at least once a week. Mum goes three times a week to confession."

"We don't believe in any o' that."

"Oh. Don't say anything to Willie about that. He might report it back to my folks. If they knew you were not God-fearing, they might stop me from seeing you."

Rob's smile was as wide as the Montrose beach below when he heard this. "Does that mean you would like to see me again?"

"Yes. I think it would be nice if that's OK with you?"

He looked at her shining brunette hair bunched up under her hat, with her smooth complexion and stunning blue eyes. He wanted to kiss the smiling rosy lips but remembered Willie on the other side of the Pavilion. "That would be just grand."

They sat and talked for a further half an hour before Willie came over.

"Time to go, Lizzie. Say your goodbyes to Corsar."

"His name is Rob, Willie."

"Ok say your goodbyes to Rob, and let's be getting home."

Much as they both wanted to kiss on the lips, Lizzie gave Rob a quick peck on his cheek. "Thanks, Rob. I'll see you again soon."

"It was grand Lizzie. See you soon." Rob had no idea how to quantify his emotions at this point. He was happy beyond anything he had felt before. Even the drizzle on his face on his way home could do nothing to dampen his joy. The thought of war never crossed his smitten mind.

ELEVEN

At the end of July 1914, the Battalion was in a training camp in Monzie, some sixty miles from Montrose.

On the morning of Tuesday, 28 July, the Battalion were on parade. It seemed like an ordinary parade. The Major marched to the front and halted.

"Everyone present and correct, Sir," bellowed the Battalion Sergeant-Major.

"Stand the men at ease."

"Battalion, stand at ease. Stand easy."

"Men, our two special service sections are missing. They have been alerted for duty. This is a precautionary move. Yesterday, Austria declared war on Serbia, and we are readying ourselves in case a war breaks out in Europe. Training will become more intense. We need to be ready should the worst happen. Thank you, Sergeant-Major."

"Battalion. Attention. Officer on parade, dismiss." Everyone turned to the right, gave a smart salute and started to mill about.

No one, least of all the politicians, thought the war would come. Still, the Guardian newspaper report on the day after the assassination in June was beginning to look like it might be in error. There was more than a faint whiff of war in the air.

"Where's Serbia?" asked Jimmy Shand.

"Somewhere in Europe," said Ian Drury.

"What's a war between Austria and Serbia got to do with us?"

"No idea, Jimmy. We go where the army tells us. What for is none of our business."

"I heard someone say that the Germans might get involved." It was Hector McFarlane speaking.

"Where'd you hear that?" asked Jimmy.

"In the pub."

"What the fucks it got to do with Germany?"

"I don't know, but this man..."

"Right, you lot. Fall in by company," bellowed the Sergeant-Major. It appeared that the intense training was to start right that minute.

While training with the Battalion, Rob got paid one shilling per day. It was slightly less than he earned in the docks, but he got three meals a day thrown in at the camp. He did not complain.

Treaty arrangements of European countries was a mystery to most. Thoughts of a war involving Britain were a long way from the minds of ordinary people. That was about to change. The dominos were about to fall. Two decades of political manoeuvring in Europe were about to bear rotten fruit. His politics revolved around the newly formed Labour party and the Trades Union movement. The rights of rural workers in Scotland were arguments that he had heard from birth. The exception was Britain's involvement in India.

Sandy was opposed to British rule there and said so frequently.

The death of the Archduke on 28 June incensed the Austrians. They wanted to punish Serbia for their treachery. They attempted to rally support from their ally, Germany. Big Austria giving little Serbia a bit of a hiding was small beer by international standards. Most of the British public was in the dark about events in Europe. Still, talk of war was not uncommon in some homes and pubs.

Rob, and the men of the Black Watch territorials, were sent on exercise again. One half of the Battalion went to Broughty Ferry. Rob was in the other half of the Battalion that went to Dundee. Both groups toiled away doing defensive work on their billets. Maybe they thought the English were about to invade Scotland again.

"If there is a war in Europe and an invasion force gets this far north, then we're all in the shite," said Donald Muir as he and Rob were digging ditches.

"If they get here, then I suppose we head for the highlands and hide in the hills," said Rob.

"I lived in the countryside for a while. It's not that bad."

"Me too, and I didn't like it much."

"Mind you, who'd want to invade Dundee. They can have it without a fight for me."

"Aye, and me as well. You can smell that jute a long way away."

During the month, Rob spent much of his time at work in the port and docks of Montrose. He was still obliged to train as a soldier. Training for territorials was voluntary. Now that a war might be coming, it was impressed on the men that they might need as much practice as they could get. Telling the men that their life might depend on it was a good motivator.

Training consisted of a lot of marching, running and hand to hand combat. Bayonet practice was farcical. There were no rifles in the Battalion, so broom handles had to suffice. They charged at a sack of straw with a broom handle that did not even have a bayonet attached.

"I don't mind the marching, running and hand to hand stuff," said Rob to his pal Davy Dewar. "Throwing yourself on that bloody barbed wire so you and others can jump on my pack is shite."

"Aye. It's bloody sore. I thought we were supposed to shoot the enemy in a war. We've had no chance to do that yet. Fucking fat lot of use we'd be in a fight. Mind you, wi all those barbed wire cuts we could drown them in our blood."

"It wid be hard for us to shoot anybody wi no bloody rifles or ammo."

"Come on, Rob, it's time ti kill a few more stooks wi our broom handles."

Rob continued to work and train. He had a few chances to meet Lizzie again, but they were still in the company of Willie. Rob and Lizzie both longed for some private time, but her parents insisted on an escort. The catholic religious strictures of the Ross family were getting on Rob's nerves. He never mentioned his atheist views to Lizzie, nor were his feelings about her parent's views. Lizzie did not need words to know she could hear and see it when the two met. Lizzie was working on her brother, trying to get him to come out with her as agreed, but go off on his own for a time.

In that year, Rob and the citizens of Montrose saw the aircraft of the Royal Flying Corps take off. They headed along the coast towards their eventual destination at Amiens in France. The planes used the coastal route to guide themselves south. They had no instruments for navigation, so they used the coast as their guide. Their destination was Farnborough in Hampshire, some six hundred miles away.

Winston Churchill, First Lord of the Admiralty, chose Montrose as the airbase. It occupied a strategic position between the Royal Naval bases at Rosyth, Cromarty and Scapa Flow. The job of the squadron was to protect the fleet. The comparison between the metal dreadnoughts bristling with guns and the tiny wood and wire aircraft could not have been starker. It was like asking a squadron of mayfly to protect a shoal of mighty crocodiles.

As the planes left Montrose to follow the coast, the pilots waved to the people below, who waved back. Many looking up wondered why anyone would want to sit in such a flimsy contraption.

"If I hit it with this stone," said one young boy holding a large pebble, "I'm sure I could knock it out of the sky."

"Why'd you want to do that?" asked his friend.

"Just to see if I could."

"Well, you can't. They're too far away now."

On Saturday 1 August, Rob and Lizzie managed to get to the film showing in the Town Hall. It was a silent film drama called Shop Girls with piano accompaniment. Willie waited for them in the nearby pub. Lizzie had managed to get Willie to consent to let her and Rob meet without him being present.

When she entered the hall, Lizzie checked to see if anyone knew her and her family. The hall was sparsely populated so, she could scan everyone. She was relieved to see no one she knew.

Sitting in the cinema, Lizzie put her arm through Robs. Her closeness, and smell of her perfume, made Rob forget the poor film. Sitting in the dark Rob, managed to put his arm around her shoulders. He even managed a full lip kiss in the darkness. Lizzie had instigated the kiss, but not before she checked again that none of the other patrons was watching her and Rob. Going out with a man was bad enough, but seen kissing in a public place would have meant curtains for her freedom to meet Rob. Rob's decision to join the army to get to the summer dance seemed to have paid handsome dividends, at least for now.

While Rob and Lizzie were canoodling in the cinema, unknown to them, Germany declared war on Russia. It was more serious, but still some way from Britain and war.

The Daily Mirror's headline on the German declaration of war was:

' The sword is forced into our hand said the Kaiser, as he makes war on Russia'.

The papers give the impression that this is a problem in mainland Europe and nothing of great concern to Britain.

On Monday, 3 August 1914, Rob went back to work in the docks. In faraway Europe, the pot was coming to the boil.

The following day the pot boils over. Rob hears on the radio that Britain has declared war on Germany. The reason, he learns, is that Germany has invaded Belgium and Britain has a treaty to defend Belgium.

"Why do we have to defend Belgium?" asked Rob to the group who were listening to the radio with him.

"It says we have a treaty to help Belgium if they're attacked," said Peter Hamilton.

"Why would we sign that? What have they done to help us?"

"Doesn't say, but we're at war."

"Fuck. My dad was right."

"What's that, Rob?" asked Steve Maitland.

"Nothing Steve. Just something my dad said a couple of months back."

The newspaper headlines are not what many in Britain want to see. It's not what Rob, Lizzie or Jimmy wanted. On the other hand, Rob remembered that he had given his oath and was training to fight, even if only with broom handles.

There seemed to be an appetite for a fight among the public. The last major war for British troops was the Boer war that ended in 1902 with a comprehensive British victory.

"We can do the same to the Germans as we did to the Boers," was a general feeling.

Each day Rob read the newspapers, and all he could see was the conflict getting bigger as more and more countries joined in. Declarations of war are now so many that they are like confetti.

In September, the company moved to Dundee. They carried out defensive works on their billets, followed by increased training. By late September

1914, there had been extensive training, but none of it with rifles. Rob and his comrades became dab hands at killing sacks of straw with broom handles, marching and running around with packs. Perhaps an enemy would die laughing at their antics.

On 26 September, Rob was both relieved and sad. He and 300 others from the Battalion transferred to a camp near Forfar. He was allocated to a reserve group of men. Some of whom could not shoot straight. Some were medically unfit for foreign service. Others, like Rob, were under eighteen and a half years of age and too young to go to war overseas.

Rob put on a brave face. "I can fight like the next man. I'm not afraid." Secretly he was partly pleased. Men died in wars. He did not want to die. By not going when the rest of his unit left, he could stay at home and meet Lizzie. Willie would have to go with the rest of the Battalion. Every cloud has a silver lining, he thought.

On Friday, 29 October, Rob was at Broughty Ferry Station helping those called for duty to pack their gear, ready for the train journey south. Some families had managed to get to the station to say goodbye.

Rob saw Willie Ross lugging bags and crates onto the train. He went to help.

"I'll give you a hand, Willie."

Willie looked around and saw Rob. "Thanks, Rob. Pick up those bags and load them onto the baggage car." He indicated a pile of bags.

"Family not here then, Willie."

"No. My folks won't come, and Lizzie could not get time off work."

"Sorry."

"Not your fault. Still, no chance to see Lizzie today?"

"No."

Orders were bellowed along the platform by the Sergeant Major. "Battalion. On the train. Move."

Willie moved to board the train. "Willie."

Willie turned to see Rob holding out his right hand. "Good luck... Willie."

Willie took Rob's hand. "Thanks, lad. Look after Lizzie for me."

"I will. They say it'll be over by Christmas. See you then for a drink?"

"Aye. We'll be back for the New Year. You can buy me a dram then to celebrate."

Willie and several hundred other men boarded the train. Doors closed with a crash, and windows let down. Men leaned out and waved to their comrades and families. A whistle blew, and in a cloud of smoke and a screech of metal wheels on metal rails, the train chugged off south towards Southampton.

Rob watched as the train puffed south towards the Tay Bridge. As it vanished out of sight, an order was shouted to fall in on the other platform to head back to Dundee. Rob was conflicted between doing his duty with his comrades and staying at home close to Lizzie.

TWELVE

On 5 August, DORA came into the picture and complicated matters between Rob and Lizzie. Far from being a woman that took Rob's eye, DORA was the Defence Of the Realm Act. It was an act of parliament.

It came between Rob and Lizzie, as well as many others. The Act gave parliament sweeping powers to do almost anything it wanted in a time of war. Rob's first encounter with the Act was at work in the docks. Employees got the news that the government had taken control of the Docks.

"It's not just us," said the owner to the assembled staff. "They've taken over all docks, factories and land. The government will tell us what to produce, and we will do it. We have no choice."

"What will that mean for us workers?" shouted Rob.

"I'm sorry to say that the working day will be longer. They want to increase the amount of equipment needed for the war, and they need it quickly. You're all going to have to work extra hours."

"Will we get extra money?"

"No. The government want to increase production but not expense. This war will cost a lot of money."

"That's not fair," shouted another man. "We should go on strike."

"The Act covers strikes. It makes them illegal, and you would be tried by a military court, not a civilian one. Different rules apply there. You might face a firing squad."

The noise of discontent rose markedly among the crowd of men. There was a lot of shouting, swearing and cursing with the occasional waving of fists. The men were not happy, but they knew in themselves that there was nothing that they could do.

"Less time to get a drink," muttered a man near Rob.

"It's worse than that," said Reg Gillman, the foreman. "They've cut the hours pubs can open. Yon Lloyd George is tea total, and he wants the rest of us the same."

"I don't know about you," said Rob to John Ramage, "but I don't have much money left at the end of the week to afford drink and get drunk. I wouldn't dare go home drunk. My dad's tea total. He'd make me sleep in the garden."

"He wouldn't do that, would he?"

"My brother Will came home drunk one night, and he got refused entry to the house. I think that's why he joined the merchant navy, to get away."

"He's not up at Scapa Flow on the big battleships then?"

"No, he's on cargo boats travelling across the Atlantic."

"When will he be back?"

"I don't think he's coming back. He left a note for us to say he might not come home for a long time. He's talked about America. He liked what he saw there. I think he might like to stay there, and anyway, they're not in this war."

"Well, good luck to him if that's what he wants."

At the next training meeting, things got worse. They got the news that training would increase. As a territorial, he did not have to attend all the training sessions. Nevertheless, he felt that he should.

"If I have to go to war, Lizzie, I want to be as ready as I can be. It's the best way to stay safe."

"Aye, love, I understand, but it might mean that we won't see each other as often."

"That's true, but I signed up Lizzie, and so did Jimmy. I need to be ready if I have to go."

"It scares me to think that you might have to go and fight. We've not had long together so far, and I don't want you charging off to fight. You never know what might happen."

"I know, love. The talk is that it will all be over by Christmas, so I might not have to go."

"I do hope so for you and Jimmy."

At the next training camp, they received a rifle. Now he was a proper soldier. Charging at a sack of straw yelling with a gun and bayonet in hand was soldering. It was practice for war, or so they thought. Volunteers were joining the battalion eager to get to the war. As a territorial, they had to choose to go abroad. There was no requirement yet for forced foreign service for territorial soldiers. Rob saw men come and go, but he was still underage for service outside the UK.

Rob had a little experience of guns on the farms, but he had never actually fired one. The first session on the rifle range was a painful experience for him. He went through the drill to load the magazine. He loaded it into the gun and put the safety catch on. Now, he is ready to shoot.

"Take your places opposite your target," bellowed the sergeant. "Get yourselves in the correct firing position as instructed. Release the safety catch. Hold the stock hard against your shoulder. Take careful aim and only fire when I give the order."

The sergeant walked along the firing line, inspecting the position and safety catches. He moved to the rear and bellowed again.

"Enemy to the front, five rounds, fire." Five rounds were all the bullets that the magazine held. The firing line erupted in noise.

Rob's first shot told him that he should have paid closer attention to the sergeant's instructions. The kick from the rifle smashed against his shoulder. It was much stronger than he had imagined. Still, he let off all five rounds. His accuracy came in for some verbal abuse by the sergeant.

"You're not going to frighten the enemy then, Corsar. The safest place for them is to stand in front of you. They'll never get shot."

After this first experience on the firing range, Rob met Lizzie the following day at the Traill Pavilion. She put her arms around him to hug him.

"Aaah." Squawked Rob in pain.

"What's up?"

"We got a chance ti shoot wi our rifles yesterday. I didn't hold mine hard enough against my shoulder, and the kick gave me a right, sore bruise."

"You're not a rough, tough soldier yet then," laughed Lizzie. "I'll take care of my brave wee man," she mocked, giving him a little hug.

"And I'll put you over my knee if I hear any more of your cheek."

"Now there's a sight that would make the other folks in the Pavilion tut or laugh."

"Aye. Best not then."

"Let's walk along Traill Drive. I'll walk on your left so as not to be accused of injuring one of our brave fighting men."

"Talking of brave fighting men, have you heard from Willie yet?"

"We had a letter the other day. He's fine but not much else in it. The Censor makes sure he gives nothing away. I hope he's OK."

The pair continued to walk along the Drive arm in arm in silent contemplation. The mention of Willie tainted the intimacy between the two.

Notices on the town hall notice board listed men killed or missing in action. Rumours began to surface about the conditions on the front. The reality of war was starting to sink in.

Rob walked Lizzie back towards her house. He left her a short distance from the building at Lizzie's request.

"I told my folks I was out with some friends tonight."

"Oh. Why's that then?"

"Without Willie around to keep an eye on me, they don't want me walking out with a man they don't know."

"That's harsh. You're old enough to make your own choices. Maybe you should introduce me to them."

"I am old enough, but it's their house, their rules. With all that's going on in the war, it's not a good time to introduce a new complication."

"So, I'm a complication, am I?"

"You know fine well what I mean. We're just getting to know each other, and it's too soon. I know my folks. They'll kick up a fuss and stop me seeing you."

"Is that a bad thing then? Do you want to keep seeing me?"

"Yes. I like you fine enough, Rob, but I need to be sure when I broach the subject with my folks."

"That's OK then. I'm a fine lad, so I don't know why your folks wouldn't like me. Still, there're your folks, and you'll know them best."

"You're my lad Robert Corsar, and you are a fine one at that. I need to go carefully with my folks.

Lizzie checked the street they were in to see if anyone was around who could see her and tell her parents. The coast clear she faced Rob.

"A quick kiss before I have to go in then."

"OK." Rob took Lizzie in his arms and felt hers circle him as they kissed. The kiss lasted a few seconds and left Rob wanting more.

Lizzie stepped back quickly.

"Someone is coming. Quick, be on your way."

As he reversed, he said, "I'll leave a note in the usual place when I'm free."

"Aye. Do that."

Lizzie hurried away into her street, worried that she and Rob might have been seen.

THIRTEEN

The war was not over by Christmas as widely hoped. At training sessions, word got around about the number of men from the Battalion being wounded and killed. It was not a lot so far, but it was unsettling to Rob and his pals.

"I know that you are finding out from friends and family in the Battalion about our casualties in France. It is sad, but we are at war." Said the major at one of the regular sessions in the battalion drill hall. "This is not information the War Department wants spreading. Keep the information to yourselves. The Defence of the Realm Act gives us, and the police, powers to stop people from spreading information prejudicial to morale. If caught, you will go before a military court. It will deal harshly with you. It's all I have to say on this matter. On with the training exercises for tonight, Sergeant."

"Right, you lot. Get fell in by company order."

The festivities for Christmas 1914 for Rob and Lizzie were quiet. Lizzie had left her job in the high street drapers shop and joined the Land Army. Fabric for civilian clothing was becoming harder to get, and the shop struggled to pay her. She got work on a farm to the south, just outside of the town. Like Rob in the docks, she worked long hours outside in the cold. She was also worried about her brother, who was at the front.

While her wages were slightly higher than in the shop, she got less money than men doing farm work. It seemed paradoxical to Rob that he had left the land some years earlier, only to be replaced by his girlfriend.

On Christmas Eve, the two met at the Ship hotel bar.

"Lizzie. You look tired. Is it the work?"

"It is. I never realised what you and your family went through working on the land."

"Do you have to go to church tonight?"

"Yes. I need to be home later to get ready for midnight mass."

"How long have we got?"

"About two hours so, best make use of the time."

"Let's have a quick drink and then find somewhere to be alone together."

The couple had their drink and warmed up a bit before they walked into the evening to find a quiet spot. They walked hand in hand to the railway station. No trains were due, so the place was empty. It gave them some shelter from the wind and benches to sit on.

Sitting on a station bench, the two cuddled. Rob kissed Lizzie, and she responded.

"I miss you, Rob. We don't get enough time to be together."

"I know, love. We're both in jobs controlled by the War Department, and I have my training."

"I'm worried. Will you be going to the front?"

"Not for the time being. I'm underage."

"When will you reach the right age?"

"In about a year. I need to be eighteen and a half before they can send me."

"I hear stories of young men lying about their age to go now. You won't do that, will you?"

"I can't now. When I signed on, I gave my correct date of birth. It's on my records so they won't send me before my time. Perhaps it'll be over before I have to go. Now that I've met you, I would not lie about my age to go."

"I hope so. We don't hear from Jimmy all that often. It upsets me, and my mum. Even dad seems to worry. Not something I've seen him do before."

"Lots of families are worried, lass. Mine are worried about my brother Will. My dad got a letter saying that he had left his boat in New York and never returned."

"Tell me he didn't die."

"Not that we heard. He told me he might want to live in America. I'm guessing that's what he's done. He'll have jumped ship and become illegal in America."

"What'll happen to him?"

"Don't know, love. He can look after himself. If the police catch him, he might end up in prison. He might even be sent back. If they do that, my dad says he'll spend time in prison here for jumping ship."

"What'll he do in America?"

"Will's a big lad, he can take care of himself. He'll find something to do for money."

A look at the station clock told Lizzie she would have to go soon. She pulled Rob closer. There followed several minutes of kissing and cuddling in the cold and dark.

"I'll need to get back."

"I'll walk you." The two started towards her house. Lizzie stopped Rob just before they turned into her street.

"I'll need to go in alone. Kiss me here."

"If we are going to be steady, we'll need to meet each other's families sometime."

"We will love, but not tonight. Soon"

"Fine, lass."

Rob stood on the corner and watched Lizzie to her door. He made sure that he could not be seen if her mother or father looked out.

FOURTEEN

Rob and Lizzie met whenever they could. They left secret messages for each other in a spot near Lizzie's house. They also contrived to meet with the help of Lizzie's workmates on the farm. She did spend some time with them. More often than not, they were her cover for meeting Rob. The pair tried to stay away from places that they could be seen together. Occasionally they contrived a chance meeting if there might be people who could report back to Lizzie's mother.

Lizzie's mum was suspicious of her, but she had a much more independent mind now. Some of this newfound independence was down to the socialist views of Rob. Most were down to the influence of her fellow women farmworkers. Some of them may have had a rustic crudeness in their attitude to men and women, but the general tone of their conversation was one of enjoying life while they were young and free.

"What about you, Rose? What do you think?" asked Lizzie.

"With all the young men at the front, there's not much chance of a bunk up."

"Rose Mitchell, you're a trollop," laughed Lizzie.

"No chance of that yet. Still, when the men get back, they'll be as anxious as me."

"That'll be a fine day Rose," said Maggie. "All us young ones will have a rare old time."

"You're a pair of trollops," said Irene. "Only Lizzie and I will be pure for our husbands."

"Pure terrified of your wedding night if you ask me," said Rose. "We've all seen the animals do it in the fields. It's nothing special. I expect the men at the front might be having a good time with some of them, local lassies."

"I hope so," said Irene. "I'd hate to think that they had not done it before they got killed."

Lizzie burst into tears.

"I'm sorry, Lizzie. I'm such an inconsiderate cow. I'd forgotten about your brother."

Lizzie wiped away her tears and walked away from the group.

In the spring of 1915, Rob and Lizzie met at a picture show. It was a much better film than the previous one. The Tramp, starring Charlie Chaplin, was a much more enjoyable film.

During the film, there was much laughter in the audience. Rob and Lizzie managed some intimate contact, some of it was intentional, and some were the result of their laughter. They were in a much better mood.

After the film, they walked and talked about how much they had enjoyed the film together.

"It was a lovely picture. It's a while since I had such a good laugh," said Lizzie.

"Aye lass. It was good. That Chaplin Fella is good. He'll go far."

"Will we go far, Rob?"

"Sorry, lass. What'd you mean?"

"What about us, Rob? We've been walking out now for half a year. You're likely to be sent to the war soon after your eighteenth birthday. What do we do then? I might love you."

"Oh. That makes me fair happy, lass. I feel very much the same for you."

They had walked to the benches on Traille Drive overlooking the dark sea beyond. They sat down and, Rob put his arm around Lizzie's shoulder. He pulled her to him, and they exchanged a long passionate kiss.

"I'm not quite eighteen yet. You're only a year older than me. As you say, I might go to war soon. What do you think we should do about it?"

Lizzie turned to look Rob directly in the eye. She looked serious.

"Do you think we might marry someday?"

Rob's eyes shot wide. He blinked several times before he answered.

"I never really thought about it. What do you think?"

There was a tear in Lizzie's eye.

"It's not what I think Rob, it's what you want. Do you want to spend your life with me as your wife?"

Rob was still recovering from the mild shock of this turn of events. He had not thought about how his relationship with Lizzie might develop. He was always pleased to see her and missed her when they were apart, but marriage had not crossed his mind. Now that she had raised the subject, he thought it might be what he wanted.

"I'm sorry that I made you cry, Lizzie, but I had not thought much about it till now. I think it's a grand idea. Perhaps we should get married."

"In that case, I supposed you'd need to ask me first. My dad would want you to ask him for my hand in marriage. He's like that."

"Oh. I never thought about that either. In my family, we just expected couples to make up their mind and get on with it."

"That's not very romantic...is it?"

"I suppose not. We're not a very romantic family. I've never seen my dad kiss my mum, even on her birthday or New Year."

"That's sad. You're not like the rest. You're sweet to me."

"I never gave it much thought. I just did what I thought was right at the time."

"Well, I liked it."

"That's nice."

"You should meet my folks at least. You never know, that might put you off me forever. Are you ready for that since you know what they're like?"

"I'm a soldier. The army expects us to front up the enemy. How would you feel about meeting my folks?"

"I've met a couple of your sisters, and they seem fine. I'm sure your parents are no bother."

"My folks are no the most hospitable of people."

"I'll need to broach the subject of a boyfriend first. I think they've guessed I have one, but I've not said. Shall we start there?"

"Sounds fine to me. Both are chapel going folk. Will they want to question my religion?"

"I don't know, but I expect they will, at some point."

"Ah well, we'll have to wait and see. I'm getting close to my birthday now. I might be off to war soon after that."

"I know. Don't let's talk about that. I don't want you to go, but you'll have no choice."

"Still, if I hadn't joined up to go to the summer ball last year, I wouldn't have met you. I can't un-enlist now. The King might need me." He said with a smile and a chuckle.

"I need you more than him. He's got lots of men to choose from now." Lizzie pulled Rob close to her and kissed him.

As they walked by the bowling green, the pair made their way to the benches nearby and sat down. The twilight changed the colours of the day and changed them to look like a black and white film.

They sat for a while, kissing and cuddling, arms entwined. As they broke a kiss, his right hand slid across her chest. He stopped it as it cupped Lizzies left breast. Lizzie did not have big breasts and, what Rob felt was mostly her coat covering her breasts. He had not planned this. It's not that it had never considered touching Lizzie's breasts. He had. He had no idea how to go about it, especially with Lizzie's strict catholic upbringing. He thought that if he tried, she might slap him, shout at him or even worse, never see him again. Hand on breast, he waited for her response.

She did not slap him or shout. She looked at Rob with love in her eyes. He was aroused, but he was also embarrassed. He had touched Lizzie's private parts in a very public place. Luckily there were no people close enough to see. Not knowing what to do, Rob quickly pulled his hand away.

"I'm sorry, Lizzie. I didn't mean to. . . do what I did. You're not too angry or upset, are you?"

"No love. I was a little surprised but not angry."

"I'm awful sorry. I don't know what came over me."

"How did it feel?"

"It was nice and soft. What about you?"

"After the surprise, I thought it was quite nice."

"I've never done anything like that before."

"Nor have I."

"Will you want to stop seeing me?"

"Don't be silly. I want to keep seeing you. Touching my breast like that made me feel very warm and a little breathless. How did you feel?"

"I felt embarrassed that I had done that to you, but I also felt excited."

"We should do it again but let's find a more private place where we are unlikely to be seen. Would you like that?" This comment made Rob very happy.

"I would. I'm awful glad that you're not angry."

"I'm not. I'm quite happy."

"I'm not sure what to do when I touch your breasts. It was the first time for me. Jean taught me how to hold a woman when we dance, but this is a very different kind of dance. Not something a sister should teach her brother."

"It was a first time for me too. When we do it again, I expect we'll have to learn together. Will, you want me to touch you. . . you know?" She nodded her head to his groin as she spoke.

"Yes. If that's OK by you."

"I think so. Now kiss me before we have to go."

All too soon, they two rose and headed for Lizzie's home.

"Take me to my door tonight."

"OK."

"It's time my folks found out that I'm old enough to have a boyfriend without having to have someone spying on me."

The gas mantle lights in the Ross house were on when they arrived. The curtain was open. Lizzie's mum observed from the window.

At the door, Lizzie kissed Rob on the cheek. Suddenly, the door swung open. Mrs Ross stood there with a face like thunder.

"You, girl, in," she ordered. Rob had heard less autocratic orders on the battalion parade ground.

"You." She pointed at Rob with a bony finger. "Away you go from my, girl. I'll not have your sort anywhere near her."

She pulled Lizzie into the house. Lizzie looked back with her face showing utter dejection. The door slammed shut, and Rob shuffled despondently off towards his own home.

Inside, Lizzie's mother spun her across the room, and the shouting started.

"What do you think you're doing with the likes of him? You'll not be seeing him again, my girl."

"I'll see who I like, mother, and you can't stop me."

"We'll see about that girl."

" I'm a grown woman, and I'll make my own friends."

"Get up to your bed and don't cheek me, girl, or you'll be out on your ear."

Lizzie looked at her dad, who motioned her up the stairs with a flick of his head. After Lizzie had disappeared, he spoke.

"That was a bit harsh, Mary. She is growing up, and we'll need to let her go at some point."

"Maybe so, George, but not to the likes of him."

"Do you know him then?"

"No, but I know his sort, and I'll not have Lizzie mixing with the likes of him."

"It's a bit harsh to convict a man without a trial, Mary. Lizzie likes him, and we brought her up the best we could. Maybe he has something we can't see. I don't think she would take up with just anybody."

"I still don't think he's the right sort of man for our Lizzie."

"Not our choice, dear. Lizzie's old enough to make her own decisions. I'm off to bed now. Are you coming up?"

"I'll be up in a minute when I've finished putting out the breakfast things."

George Ross just looked at his wife and climbed the stairs to their bedroom. He was wondering how to deal with this problem. Perhaps he would have a better idea after a night's sleep.

On his way home, he was still surprised by her suggestion. He wondered how her strict catholic upbringing could allow her to suggest it. She said that the girls on the farm had talked about sex while they worked together. He wondered if that had influenced her. Whatever had happened, he was pleased that they might do it again. He also remembered that she was the one who had kissed him on the night of the Summer Ball. She was also the one who suggested he return her kiss that night.

She had not flinched when he had touched her breast. He half expected a slap on the face or at least harsh words, but none came. Her parents were strict Catholics and insisted on a chaperone when she was out. How could someone from a background like that let a man touch her intimately? He did not know what to make of the situation.

If they were going to do it again, he was also worried that he would make a mess of it because of his lack of experience.

FIFTEEN

Working long hours on manual jobs gave Rob little time to think about Lizzie. On the battalion firing range with a rifle in hand, Rob could only see the dark scowling face of Mrs Ross in the centre of his target. His hatred of the woman gave him a steely determination when shooting. It did not take him long to become a good shot. He never considered how his newfound expertise might help him in the years to come. He just wanted that witch gone.

About a month after the doorstep incident, Rob came home late one evening. A woman he recognised was walking towards him. She was Rose Mitchell, who lived in his street.

"Hello, Rob."

"Hello, Rose. How are you?"

"I'm fine, Rob."

As he was about to walk on, Rose spoke again.

"I have a message from Lizzie for you."

"Lizzie? How do you know her?"

"We work together on the farm up the road."

"How is she?"

"She's miserable, just like you seem to be."

"Aye, well, her mother saw to that."

"She told me what happened."

"Cantankerous old witch."

"She's not the most hospitable person. I've been to the house a couple of times. Full of crucifixes, pictures of saints and the like. She's a bit of an ogre and keeps a strong grip on Lizzie. Thinks all men are out to do no good."

"She certainly thinks I'm up to no good."

"I don't know how she felt about her son, Willie. He was not as righteous as she might have thought. Still, he's at the front now, so not much fun for him there."

"No. I've heard it's a bit grim, but not much useful news gets past the censors."

"I'll need to go, Rob, but Lizzie gave me a message for you. Can you get away on Saturday afternoon and meet her at the Traille Pavilion?"

"I should be able to manage that. Did she say what time?"

"No time but late afternoon or early evening. She'll get away from work early and meet you there."

"Grand. Tell her I'll wait."

"I'll do that tomorrow."

"Thanks, Rose."

"No trouble Rob. Goodnight."

"Goodnight, Rose, and thanks again."

Rob moved off with a spring in his step and a smile on his face.

SIXTEEN

Rob's back-breaking work seemed a little lighter the rest of the week. He was eager to see Lizzie again. He needed to find out what had happened that night. Was what her mother said going to stop her walking out with him. Maybe this meeting would tell him whether she wanted to keep seeing him. On the other hand, her mum was the ruler in that house, so she might dictate what Lizzie could and could not do.

As the day drew closer, Rob started to worry. What if the old witch had told her to end it all? Perhaps that was the reason for the meeting. No. She would not have asked Rosie to pass a message on if that was the case. He convinced himself that she wanted to see him, despite her mother. For the whole of the Saturday, Rob flipped between joy and fear. He had not got the idea that this might be the end of their relationship totally out of his mind.

It was late in the afternoon when he finished his shift. He quickly washed himself down in the sink in the dock restrooms. It would take him a while to get home, wash and change before his meeting. He was worried because there was no time given for the meeting. What if she turned up, waited and then left because he was late. Best get there quickly, roughly cleaned than not get there on time.

The sun was shining but was low in the sky behind the town. There were a few clouds on this decent late spring evening. There would be a fine sunset tonight, thought Rob, as he headed to Traille Drive across the bridge over the River South Esk. He could see the setting sun reflected in the waters of the Montrose basin on his left. Rob hurried along Hill Street and on towards the seafront. When he arrived at the Pavilion, he was sweating from his exertions. She was nowhere around. He wondered if he had come too late. He sat for a short time on the grass before he saw her hurrying towards him. His heart pumped, and his mood rose.

She was with another person. As she got closer, he could see that it was Rose. He became more worried. Had she brought Rose along to give her moral support as she broke up with him?

The two women stopped in front of Rob.

"Hello, Rob," said Lizzie quietly. She seemed nervous.

"Hello, Lizzie, Rose."

Rose just nodded towards him. There was an awkward silence for a few seconds. No one seemed to know what to say.

"Well, get on with it, Lizzie," said Rose. "You came to talk, so talk."

"Aye. Sorry." There was another short pause that heightened Rob's anxiety. "Can you give us a minute Rose?"

"I'll sit over by the Pavilion while you talk. Mind and get a move on, there's not much time."

"Do you two have somewhere else to go?" Asked a somewhat dejected Rob.

"No. It's just that I lied to my mum about what time I'd finish work today. I got away a bit early so we could meet."

"Let's stroll a bit while you tell me what it is you need to tell me."

Rob was not sure whether he could take Lizzie's arm. She might have bad news and turn away. The sun was setting over the town on their right. There were a few spots of rain from the dark clouds coming in over the North Sea. It was not cold, but Rob was shivering from anticipation.

"I'm sorry about my mum and what she said to you the last time."

"You don't have to apologise for your mum. Unless what she said is what you feel, and that's what you want to say to me."

"No. No, it's not. I was angry because that's not what I want."

"What do you want then?"

"I still want to see you, Rob. I just hoped that my mum hasn't put you off me."

"I don't care about your mum, Lizzie. It's you I care for, not her."

"I'm awful glad you said that. If you want, we can continue to see each other?"

"I'd like that. What will your mum say to that?"

"She won't like it. I'm going to have it out with her tonight."

"What are you going to do?"

"While I live in her house, I'll have to abide by her rules indoors. Outside the house, she needs to know that I'll make my own rules. I'll have my own friends and not the ones she thinks are suitable."

"That's a bit strong. Are you up to how your mother might react? You said she was a strong Catholic. Will she accept what you are saying? Perhaps she'll throw you out for going up against her."

"She said that the last night you took me home. She was angry and tried to get me down to the chapel to talk to the priest, but I didn't go."

"What if she does throw you out? Will your dad agree?"

"My dad doesn't say much. He seems to go along with whatever my mum says. Anyway, Rose says they have a spare room that I can use. Her folks have said OK. I don't want to leave my home, but I will if it comes to it."

"That's a bit radical for you, Lizzie. I've not heard you like this before."

"It's working with Rose, Maggie and Irene on the farm that's done it."

"How so?"

"Things are changing for us women, Rob. Rose and Irene have attended the women's movement meetings. Women are just as good as men."

"You'll get no argument from me. I've watched my mum and older sisters working and working at men's jobs."

"Things are going to have to change after this war. We, women, are doing the men's work. I've heard that women work in factories and engineering in Dundee. We're even making shells for the guns. That's dangerous work. We'll need to have a say in things after this war. We won't stand for being treated this way anymore."

"That's a bit radical for you, Lizzie. Have my family's attitudes rubbed off on you?'

"I think it's working with Rose and the others that have done it. They've attended women's meetings and come back with ideas. I'd never thought about it before I met them and you. They're right things need to change for us women. After this war is over, we women won't stand for being ignored. We want fair treatment."

"Me and my family would agree, as you know. My dad's agitating for votes for women. I've seen how hard women work in the docks. They're doing their bit, and it should be recognised. What about your mum? What will she think?"

"She'll listen to my dad and the priest. I expect she'll not like it, but she'll have to get used to it because I think it's right, and I'll not change."

Lizzie's voice had risen as she spoke. She was standing on a metaphorical soapbox. Her face was glowing.

"Your mum's one thing, what about your dad? He works for the council. Might he put his foot down?"

"He'll be fine. It's my mum that rules the house. You told me about your folks before Rob. It's time for action in my house. I'm sure some of my mum's anger is to do with Willie being at the front. She's worried, as are my dad and me. We're just hoping he's safe."

"Any news from him?"

"The usual stuff that the censors allow. Nothing about what it's like out there. He says he is fine, so that's good."

"Lizzie, we haven't much time," shouted Rose from behind the couple.

"Coming, Rose."

"What's the rush?"

"I need to get back when I said I would. Show that I keep my word. Also, If I get thrown out, I'll need time to get to Rose's house. We'll meet again, next Sunday night if you're free. That's the first time I'm going to have off."

"OK. Sunday at say six pm. Is that OK with you?"

"Aye. Where shall we meet?"

"How about the town hall steps? That OK for you?"

"That'll do fine. I'll be off now to face my mum. Wish me luck."

"Good luck, love. Be strong." Rob kissed Lizzie.

"Come on then, Rose. Let's be off to meet my fate. Bye Rob."

"Bye, love. Bye Rose, and thank you."

"No, bother Rob."

The two women hurried down the road. Rob watched them until they disappeared. He secretly harboured a desire to go and sit outside the Ross house to see what happened.

"No. If the witch sees me, it'll be all the worse for Lizzie." He strode off home.

SEVENTEEN

Lizzie said goodbye to Rose at the end of the street. It was getting dark as the two parted.

"Will you be all right?"

"I hope so. My mum can be terrible fierce if she has a mind to. I'll need to stand my ground."

"Will she throw you out tonight or wait 'til the morning?"

"Could be either way. I suppose it depends on how angry she gets and what my dad does. I've never seen him stand up to her yet. She's his wife, so, he might side with her. I don't know.

"Well, you know where to come if she does."

"Thanks, Rose. I hope I don't see you later if you know what I mean."

"Aye, I do. Good luck, Lizzie."

Lizzie pushed the door of her house open and started inside. Her fears about her mother were immediately confirmed.

"You're late. Where have you been?"

Lizzie paused to draw her breath and summon her courage. She was about to speak.

"Well, girl. Out with it. What's your excuse?"

"I've been to meet Rob..." She never got a chance to continue.

"What?" The question was bellowed loud enough for the whole street to hear. Her mum's face went red with anger. "I told you to stay away from that boy. He's no good. He'll be nothing but trouble. While you're in this house, you'll do as you're told."

"I will, mother." Lizzie had hoped to stay calm, but her mother's anger washed that away. "As soon as I step over the door, I'll lead my own life." As she spoke, Lizzie's pointed towards the front door. "I'll pick my own friends, men and women, and I'll see whoever I please when I please. While I stay in this house, I'll abide by your rules. Outside, I'll have my own rules."

Lizzie's mum's jaw dropped open like a goldfish in a bowl, mouth opening and closing without uttering a word.

"Don't you dare disobey me, girl, or you'll be out on your ear," she eventually shouted. "You'll do as you're told."

"While I'm indoors, I'll obey your rules. Out there," Lizzie's arm and finger shot out again towards the door, "I'll obey my rules, not yours."

"You ungrateful little hussy. That boy and his family have infected you. They're the devil's agents. Turning you against your own family."

"No, they're not. The Corsars are honest, decent, hardworking folk."

"They're trouble makers. I know his parents. They've been trouble makers all their lives with that workers' rights and Labour Party rubbish." The volume of the argument was rising by the minute.

"That's rubbish. Rob tells me that his dad's motto is a labourer is worthy of his hire. That means a fair days pay for a fair day's work."

"They're against God's law. They want common people to be telling the bosses what to do. They even want them in parliament. Bosses boss and workers work. That's the way of things."

"Not any more, mother. Things are changing."

"Don't you cheek me, girl."

"I'm not cheeking you, mother. I'm just pointing out the new reality."

"The new reality according to those Corsar devils?"

"In part, mother. Things are changing all around. We're working on farms, in factories and making shells. We're helping keep the country going while Willie and our menfolk try to save it from the enemy. We'll need to have a say when this is all over."

"Don't you dare bring Willie into your argument? He's putting his life in jeopardy for the likes of you. What do you mean, have a say?"

"Yes, he is mother, and I am more than grateful. I'm also scared for him. I want to do my bit to help him come home safe to a place I have helped keep going. We women will need to get a vote after this war."

"I'll not have you talking like that to me. Out you go, my girl."

"Fine. I'll pick up my clothes and be gone in a couple of minutes."

"And where do you think you'll go?"

"Rose says they have a spare room that I can use. I'll lodge with the Mitchells."

"Does she now? And what do her folks think about that?"

"They're fine with it. Rose talked it over with them, and they'd be happy to take me in."

"You've planned this! How dare you?"

"Mary. Hold your tongue."

Both women looked around to see George Ross sitting in the chair by the fire. His voice was strong but not loud. It had an air of authority that Lizzie had not heard before.

"What are you saying, George?"

"I'm saying hold your tongue, Mary. I've heard as much of this as I want to hear. There'll be no throwing out tonight. You and I need to talk."

"In front of this hussy?"

"No, Mary, and she's not a hussy. She's our daughter. Lizzie, will you go to your room please while I talk to your mum. You and I will talk tomorrow."

"OK, Dad." Lizzie headed for the stairs. "Good night Dad."

"Good night, lass. Sleep well."

George Ross looked at Lizzie and motioned with his eyes to her mum, giving a curt nod.

"Good night, mother." Using mother rather than mum helped convey Lizzie's feelings without saying anything specific.

George looked at his wife and gave her a similar eye signal.

"Good night Elizabeth." The use of her full Christian name showed her mother's anger.

Lizzie shot daggers at her mum as she walked up the stairs to her room. She never heard her father talk as forcefully as that, especially not to his wife. She wondered what would happen.

"Make some tea, Mary, and we'll talk."

"George." Mary started to say something, but George stopped her.

"Hush now, Mary. Just do as I ask, please."

Mary filled the kettle and put it on the fire. She laid out two cups and got the milk from the larder. She made the tea and poured two cups through a strainer. She put one sugar in her teacup and two in George's. By the time she had set the cups down, her anger had abated a little.

"George."

"Sit down, Mary and drink your tea."

"George. You've never spoken to me like that before."

"I've never seen the need before."

"Why do you need to now? I've never heard such cheek before from the girl."

"She's a woman Mary. She's not a little girl anymore."

"She's a child, George."

"Mary. Willie and Lizzie will always be our children. Willie is a grown man at the front, and Lizzie is not a child anymore. She's a young woman. She'll be nineteen soon."

"I know, George. I'm worried for Willie, and I worry about Lizzie. She's in with that Corsar family. They're trouble makers."

"I never met this lad, but I have met his father on many occasions. He came to the council offices to register the birth of another child. He's dour but seems polite and honest. People I've spoken to say he's a hard worker."

"What about all that worker's stuff and this new political party?"

"Well, Mary, the parents are only trying to help ordinary working men get enough money to put a roof over their family and food in their bellies. That's not a crime. That phrase Lizzie said 'a labourer is worthy of his hire'. I like that. Work should enable you to take care of your family. You might consider them trouble makers, but they should remind you of someone you know well."

"Who?"

"What about Jesus. He was considered a trouble maker in his day. He only tried to help the poor, sick and disadvantaged. Alexander Corsar, in his own small way, is only doing the same."

Mary's face had gone pale. "You're not suggesting that this man is a new saviour? God forgive your blasphemy." Mary was crossing herself as she spoke.

"Calm yourself, Mary. Corsar is not a new messiah. He's only like Jesus in that he wants to help others, and himself, of course. He's also very committed to his cause."

"How do you know George? Are you a secret socialist?"

"No, Mary. I'm not a secret socialist, but I understand Corsar's views, and I respect them. He's not violent and can argue his point well."

"Have you heard him?"

"No. It's just that some folk in the council turn up at meetings and report back. We need to know what's going on. There might be spies in the town."

"George, what's the world coming to?" Wailed his wife. "Is that man a spy?"

"No, Mary. He would appear to be just a committed socialist."

"Is that not the same thing, George?"

"No, it's not. It might be a flash in the pan. Who knows what might change after this war. We hope we'll win, but we might not."

"Why would there be spies in Montrose, George?"

"We have the flying base, and there's a good view out to sea on a clear day."

"Why would spies need a clear view of the sea?"

"Ships, Mary. They might want to report ship movements."

"God save us, George. Are things that bad?"

"Lizzie is right, Mary. Things are changing, and it's not just the war. Lizzie and lots of young women are doing men's work. You keep her on too short a rein. You need to let it go a bit."

"I'm frightened for her. She's only eighteen."

"She'll soon be nineteen. Remember when you were nineteen." Mary nodded. "We were married, and you were expecting Willie. Many young women of nineteen are married with kids. We've brought both our kids up the best we can. Let Lizzie lead her life. She's smart and responsible. If you don't, we could lose her. You don't want that do you?"

"No, George."

"Think on this, Mary. Young Corsar is in the army territorials. He must be too young to go to war just yet, but he might be off to France to join Willie soon. He and Lizzie will be separated. Let's see what that brings?"

"I never thought of that."

"Right. Tomorrow night when she comes in from work, we'll talk to her. Let her know what we've decided. Tell her we trust her. Is that fine by you, Mary?"

"Yes, George."

"Good. Now off you go up to bed. I'll be up in a minute when I've washed up the cups."

EIGHTEEN

Breakfast in the Ross household had never been a lively affair. It was spring when the daffodils were blooming, birds courting or nesting and trees starting to show their vibrant green leaves. None of this was visible as it was dark outside. It was half-past four in the morning when Lizzie rose to have her breakfast. Her mother had always been first up to prepare breakfast. Today was no exception. She always considered this part of her wifely and maternal duty. Despite the spring, the atmosphere in the room was glacial. The quick meal passed with just a few grunts of 'Ta' or the even less frequent 'Please'.

Lizzie had an early start on the farm. She arranged to meet Rose and walk to work together. She rose from the table, grabbed her bag, and headed out of the door at around quarter past five.

"I should be home by about six tonight."

"Same time as your dad."

"Aye. Bye." She was gone into the street before her mother had any chance to respond. The dark sky was beginning to show the first glimmer of daylight. It took about ten minutes walking to the meeting with Rose.

"Morning, Rose."

"Morning, Lizzie."

"I think it might rain today. That'll not improve my mood."

"What happened? You didn't turn up at our house. I assume you did not get thrown into the street?" Rose was chattering excitedly.

"No."

"Come on, Lizzie. What happened? Did you get it sorted then?"

"I'm not right sure."

"What'd you mean you're not right sure?"

"That's because I'm not."

"What on earth does that mean. You either got it sorted, or you didn't. Which is it?"

"I suppose it's neither."

"That's no answer, Lizzie. Tell me what happened."

"Nothing got sorted."

"Did you not say anything when you got home? Were you afraid?"

"I was afraid, but I did say what I wanted to say."

"That's more like it. What did you say?"

Lizzie pulled her coat collar up, and her head shrank into it to protect her from the rain. It was only a few seconds before she spoke again, but Rose was getting agitated to hear the outcome of the previous night's events.

"My mum was at me the minute I walked in the door."

"And?"

"Well, we were well into it when my dad told the two of us to hold our tongues."

"Both of you?" Asked an incredulous Rose. "You and your mother?"

"Yes."

"Was he angry as well?"

"I think so, but I couldn't tell from the tone of his voice."

"What did you do?"

"We both shut up and stood open-mouthed. I've never heard him talk like that before, not even when Willie or I got into trouble as kids."

"Did your mum shut up as well?"

"She did for a few seconds. She was as shocked as me. Then she started to speak. He put a finger to his lip, and she stopped. He said that there would be no putting anyone out on their ear this night. He told me to go to bed and get some sleep. He was going to talk to my mum before they went to bed. He says he'll talk to me tonight."

"Did you sneak an ear at their conversation?"

"No. I was tired, so I went to bed and went to sleep. I'll have to wait and see what happens tonight."

"So, you might still be out on your ear."

"I don't know. I might be. Are you and your folks still OK if I turn up with my things?"

"We were kind of expecting you last night so, tonight will be fine."

"Thanks."

As they walked, the sky had become lighter, and the clouds above them became visible.

"Looks like you were right, Lizzie. Those are rain clouds. This drizzle's going to get worse, bugger."

"Rose, that's not ladylike language."

"That's OK, Lizzie. I'm no lady," Rose laughed.

"What were we supposed to do today?"

"We're planting some oats. Might need to go and check some of the new lambs and calves. He'll be mad as hell if any die outside."

"Could be worse."

"Could it?"

"Aye. We could be at the front with the men."

"I sometimes wonder if that wouldn't be better than old McArdle in a bad mood. Still, best be thankful for small mercies."

NINETEEN

"We're off, Mr McArdle," said Rose.

"Already?"

"It's gone five when we're supposed to finish."

"I suppose you'd better go then. What's the rush?"

"Lizzie has a meeting."

"One of these suffragette meetings, I expect. I expect that from Rose, but I thought better of you, Lizzie."

"It's not a woman's meeting. It's a family meeting, Mr McArdle."

"OK. Off you go then. Mind you both be on time tomorrow."

"Have you put that oilskin Rob got you in your bag?"

"Aye."

"How did he get it for you again?"

"I told you before, Rose Mitchell, best not ask."

The two walked home the same way that they had come that morning. There was not much talking. The day had been hard work. Planting in the rain was no joy. On sunny days, working outside was pleasant if hard. North East Scotland was a fine place to grow oats as it was cool and damp. Occasional long summer days helped the growth. When the two reached the point that they always met, they parted.

"Good luck Lizzie."

"Thanks, Rose. I don't know what my dad will say."

"Remember. If you're out on your ear, come around to us. We'll put you up."

"I hope I don't see you before tomorrow. If I get kicked out, I should be round to you before nine tonight."

Lizzie knew that her father got home every night at about six. She arrived in her street about fifteen minutes early. She did not want to go into the house before he arrived, so she waited at the corner. When she saw him coming, she walked out from her hiding place to meet him and walk the few final yards with him.

"Hello, lass."

"Hello, dad."

"Have you been waiting for me?"

"Not really."

"That suggests a yes. Did you not want to go in on your own then?"

"No, dad."

"OK, lass. Best get home and have our tea. We'll have a wee talk after that. Best not to talk on an empty belly."

Lizzie clung to his arm. The way he had just spoken to her made her believe that he was not going to say anything terrible to her. She felt less anxious than she had been on the way home with Rose.

The price of food had risen dramatically since the start of the war. Some of the rises were due to shortages, but some were due to profiteering. There were heavy fines for profiteering. Working on the farm gave Lizzie access to some supplies. Her mother also grew some vegetables and fruit in her back garden. It wasn't much, but it supplemented the meagre diet.

The meal that evening consisted of a bowl of homemade tattie soup. The soup was a mixture of potatoes, a leek and a carrot. The stock was also homemade. It was no watery concoction. It was thick with lumps of potato and carrot to give it some semblance of a body. There were also thick slices of bread. These were dipped into the soup and eaten.

The meal passed in awkward silence. At the end of the meal, George Ross spoke.

"Mum, you and I will wash and dry the dishes. Lizzie, you wipe the table and put the kettle on for a cup of tea. Then we all sit down around the table."

Lizzie placed three cups of tea on the table along with three homemade scones, a sliver of grease and a bit of crab apple jelly, also homemade. Once they were all settled, George spoke.

"Lizzie. As you know, your mum and I talked after you went to bed last night. I must say that I am disappointed with the way you spoke to your mother. It was disrespectful and rude."

"Sorry, dad."

"It's not me you should say sorry to Lizzie. You should apologise to your mum."

"Sorry, mum."

"I'm sorry, lass, for the way I spoke. We both said things in anger and haste. We've not heard a word from Willie for a while. I'm worried and upset. What little news comes through is not good."

George continued. "What you said last night, Lizzie, is about right. It is our house. While still living in it, you must abide by our rules." Lizzie nodded. "What that means is that your mum needs to know your comings and goings. She needs to know when to make meals and the like."

"You are nearly nineteen, and someday in the future, you will move out to a home of your own with a husband and possibly a kid or two. When you are a parent, you will understand how parents feel for their kids. We have done the best we could for you and Willie. Like Willie, you will have your independence someday."

George reached for his knife and split the plump scone. He greased both halves and put a lick of crab apple jelly on top. The two women realised he had more to say and filled the silence by cutting their scones.

"Things are changing. It is not just the war, as you said. Women are taking the place of the men who are away, and no doubt when this war is over, you lassies will want your say. People like your lads father will agitate for it. In the meantime, when you walk over the door, you'll have the right to make your own decisions. You're a bright lassie Lizzie, so I've no doubt you will remember that all decisions have consequences, bad as well as good. You'll have to live with them, so make sure that you weigh up the pros and cons. As for that Corsar boy."

"His name is Rob, dad."

"Aye. Rob Corsar. He is your choice for the moment."

"I'm sure it'll be longer than that."

"Maybe so, lass. Remember, he is in the army and will be sent to the front to join Willie and the rest if this war does not end soon. He might be away for a long time. Remember, we've not seen Willie since he left. The same will be true for Rob. A separation will test you both. I hope you're ready for it."

"I worry about him going, dad, just as I worry for Willie. Maybe the war won't last that long."

"It might take a while yet, lass. There's no sign that it's going to end soon. They keep saying it'll be over by Christmas. I'm sure we all hope that it is and our lads come back safe and sound. I've met Rob's father, but we've not met him. Perhaps it's time we did. What do you think, Mary?"

"Aye. Perhaps it's time we did. You should invite him for tea one day, Lizzie. We might get to know him better."

"He might get to know us as well, Lizzie. Will he come if you ask?"

"I'm sure he would, dad."

"That's fine then, lass. Invite him round and see what gives. Make sure your mum has plenty of notice so she can bake one of her cakes."

"It might be some time. We are both working long hours and days now. He works in the docks on the Ferryden side of the river. They're under the government rules for hours as they're a vital industry."

"Aye, I know, lass. Only a few like us in the council offices can keep more regular hours. Do what you can. Are you OK with that, Mary?"

"Aye, George. I'll do Lizzie proud when the lad comes."

"I know you will. Thanks, mum."

"I've got some paper and a pencil. Would you like to write Willie a letter? When did you last write to him? Tell him what's going on. I'm sure he would be happy to have a word from you. Might make him feel better," said George to Lizzie.

"I'll do that, dad."

"I've also got a newspaper and a couple of magazines in my bag if you want to read."

Lizzie took the paper and pencil from her dad's bag. She sat down and started to write to her brother. She told him that she had also joined the Land Army working on McArdle's farm. She finished by telling him about walking out with Rob and reminding him that he was the lad he used to chaperone.

TWENTY

On Sunday, following the meeting in the Ross house, Lizzie got to the town hall steps at six, as arranged. Rob was already there. The walk for Rob was shorter from the docks than the walk for Lizzie from the farm.

Rob gave Lizzie a quick peck on the cheek. It would not be proper to kiss her full on the lips in public. The Scottish kirk still had a stronghold on public morality.

"I was worried whether you would come or not. How did your meeting go?"

"Better than I thought it might."

"So, what happened? Were you thrown out?"

"No. My dad saw to that."

"Your dad? I thought he just did what your mum wanted?"

"That's what I thought. This time I was wrong."

"So, tell me, love, what happened?"

"When I went in, my mum was at me before I had a chance to breathe. She was in a right old rage. I lost my temper, and we started to argue. She was laying down the law, and I started shouting my point of view. She got right fired up by that. I thought she might explode."

"So, how did it end?"

"My dad ended it."

"How?'

"He told the pair of us to hold our tongues. It was the way he said it that shut us both up. I've never heard him talk like that before, especially not to my mum."

"Did she shut up then?"

"She did."

"How'd he manage that then? From what you said, that is not an easy task to achieve?"

"He did not shout. His voice was commanding. Yes, that is what it was, commanding."

"What happened next?"

"He said that he and my mum needed to talk. He sent me upstairs to my bed. I was glad to go and be out of it. He told me that we would talk the next day."

"Did you?"

"We did."

"What'd he say then?"

"It was weird. He said that everything that I had argued for was right. I would obey mum's rules indoors, but I would have my freedom outside. He said that I still had to tell mum where I was and when I was coming and going. They worry about me, and my mum needs to know when to make my meals. They said that I was a young woman now and could choose who I saw outside. I just had to be cautious and live by the consequences of my decisions."

"That's it then? We can meet when we like? Or at least when our work permits?"

"Yes. There was one further suggestion you may not like."

"Oh aye? What's that then?"

"They suggested that you come to tea so that they can meet you."

"Did you tell them my name is Rob, not Daniel?"

"What?"

"Daniel. The man who put his head into the lions' jaws."

"All that church upbringing and I missed that. Maybe I'm not as wise as I thought I was. Anyway, Rob Corsar, why are you, an unbeliever, quoting religion to me? You'll be struck down by lightning any minute now."

"Just because I don't believe doesn't mean I don't know. My dad always says that if your argument is to be convincing, you need to understand the other fellow's point of view. My mum and dad don't believe, but they said we kids should make up our own minds. Like my brothers and sisters, I read a lot and made up my own mind."

"So, why don't you think that God doesn't exist?"

"I don't see the hand of God in this war."

"The Germans are the enemy and are heathens. God must be on our side."

"Is He? The German soldier has a phrase on his belt buckle. It says, Gott Mit Uns. I'm told that means that they believe that God is with them. If there is a God, then He can't be on both sides unless that is His plan, which I doubt."

"I'm sure the priest has an answer to that."

"I'm sure all priests, ministers or parsons have some answer, but so do the German ones. No, I'll stick to there is no God until proved different."

"So, if someone could prove it to you, you'd change your mind?"

"If it could be proved, but no one has so far."

"Never mind you blasphemous heathen, I'll still love you."

"That's OK then."

"What shall we do with our time tonight?"

"It's Sunday, and everything is shut. That's your lot's fault. Let's take a walk around the town and down to the links. It'll stay light 'till about nine. What time are you going home?"

"I said I'd be home about nine. I've had sandwiches, so no need for a meal from my mum. Hers might well have been sandwiches as well. The price of everything is rising, what with the shortages and profiteering."

"The profiteers are the worst. They should be hung for taking food out of ordinary folks mouths."

"My dad has something to do with that in his job at the council offices. I don't think he's strung anyone up, but I'm sure he would be tempted if it was up to him."

"Sounds like a good man, your dad. I'd be glad to meet him. See what we can arrange for tea at your house."

"I'll need to give my mum plenty of warning. She'll want to make a show."

"Just for me?"

"No, stupid. She does it for every visitor we have."

The couple walked down the high street arm in arm. They turned down a side street and headed towards the links. The sky was overcast, but it was not raining, and that was a bonus. They chatted as they went.

"How'd you feel about coming to see my folks?"

"From what you've said, seeing your mum is like going to the front. I don't fancy either. Still, I only have to spend an hour or so with your folks. I'll put my head into the lions' mouth for you." Rob was smiling as he spoke, gently poking fun at Lizzie.

"For your cheek, I'll wind my mum up before you come."

"Seems it doesn't take much to do that from what you've said."

"No. She'll be on her best behaviour to please dad and me. She'll also make a big effort with the tea. What she can bake will depend on what's in the shops and its price. Is there anything you would like?"

"A pleasant evening would be nice."

"That's not what I meant, and you know it. What about food."

"I can eat pretty much anything after what we went through a few years back."

"What happened then?"

"I'm a bit ashamed to say."

"It can't be all that bad. Can it?'

"Yes."

"If you want to tell me, I'll listen. Don't tell if you don't want to."

"You might as well know."

"You were not in jail or anything like that, were you?"

"No. Jail might have been easier."

"That sounds bad."

"It is. Do you want to know?"

"Only if you want to tell me."

"OK. My dad had lost his job again. The rest of us were struggling with jobs and wages. Even between us, we didn't have enough money coming into the house to pay the rent and food, so we were tossed into the street, bag and baggage. There were nine kids, my mum and dad with only a few coppers coming in from Will, Jean, Me and Annie."

"That's not all that bad, Rob. Plenty of folk have lost their houses. Where did you all go?"

"That's the thing Lizzie, we had nowhere."

"Did you end up in the poor house?"

"My dad would not have that, so, no. My dad knew of disused old bothies in the hills outside Brechin. We went to one of them."

"Disused and old is not bad for a wee while. How did you manage there?"

"My mum and the girls cleaned the place up a bit. Dad, Will and me did a load of repairs to the roof, doors, windows, outside cludgie and a water pump."

"How did you live? Where did you get money?"

"All of us went out and tried to find any jobs that we could. Even young Frank and Mary tried their hand. We mostly worked for food, although sometimes we got a penny or two for some work. We did anything that paid, mostly day work. We were not proud."

"That sounds hard. How old were Frank and Mary?"

"It was hard. Frank was six and Mary nine. What was worse was the cold winter. We had little in the way of blankets, so we slept in our clothes, the same ones we worked in. There was plenty of wood for the fire, but there was eleven of us. No baths, just a wash in cold water. Sometimes we washed in the local burn."

"Did you manage to get enough food for you all?"

"Not always, so we stole eggs, potatoes and turnips. We did what we could to survive."

"That's tough."

"There was worse."

"What could be worse?"

"My mum got pregnant again."

"So, what happened?"

"My dad got a job as a carter working for the Montrose brewery."

"That was good."

"It was. The strange thing is he's teetotal. He would only cart soft drinks for the brewery as he didn't hold with drink."

"Does he know that you drink beer?"

"He does. When he's mad at me, I often get the lecture on the evils of drink. All his kids drink."

"He knows and puts up with it?"

"He doesn't like it, but what we do outside is our affair. He won't have drink in the house, and if we come home the worse for a drink, we have to sleep outside."

"He's a hard man, your dad."

"He is, but he's fair. We all know how he feels, and we all accept the consequences of coming home drunk. We've all slept the odd night in the back green."

"Even the girls?"

"Aye. They get treated just the same as us men. We are all equal in our house."

"That's a hard story, Rob. I never knew."

"Why should you lass? It's not the sort of thing you want to brag about."

"You're nearly eighteen now. Have you heard anything about if you might go to France?"

"Nobody knows. If the war continues, I'm sure to be sent. I took the King's shilling, so I'll have to do as I'm told. Maybe I should have done what my brother Will is going to do."

"What is that?"

"He joined the merchant navy. The first chance he gets, he will jump ship in America. They're not in the war and plenty of work for the like of him."

"Isn't that illegal?"

"Yes, but once gone, who is going to go looking for him in such a big country? We have enough problems here to keep us busy. Best not tell anyone, especially your dad. He works for the council, and he'd be bound to tell."

"My dad's not a clipe. He'll not tell."

"He works for the council Lizzie. He has a position of responsibility. What would happen to him if they found out he knew and didn't tell? He might lose his position."

"Aye. I see what you mean. I'll not say a word to anybody. Not even the lassies on the farm."

They strolled onto the links by the shore. The wind off the sea was chilly, so they did not tarry. They passed the golf links as they headed back towards town. A few hardy souls were finishing off their rounds before it got dark.

"Never really understood that game," said Rob as they passed the course.

"It's been around a very long time."

"Has it now? Are you a player?"

"No, but my dad is when he gets a chance. He says this is one of the oldest courses in the world."

"It looks it. Still, the greens look quite nice in good weather."

"I should be getting home now, Rob."

"OK, lass. When are you next off work?"

"I've got a free day a week on Tuesday. Can you get away then?"

"I've got an army training camp near Brechin the weekend before. I'm not sure if I can, but I'll try."

"It'll soon be your birthday. Maybe we could do something special that day."

"That'll be three weeks on Tuesday. I would like to spend it with you. You won't arrange anything with your family for that day?"

"No silly. I wouldn't do that. We'll fix that up sometime later."

The pair kissed at the end of the street. They did not want to be seen outside her house. Rob walked her to the door and hugged her before he left.

TWENTY-ONE

Rob and Lizzie decided that it would be best if Rob visited the Ross house after his eighteenth birthday. They picked a day two weeks after that.

Rob tried with his appearance. His hair was in the regulation army 'short back and sides. Before he left, he washed, shaved, combed his hair and polished his shoes. His jacket, shirt and trousers, were borrowed from his elder brother. His two sisters also inspected him. They were the only suitable garments in the house. He usually spent what little extra money that he had left on workwear.

"You'll do fine," said Jean.

"Don't know what she sees in you," joked Annie.

Emma, who was three years younger and shared her birthday with, Rob was more supportive.

"Show them what we Corsars are, Rob. Just 'cos old man Ross works for the council; doesn't mean they are any better than us."

"Right then. Into the lion's den, I go. Thanks, girls."

The three girls wished Rob well as he left. His mother and father said nothing, not even goodbye. Since he did not expect anything from them, he was unsurprised. Rob left the house and strode purposefully away. When he entered the street and saw the house, he was less confident. The tongue-lashing Mrs Ross had given him that night as he left Lizzie on her doorstep gnawed at his nerves. His joke about being Daniel striding into the lion's den was less funny to him now that he was about to do it.

Lizzie had been waiting and watching for him because she had the door open before he knocked.

"Come in, Rob."

Rob was careful to wipe his feet before he entered. It was polite, but it also gave him a second to gather himself for meeting her parents. He strode forward towards her mother with his hand outstretched.

"Pleased to meet you, Missus Ross."

Mary Ross lightly took the rough hand offered to her. Both she and Rob remembered the tongue-lashing she gave him, and that knowledge created a tense atmosphere. It did not go unnoticed by Lizzie and her father.

"Nice to finally meet you, Robert. Come away in." From the tone of the greeting, it would have been hard to know that the two had an unpleasant history. The tension showed in their body language and her use of his given name.

"Rob, this is my dad."

"Pleased to meet you, Mister Ross."

"I'm glad to meet you, Rob." A much better reaction, thought Rob.

There was a short awkward silence in which no one knew what to do next. Lizzie broke it.

"Why not sit around the table with mum and dad and get to know each other? I'll put the kettle on for tea."

Mr Ross indicated a seat for Rob on the long edge of the table. He seated himself on the opposite side. Mrs Ross sat to his left. Rob now noticed the spread laid out before him. Lizzie was correct. Her mother had made a great effort with sandwiches and cakes. Each place setting had matching cups and saucers. There also a matching side plate with a linen serviette that matched the table cloth. There was also matching cutlery. Rob could never remember seeing anything like it in his life. The Corsars drank and ate from whatever was available.

"That's a wonderful spread Missus Ross," was all he could think to say.

"I'm glad you like it. Help yourself to the sandwiches."

"Thank you." Rob reached over and picked up a small triangular sandwich. He was amazed that someone would do this. In the Corsar household, a sandwich was something slapped between two slices of thick bread. These were small and delicate, just about enough for one mouthful. Lizzie arrived with the tea and started pouring.

"Milk and sugar, Robert?"

"No, thank you, Missus Ross. Just as it comes."

Lizzie sat down on Robs right.

"Well, Rob, Lizzie tells me that you work at the shipyard over on Ferryden side."

"Yes, sir, I do."

"That must be hard long hours, what with the war and the defence regulations."

"Both, sir. And we got our wages cut."

"I heard. I expect that upset all the men."

"It did. Still, with a war on, and we need the boats. We were not happy, but we understood. Not my dad, though. He wanted to argue the toss with the owners. In the end, he accepted the fact, as many of the men said, it was for the best. What with the war and all."

"I've heard that he is a very vocal supporter of workers and women's rights."

"He's fought for both most of his working life. It's something he and that man Hardie talked about every time they met."

"Do you mean Hardie, the MP for that Welsh constituency?"

"Aye. That's the man. He came to our house whenever he was up this way."

The information made Mrs Ross stare. It was one thing for an ordinary working man to be part of this new Labour Party. What else could you expect? On the other hand, hob-knobbing with members of Parliament was not what she had expected. It was only a Labour member of Parliament, not a proper Liberal or Unionist member. As she looked and thought about what he had said, she remembered that the Labour Party had propped up the Liberals to form a government. Some Labour Party members had served in the government. Hardie had campaigned to stop the war. Remembering her son, she suddenly thought him not so bad. Perhaps the Corsars are not as bad as I thought, she mused.

"Some think him a trouble maker," said Mr Ross.

"Him and my dad, both. Not everyone is in favour of workers' rights or votes for women. They also want us to leave India and end the war. I've lived as the son of a poor farm servant. I'm for workers' rights. I know what it is like to be very poor and not have enough to live on after a hard day at work."

Rob reached over to take another sandwich. He suddenly remembered he was not in his own house where you were either quick or hungry. He looked at Mrs Ross, waiting for approval for what he was about to do. His hand hovered near the sandwich plate.

"Go on. Help yourself," she said.

Rob did. He put the sandwich on his plate and took a mouthful of tea before he resumed.

"I'd like the war to end now so I don't have to go and so that Willie and my other pals can come home safe. Women are doing as much work as men now. They should have a say in things after the war. My dad always said, being right isn't always popular. He learned that to his cost. The landed gentry stopped him from working on the land. His agitation for rights did not go down well with them. He didn't like it, but he knew the consequences of what he was doing, and he still did it. He made his choice."

"That's a brave speech, Rob. You are not a conscientious objector, are you?" Asked Mr Ross.

"No, Sir, I'm not. I'd rather not go to war, but I signed the contract. I'll do my duty if I have to go."

"I'm sure we'd all prefer that there was no war."

"Do you think that women should have the vote, Robert?" said a sceptical Mrs Ross.

"I see no reason why not. They're doing the same work as men now, so why not let them have a say in how the country is run?"

"You think that women should have a say in running the country. That's a bit radical, is it not?"

Rob thought for a moment.

"Not really, Missus Ross. After all, it is not all that long ago that the country was run by a woman, Queen Victoria."

"That is different. She was of royal blood."

"True. She was raised to rule with all the privileges that come with the position. No reason why other women could do the same in those circumstances. After all, women run households?"

"You'd live under a woman Prime Minister if that were to happen?"

"It's not going to happen any time soon. Women have to get into Parliament first. That'll take time, but there's no reason why we won't have a woman Prime Minister someday in the distant future."

"You're right, Rob. That won't happen anytime soon. Certainly not in our lifetime. Now, dig in and let us do justice to my wife's excellent spread."

Mrs Ross was taken aback by his speech. Her view of the labour movement was still very firmly held. That her daughter was walking out with a man who held these views troubled her. She agreed with his wish for an end to the war. With her only son at the front, how could she not? As for women having the vote, she had not thought much about it until her daughter had mentioned it that night. She had said that she got the notion from her fellow workmates. That may have been so, but young Corsar's attitude only helped cement her view. Her view of the Corsar family was still firmly held, but she was less certain now.

Mr Ross helped himself to sandwiches and tea. He looked at Rob and admired his conviction even if he might not agree with all his views. After this war, things would probably change. Perhaps Lizzie and her young man, indeed all the young men and women, would see to that. He's no fool this lad, he thought.

Lizzie, sitting on Rob's right, smiled. She was full of pride for how Rob had expressed his views. The ice had been broken, at least a little. Perhaps her parents would come to accept that she could make good choices.

The evening went well. They were impressed by Rob's ability to articulate his views, even if they did not agree. Daniel had survived the lions, or at least Lizzies family.

TWENTY-TWO

The day that Rob and Lizzie both dreaded finally arrived. Rob got his orders to head for France and the front line. It was late November 1915, and the carnage at the front was well known. There were only a few widows and orphans in the Montrose area. Men with terrible wounds were more common. All around the county, there were many bereaved families. There were even more living in dread of the buff telegram. The newspapers tried to be upbeat about the war. Letters home from soldiers in the trenches gave an altogether bleaker picture. Families with men at the front knew that the war was not going as well as the papers said.

"When do you have to go, Rob?"

"Next month."

Lizzie was afraid. Rob was not happy either, but he tried not to show his feelings too much. A typical Corsar trait.

"Next month is only a few days away, Rob. It's so soon."

"We always knew that this was coming, Lizzie. I never thought that getting to the summer ball would lead to this."

"Nobody did."

"I think my dad had an idea."

"What makes you think that?"

"When I joined up to go to the dance, he said I'd soon be dancing to a different tune. I think he saw that war might come."

"Did he say that?"

"No. He said what I just told you. Maybe the folks at his political meetings had some inkling and talked about it."

"He didn't tell you then." Lizzie was trying to understand. She was close to tears but tried not to show it. She pulled Rob closer to her and hung tightly to his arm.

"I don't think he knew. He just guessed based on what he was hearing."

"We haven't much time then before you go."

"No. I've been thinking about what to do since I got the order. Should we become engaged then?"

"Are you asking me to marry you?"

If a picture is worth a thousand words, then Rob's face was a blank page. He had asked his question without looking at the next step and its consequences. He realised that Lizzie's question was the next logical step.

"I suppose I am." Rob meant what he said, but his delivery was almost apologetic.

"That's not a very romantic proposal. Aren't you supposed to ask my father for my hand in marriage and get down on one knee to me?"

"Am I? I never really thought about it. Is that what you want?"

"No."

"No, you won't marry me or no, that's not what you want?"

"I will marry you. You don't have to go to my dad and ask."

Rob's face was now a picture of astonishment. It was another step he had not considered. He thought for a second.

"Would you not want me to ask your folks? I'm sure your mum and dad would want the courtesy of being asked."

"I'm sure they would, but I've made up my mind."

"What if they said no?'

"I'll do it anyway. I'm old enough to make up my own mind."

"Perhaps it's best we wait till after this war is over."

"You're right. Best we wait till then."

"Aye. You're never sure what might happen."

"Oh, Rob. Don't say things like that. I can't stand the thought of you going."

"Sorry, love, but that's the way of things. They keep saying it'll be over by Christmas. Maybe this year it will."

"I think my folks would want me to get married by our priest in the chapel. He will want you to become a catholic before he does the wedding."

"You know I won't do that, Lizzie. I'll marry you in your chapel because I know that's what you and your family would like. I'll never convert, not even to marry you."

"You could always say that you believed."

"That's a lie I'm not prepared to tell. I couldn't even begin to pretend to be a catholic. I wouldn't know how."

"You won't do that for me?"

"Surely, I would have to undergo some catholic religious test to convince the priest that my conversion was true. What would we do then?"

"Perhaps leaving it till the war is over is the only option. Who knows what things will be like then."

"I'd like to buy you a ring to show my feelings and intentions. Would you like that? What would your folks say if you wore it?"

"That's a lovely idea. You can be a real romantic when you like. My folks already know how I feel. They'll have to accept me wearing your ring. You don't have much money; how will you afford a ring?"

"I'd not thought about that. I don't know how much rings cost."

"They can be terrible expensive. I don't want one like that, I'd be afraid to lose it in the fields."

"There's a man at the yard who makes rings from brass. Would that be good enough for you?"

"That would be better. How long will it take him?"

"A day or so at most."

"I'll need to give you a measurement of my finger so it'll fit."

"Of course. I never thought of that either."

"You've not had much of a plan, Rob. Did you give any of this a thought?"

"No."

"Why'd you do it then?"

"It seemed like a good idea at the time. I'm going to be away for a bit. I don't know when I'll be back, if ever..."

"No, Rob. Don't say that." Shouted Lizzie, who was now in tears. "We shouldn't think like that. It makes me so unhappy."

"Sorry, Lizzie. Still, we have to consider the possibility that I might not."

"OK. It's a possibility, but I'm not going to think like that, and neither are you. You'll come back soon, and we'll be married, and that's an end to it."

"I'll get Eric to make a ring. How'll we measure your finger?"

Lizzie fished a piece of binder twine from her pocket and held her left hand out with her fourth finger slightly raised.

"Wrap it around this finger and tie a knot. Make sure it's not too tight as I'll need to be able to put it on."

Rob tied the string around her finger, and they tested getting the loop off and on. When they were satisfied, Rob put the loop into his pocket, and they walked hand in hand.

"I love you, Lizzie."

"I love you too, Rob."

For Lizzie, the joy of having an engagement ring became diluted by the talk of leaving the following week. She didn't know whether to laugh or cry. She did neither as she was still quite numb. The couple arranged to meet in three nights' time.

TWENTY-THREE

Rob arrived at the Commercial Hotel ahead of time. He was anxious not to be late. Rob was as excited as he had ever been before in his life. It was something extraordinary, and he was nervous. He had not been anxious when he talked about getting married a couple of days ago. Today was different. He had the brass ring made by Eric. It had a couple of decorations put on by Eric without Rob asking. When he saw them, Rob was delighted. He tried to give Eric a couple of bob for his trouble, but Eric refused to take any money.

"If you're thinking of getting married, you'll need all your money, lad. Consider this a present from Edith and me."

"Thanks, Eric. It is better than I had hoped. Has Edith seen it?"

"She has. She helped with the design."

"Thanks to you both. I'm sure Lizzie will love it. Don't let people know, please."

"Why not, lad?"

"Her family are catholic, and I've no intention of converting. It'll cause trouble in her family if they get wind of it. Lizzie hasn't told her folks yet, nor have I.

We thought we should wait till after I get back from the war. If I get back."

"OK, lad. You have my word. You're off next week, aren't you? I wish you the very best of luck." Eric shook his hand with a firm grasp. "Keep your head down, trust your pals, and we'll see you when you get back."

"You sound like you know all about it. Were you in the army?"

"I was, lad."

"You never talk about it. When did you serve?"

"I was out in South Africa fighting the Boers."

"I heard that was easy for us."

"That's a load of lies put about by politicians. It was hard, bloody hard. That's why I don't talk about it."

"We won, didn't we?"

"Eventually, we did."

"Eventually. What do you mean by that?"

"The Boers were hard and smart fighters. We had hundreds of thousands of men out there, and they had just a few thousand. It took us four years to beat them."

"I never knew that." Rob was taken aback by this information. A few thousand men held up the might of the British army for four years. How could this happen?

"Do you mind talking to me about what a battle is like so I have an idea before I go to France?"

"If you like, lad." There was a short pause while Eric thought. "The thing about a battle is that you don't see it. You hear and smell it." Eric seemed to drift back in time as he spoke. "You hear the crack of the rifles and then the thump and plop of bullets quickly afterwards as they hit a target. You hear the roar of the cannon and the almighty crash as the shells land, shaking the ground under your feet. You hear the screams of

141

wounded and dying men. Then there is the smell of cordite. After the battle, you can still smell it as it clings to your uniform and kilt." Eric seemed to jolt back to the present. "War and killing are a dirty business, lad. Keep your head down. Trust your training and your pals."

"I'm sorry, Eric." Rob saw that Eric was upset when he talked of the war. His description of a battle was nothing like he might have imagined. Eric's description made Rob wonder what he had gotten himself into by joining up. It was the first time he started to question his decision.

"What for, lad?"

"Asking you to talk about it."

"That's OK, lad. I could have said no. Now, off you go and see that lassie of yours."

"Thanks again, Eric. See you when I get back."

"Good luck, lad."

With that, Rob walked out of the shipyard for the last time. He headed for the Commercial Hotel, where he had arranged to meet Lizzie.

Rob waited for Lizzie at the entrance to the hotel. Unescorted women in a hotel were frowned upon and often refused entry. He kissed her on her cheek when they met.

"Shall we go in and have a drink, Lizzie?"

"Yes. I'd like that."

They went into the bar, which was only half full. Finding a table, they sat down.

"What do you want to drink, Lizzie?'

"I'll have a small beer, please. I'm thirsty after today on the farm."

Rob went to the bar and purchased the drinks. He laid one in front of Lizzie. Raising his glass, he said. "Here's to us, Lizzie."

"Aye. To us Rob, and the future."

"I've got the ring, Lizzie. Do you want to see it now?"

"Yes, please, Rob. I thought that's what we're here for." Lizzie was excited.

Rob pulled a small piece of linen cloth from his pocket and placed it on the table in front of Lizzie, opening the linen cloth carefully as if he were revealing an enormous diamond ring. It glinted in the soft light.

"Can I pick it up?"

"It's going to be yours so, why not?"

Lizzie fondled the brass ring lovingly. Eric had polished it and inscribed something on the inside. Rob only noticed it when Lizzie pointed it out.

"What's this say, Rob?"

"What's what say?"

"There's an inscription on the inside." Lizzie held it up to the light. "It says ER and RC with a heart in between."

Rob squinted in the soft light. "So, it does. That's us, Lizzie. ER, Elizabeth Ross a love heart and RC, Robert Corsar. I never asked him to do that. What do you think, love?"

"I think it's sweet. He must be a very nice man, this friend of yours."

"He said his wife gave him an idea. Do you like it?"

"Yes, I think it's just right for us."

"Can I put it on your finger to see if it fits?"

"Yes, please." Lizzie held her left hand out, and Rob placed the ring on the engagement finger. "It even fits. He's done a wonderful job."

Lizzie held her hand out, and Rob slid the ring onto her finger. It fitted, and Lizzie flourished her hand around, showing off her new ring. She got caught up in the excitement of the occasion. Rob felt sure that the feelings he had for Lizzie were love. He had had no exposure to affection or love in his life, but his heart quickened, and he got excited in her presence. He assumed this was love.

Until he met Lizzie, Rob knew love only as a word. There was no affection shown to him, or any of his siblings, by his parents. Born into poverty, worked as children, bought and sold as farm labourers. Love and affection were for those that could afford the luxury. His parents did their best to provide shelter, food and clothing for their many children. There was no time for love. His feelings for Lizzie were the strongest he had had for anyone. He wanted to spend his life with her, so he assumed he was in love. It was a pleasant warm feeling on this cold November night. It made him happier than he thought he had a right to expect. Her pleasure in his simple gift made him very happy.

"I'm glad you like it. Will you wear it while I'm away?"

"I should if we're going to get married when you come back."

"What'll your folks say?"

"I don't know, and what's more, I don't care."

"You can always take it off and keep it in your pocket if you think it'll be trouble."

"No. I said I was going to make my own decisions. This is one of them. They'll need to get used to the idea that I'm going to marry."

"If that's what you want?"

"I don't think my dad will mind. He talked about me growing up and getting married that night we talked. I'm sure he'll keep my mum sweet."

"What about another drink? Same again?"

"Yes, please. I'll keep the ring on for the time being."

They sat and chatted while they drank. It was soon time to go.

"I'm off to a camp near Southampton on Thursday. Will you be able to come and see me off on the train?"

"I'm sure old man McArdle would give me time off for that. If not, I'll leave anyway. I wish you didn't have to go, Rob."

"I don't want to leave you either, Lizzie, but I signed the forms and gave my oath. I need to keep my word, else what kind of husband will I make?'

"Damned army. I wish you were not in it."

"It's not all bad, Lizzie. If I had not joined up to go to the dance last year, we would not have met."

"That's true, but it doesn't make me feel any better about what's going on now."

"Nor me lass. My dad would be livid if I refused to go."

"I thought he was a pacifist."

"He is. All his life, he has fought for what he believes. If he gives his word, he keeps it no matter the consequences. I gave my word, and he expects me to keep it. He and my mum would probably disown me if I tried to back out now."

"He's a hard man, your dad."

"That he is. My mum is every bit as hard. She had to be bringing up ten kids on little or no money. We survived, and I will do the same. I'll come back to you, Lizzie."

There was a steely surety about the words and the way he said them that made Lizzie believe him.

"I'm sure you will, Rob."

"Thanks, love. Be careful about wearing that ring if you think your folks will disapprove."

"They'll just have to lump it then. I don't think they're that hard-hearted. They've got my brother in France. They know how I feel about you, so they'll have a good idea of how I feel about seeing you go."

Finishing their drinks, Rob and Lizzie walked back to the Ross house arm in arm, chatting excitedly about their future together. The ring, two drinks and a loving arm pushed the thought of parting to the back of their minds. At the door of her house, Lizzie pulled Rob to her and gave him a long passionate kiss. It was not just a show of love. It was also a statement of intent for her parents if they were watching.

TWENTY-FOUR

Wednesday 1st December 1915 was a cold, wet, miserable Scottish day. Rob had been up early and gone to the Black Watch barracks to join the others leaving on that day. The group of eight consisted of six men and two new second lieutenants.

Rob's father had given him a handshake. He also wished him good luck. His brothers did the same while his sisters hugged him. His mother made him breakfast of porridge and coffee. There was no hug or kiss from her, just a cheerio and good luck. It was almost like a lodger was leaving the house to work rather than a son going to war.

At the barracks, They went through a full kit inspection. It was to make sure they had everything, and it was in good order. The six men marched to the station behind the two officers and waited for the train coming from Aberdeen. Unlike a year previously, there were no cheering crowds in the streets to see the men off. The terrible reality of the war was beginning to sink in.

Lizzie was at the station, as were several other women. Some, like Lizzie, were sweethearts. Others were concerned mothers and sisters. There were also a few male relatives and friends of the soldiers leaving. None of his friends or relatives was present. He had expected none, so was not disappointed.

After setting his kit down with the rest, he immediately went to Lizzie. They hugged and kissed. Lizzie wanted to cry but did not. She wanted Rob to think her strong. She hid her face over his shoulder, trying not to show the tears that were welling up in her eyes.

Soon, the noise of the approaching train was heard in the distance.

It was a noise that no one on the platform wanted to hear. The train chugged into the station and squealed to a halt. The old senior NCO barked his order to get on the train. He would not be going. He had done all the killing he ever wanted to in the Boer War. He had no desire to repeat that horror.

The men quickly boarded third class on the train, stowed their gear and immediately returned to their loved ones for one last goodbye. The officers travelled first class. Now, as the reality sank in, Lizzie broke down as Rob kissed her one last time, and the train started to move away.

"I'll write as soon as I get there," Rob said as his hand gradually slipped from Lizzie's as the train chugged off.

"See that you do," sobbed Lizzie.

"Maybe the war will be over by Christmas, and I'll see you then. I love you, Lizzie."

"I love you, Rob." Rob could see her mouth but could not hear what she had called over the sound of the steam engine. The outline of her lips and the kiss she blew said it all.

As the train moved further away and started to head round the bend following the outline of the Montrose basin, Rob lost sight of Lizzie, who was still waving.

She felt empty. Her sweetheart was off to war with no certainty of what would happen to him. The emptiness also came with dread. She had always feared this day, but the fear that now engulfed her was something new. She slumped on the bench sobbing. She was not alone. Two of the three other women on the platform were also crying. The third, an older lady, looked wistfully at the departing train.

"Bloody war,' cursed the older lady to no one in particular.

"Bloody, bloody politicians," cursed a younger woman sitting at the far end of the bench. She spat it out with all the venom she could muster between sobs.

"Lassies, I'm awful sorry if I upset you all," said the older woman.

"No, missus, it wasn't you that upset us," said Lizzie.

"That's the second son I've sent off to do his bit for King and country. What's the King ever done for him except teach him to kill or be killed."

"Is your other boy OK, missus?" asked the third young woman.

"The last we heard he was."

"My older brother went to France at the start. He says it's hard but is OK the last we heard," said Lizzie.

"That's good," said the older lady. "Where there's life, there's hope, and we can but hope."

The four women started back into town together. They did not know each other, but their situation had given them an unseen bond of comradeship. The younger women were drying their eyes as they talked and walked.

When he lost sight of Lizzie, Rob slumped back in his seat. The carriage contained the five other men, all known to each other. Three, like Rob, were only just old enough to go to war. Three were relatively new volunteers. They looked at each other but said nothing. Each man was lost in his thoughts. They had heard stories of the conditions in France so knew it would be tough. Harsh conditions did not bother any of them. They were, for the most part, itinerant labourers. Long hours, bleak conditions with little money, had been their lot in life.

Rob was the youngest of the group, and he was in the army and off to war because he wanted a bit of entertainment at the 1914 Black Watch summer ball. If he had not gone to the ball, he would not have met Lizzie, the girl he would marry at the end of this madness. Still, being shot at by unknown people trying to kill him seemed a high price to pay.

Rob's father was still advocating peace and an end to the war. He had never wavered from his belief. Having a son thrown into the conflict only gave his argument more strength. Sitting in the carriage on his way south, Rob remembered his father's prophetic words eighteen months ago when he saw Rob in his uniform. "You'll soon be dancing to a different tune, my lad."

"Fuck." The word slipped out of his mouth without him noticing.

"What's that?" asked John Christie.

"Sorry, John. I remembered something my dad said last year."

"What was that?"

"It was nothing."

With that, the group returned to silent gazing out of the window. They were looking at the sea on one side with the water in the tidal basin on the other. Soon, Montrose Basin disappeared behind them. The sight was replaced by rolling farmland. The train would follow the coast to Edinburgh, a place Rob had never seen.

TWENTY-FIVE

With Rob in the carriage were Ian Walker, John Christie, Tommy Douglas, Terry Greig and Joseph Murray.

Rob, Ian and Joseph were only old enough to go to war. Unlike Rob, Ian and Joseph had joined the Black Watch when the country got gripped with war fever in 1914. Not old enough to fight, the army trained them until they were. The news from the front had made them wonder about their youthful enthusiasm. Still, it would all be over by Christmas, and they could come home without firing a shot, they hoped.

Tommy explained his decision to join up on the journey to Dundee.

"I got caught poaching on the Lairds land. We were starving, and so I caught a couple of rabbits and a trout out of his river."

"Did you get jailed?" asked Ian.

"No. The Laird had me dragged into his house by the gillie. He gave me a choice. Join up or go to jail. The Laird is the magistrate, so I knew he would give me a long stretch in Craiginches in Aberdeen."

"This war might go on for some time yet," said Terry. "Surely you might have to spend less time in prison for poaching?"

"I'd been in prison before for the same offence. That bastard Laird gave me a long sentence then. This time he promised me a longer stretch and hard labour, so I joined up."

"We've just passed Lunan Bay," said Ian. "Are we going to stop before we get to Edinburgh?"

"Don't know," said John. "The railways are under the control of the army, so we'll stop where they want to stop."

"We'll need to stop somewhere before Edinburgh, or I will need to pee out the window."

"Bugger. I never thought of that," said Terry. "They might have given us a pot to piss in at least."

Despite their worry, the train stopped at most of the stations on the way south. The men occasionally stuck their heads out of the window, curious to see who was getting on and off.

When stopped at Dundee, the young second lieutenant called Fraser opened the carriage door.

"We're stopped here for about ten minutes. Best relieve yourselves before we move off. The toilets are over there." He stretched his arm, pointing to the sign some yards up the platform. "See that you're back in time to move off."

There was a chorus of "Yes, Sir," as the men scrambled out. No toilets on the train meant that the queue was quite long. Naturally, officers peed first, even before civilian passengers.

Before the train pulled out, Fraser returned to the third-class carriage and counted the men. "Next toilet break is in Edinburgh. If you need to go before that, you can improvise. It's what soldiers do." He marched back to his first-class compartment and jumped aboard as the train pulled away from the station.

"That is a right old sight," said Joe Murray. "I've seen it from the shore when we were on exercise down here, but never been on it." The sight Joe was referring to was the Tay Bridge.

"I understand it is nearly three miles long," said John.

"Is that so?" said Tommy in a somewhat disinterested tone.

"It is. The original bridge collapsed in high winds in December 1879, killing everybody on the train crossing the bridge."

"What a cheery thought. Imagine our epitaph. On the way to war, killed when his train fell from a bridge. Not very heroic, is it?" Said Ian.

"There is not much wind out there today, and this is a safer metal construction than the one that collapsed. We'll be alright," said John.

"How'd you know that then?" Asked Rob.

"My dad was an engineer before he died in an accident. I learned a bit from him when I was growing up."

"Fuck." Cursed Tommy. "All you seem able to talk about is death. Will you no give it a rest?"

"Sorry," said a chastened John. From that moment on, they all watched the crossing in silence. They might have considered it a wonderful sight on a warm sunny summer day. This was a cold, wet miserable winter day. The bridge was black with soot from the belching of hundreds of train stacks. The sky was dull and the water in the river a dirty grey colour.

The train chugged its way south towards Edinburgh. There was some idle chatter about football, family, jobs and friends. For the time being, talk of heading to the war was missing. Boarding the train made the possibility of fighting in France a grim reality. No one was yet ready to talk about it.

"That's a better sight." Joe Murray was eulogising about the magnificent Forth Bridge.

"That's not going to fall in any wind," said John.

"All that ironwork obscures the view," said Ian. "On a day like today and in this weather, probably just as well."

"I expect we will soon be in Edinburgh," said Rob. "I've never seen it."

"We're staying overnight somewhere before we head south tomorrow," said Tommy. "I wonder where they will put us?"

"Maybe they'll put us up in the barracks in the castle. That would be something," said Ian.

"You won't want to stay there," said John. "It the headquarters of the Royal Scots. A royal pain in the arse if you ask me."

"What's wrong with them?" asked Tommy.

"They're the lot that got killed in the train crash at Quintnshill earlier this year." Said Joe. "They lost over two hundred in that."

"I'd forgotten that," said Rob.

"We'll have to wait and see where they put us. Won't be long now, I expect," said Joe.

About half an hour later, the train pulled into Waverly station. The men were to disembark, so, collected their kit bags and got onto the platform.

"Right, you men," said the other new second lieutenant called Robertson. "Get yourselves and your kit over to that Sergeant there." He was pointing down the platform to the man in question. He standing just the other side of the platform gate.

A chorus of Sirs greeted his command. The six men started to meander down the platform.

"Smarten yourselves up. Get fell in and march like proper soldiers. You're not out for an evening stroll," shouted Fraser.

The men quickly fell into two lines and marched off as ordered.

"You'll be the six Black Jocks then?" grunted the gnarled old Sergeant Major.

"Aye, Sir," responded Terry Greig.

"Right. At ease. You're staying the night at Glencorse barracks. You'll get a hot meal, tea and a bed. Reveille is at zero five hundred. Get washed, shaved, and dressed. Breakfast is at zero five-thirty. Transport back here at six ready for your train south at half-past seven. Got that?"

"Yes, sir," said the group in unison.

"Right. The truck is out there up the ramp on the Waverly Bridge. Even you lot o' teuchters can't miss it. Wait in the truck for your officers. Right. Attention. Move to the right, right turn. By the left, quick march."

The six men completed their drill movements as ordered and marched up the slope to the street. There they found a truck.

"In you get," said a Private who had been standing by the truck smoking. The back was down, and the men clambered in.

"Where's this Glencorse barracks?" asked Terry.

"It's outside the city to the south."

"Is it far?"

"About three-quarters of an hour. You might have to push this wreck up Liberton Brae."

"What's that?" asked Tommy.

"It's a bit of a hill on the way to Glencorse. This wreck might have a wee bit of trouble getting up it with all you lot in it."

"There are only six, plus our two officers."

"I'm expecting a few more before we leave."

"There's the castle." Said Ian.

"You'll no be having any time to sight-see. It's straight out tonight and back tomorrow morning. You might get a wee glimpse tomorrow as you leave the station. It'll only be by lights as it's still dark at seven."

The two officers and three more Privates climbed into the truck before it drove off. It headed onto Princess Street with its array of expensive shops. As it turned the corner onto Princess Street, the men saw Jenners department store, the Harrods of the north. It looked the part. The truck turned right along the Bridges and headed out of the city. The street they were on had a few shops and long lines of large, grand, dirty granite mansions. Homes for the hoi polloi of Edinburgh.

Soon, the built-up streets of Edinburgh were left behind, and still no Brae. It was not long before Ian Walker, looking out the front of the truck, saw a hill. It did not look steep at first. It was not long before the vehicle was labouring as the incline increased. They were soon travelling at a slow walking pace.

"You lads in the back better get out and walk alongside," shouted the driver above the din of the engine which was labouring noisily.

"Out you go, men," ordered Fraser.

The nine men dropped out of the back of the truck and walked alongside. The pace was a little faster but still slow enough for the men to keep up without much effort. By the time they got to the brow of the hill, the brisk walk had taken its toll. The men were breathless.

"In you get," shouted the driver. The men scrambled up the back of the truck as it continued to move more quickly.

"Everyone on board," shouted Robertson.

"Thanks, sir," replied the driver and the truck began to accelerate.

About three-quarters of an hour after leaving the station, the truck turned left through the wrought iron gates of the barracks and stopped at the guardroom. It looked like an impressive building because it had once been a mansion. It had also been a prison in the previous century.

The nine men were processed through the guardhouse and marched off to the main buildings. They were each allocated a cot bed. A quick trip to the ablutions, was followed by a walk to the cookhouse. The men joined many more queueing for a meal. There were men from all Scottish regiments here, like Rob and his troop, bound for France.

A hot stew, containing meat of uncertain pedigree, was washed down with hot tea around rows of trestle tables and wooden benches.

"Is there anywhere around here to get a drink?" asked Terry.

"There's a village up the road a bit, but it's not much for entertainment unless you're a local." The information came from a Gordon Highlander sitting across the table. "It's a bit of a walk, and the guards won't let you go if you're leaving early tomorrow."

"Why not?" Asked Joe.

"Might get drunk and miss the early transport to the station. Absent without leave in a time of war. Could get you shot."

"Well, that's as good a reason as any not to chance it," said Rob. "Shot in Scotland or shot in France. Not much choice, except a firing squad, only has one victim, and he's tied up in plain sight. Can't miss him."

"You lot are a cheery bunch of bastards," cursed Tommy, who was repeating his gripe from earlier in the day. "I'm off to bed to get some shut-eye."

With that, the men cleaned their eating equipment and strolled back to their cots.

TWENTY-SIX

Awoken at five, the men all made their way to the ablutions. After the first order of any day, urination, they headed to the rows of sinks and mirrors for their wash and shave.

Smartened up and dressed, they all made their way to the cookhouse, where they got bacon, sausage, bread and tea. The bacon and sausage were hot, but the contents of the sausages were questionable. Still, it was a hot meal, and the men did not know when they might get another.

Afterwards, they returned to their cots, folded up the blanket, checked their kit and headed out to the guardhouse to await the transport. There they found rows of trucks and lines of men milling about waiting.

"Right you lot, get fell in," bellowed a sergeant. The men shuffled into three lines. "Get a bloody move on you idle shower of shite. Come on, come on. We've not got all day."

A group of officers appeared from their quarters. Fraser and Robertson strode towards Rob and his troop. Fraser pulled out a clipboard.

"Answer your names when called. Christie."

"Sir."

"Corsar."

"Sir."

"Douglas." There was silence. "Douglas. Answer your name. I know you're there."

"Sorry, Sir."

"Bloody impudent. Greig."

"Sir."

"Murray."

"Sir."

"Walker."

"Sir."

"All present and correct, Archie," said Fraser to Robertson.

"Right," said Archie Robertson. "We're on this truck here. Pick up your kit and get onboard."

The assembled men mounted the trucks. They headed through the gates, turning right to make the return journey to Waverly station. It was cold and dark, with a slight fall of snow as they left.

"I hope the brakes on this truck are fine," said a voice from the rear seats.

"Why do you ask?" said Robertson.

"That brae's real steep. If it is coated in snow or ice, we might be in trouble."

"Oh." The surprise in Robertson's voice showed that he had not thought of that difficulty. Like many other officers in the British army, Second Lieutenant Robertson had his commission based on his social station. Sons of landowners, who went to private schools, were not meant to be ordinary foot soldiers.

"What's with you lot?' grunted Tommy. "We're nowhere near the war yet, and all you can talk about is death and destruction. Give it a bloody rest."

There was snow on the Liberton Brae. The driver slowed right down and eased his way slowly behind other trucks.

"If our brakes fail, we won't have far to go. We'll hit the arse of that truck in front," said the voice from the back of the truck. Tommy Douglas muttered something inaudible under his breath.

The reverse journey to the station took less time than the outward one. It was mainly due to the trucks going down and not up, the steep brae.

The trucks stopped on Waverly Bridge, and the men flowed onto the pavement like water breaking a dam. Rob and his pals had no idea how many trucks there were. Why would they? They were only Privates, trained to do as they were told, without question. Good eyesight, strong will and courage were what was required. Having a brain was of no benefit. Not that many of the officers were overly endowed with intellect. Like Robertson, many were officers because of their station in life. Sons of Lairds or other worthy gentlefolk put them immediately above the lower classes.

Rob looked at the officers wandering about barking orders at the disorganised tide of men in army uniform. They all shouted with a posh voice as far as he could tell in the noise. They're trying to be leaders of men, thought Rob. They are shouting, to let the men know who's boss. I wonder how many are going to show that they are leaders. Rob was sure that they all had good manners. They would know the right knife and fork to use, bred into them because of their station in life. Rob remembered Eric's words during a tea break in the docks.

"Officers are officers because of who their families are or because they had enough money to buy a commission. Some are OK, but many are terrible commanders. Listen to your sergeants. They're where they are by bloody hard work. They know what they're doing."

Men marched down the slope to the platform where the military express train sat waiting for them. Ordered onto the train, the men stowed their gear and took their seats. The train moved off in the dark. Sunrise was not for another hour.

As the train left the station, the men on the left side could see the castle lights on the hill above them. The view was brief as the train chugged into a tunnel. It then made its way south towards Carlisle.

The train ran out through Eskbank and Dalkeith towards Galashiels. From there, it sped on to Hawick and then Newcastleton. Some miles past Newcastleton, the train slowed down. None of the troops on the train noticed much change. The army troop dispatcher, and his civilian counterpart in the guards' van noticed. They knew why the train had slowed.

"We must be near that place where the train crashed earlier this year," said John. "I heard that the drivers slow down as a mark of respect."

"Maybe it's because the line is damaged, and they don't want us killed as well," said John.

"What the fuck is it with you lot," grumbled Tommy. "Always talking about fucking death. Give it a rest, will you?"

A short while later, in a departure from historical precedent, a small army of Scottish soldiers crossed the border and invaded England. They were unobserved except for a few sheep in an adjoining field.

John Christie said nothing, but he had a weird thought. Here are us Scots crossing the border into England. Instead of fighting the English, we're going to fight their war, yet again. John was a student of history, and the irony of Scots fighting an English war was not lost on him. Despite being the United Kingdom, John still thought that this war had started in the English parliament in London. He accepted that there were Scots MPs in parliament. He had learned that none had dissented, so it was not an English war. Still, there were many more English MPs than Scottish ones. If they had voted against the war, they would have outnumbered. I'm a soldier now, so I'll do my duty as best I can.

The journey to Carlisle took three hours non-stop. There, the men were let out for twenty minutes to stretch their legs, buy tea or whatever the station provided in the way of food and relieve themselves.

A few of the men bought papers to read on the train. Others posted letters that they had already written to their loved ones and family. Many of the men bought food and hot tea from the station vendors. It was stuffy in the carriage but still cold outside.

Back on the train with a few more soldiers picked up at the station, the train steamed off south.

There were further stops at Preston, Crewe, Stafford and Birmingham. At each station, the men had another chance to stretch their legs. Rob and his team had been on the train for over six hours. Their backsides were sore from sitting on the hard-wooden seats.

Onwards through Warwick, Oxford, Didcot before another shorter stop at Reading. More troops embarked before the short run to Winchester, their final destination.

Every single soldier climbed out of the train with their kit bags over their shoulders. Fall in outside the station in lines of four was ordered. It took quite some time as men did not know where they were supposed to stand. There were no regimental groupings, just a mass of grumpy soldiers.

There were the usual bellowed orders to dress from the left, stand to attention, at ease, attention before a left turn and march up Giles Hill to the army transit camp at Winnall Down.

At the entrance to the camp, Ian muttered to his pals. "This place is bigger than Montrose."

"So, it is," said Joe in astonishment.

"Quiet in the ranks," came a bellowed order from somewhere just behind the group.

The camp was several camps around the one small English town. It was clear from the number of huts on the sites that the camp population outnumbered that of the town. It was to be the Black Watch soldiers home for a few days before moving on to France.

Routine in the camp was familiar to all of the soldiers. It mirrored the training camps they had attended before this trip.

Mornings started with ablutions, washing and shaving, breakfast and then out on the parade ground. Here they practised close-order drills, hand to hand fighting and bayonet practice. There was one extra drill to learn. The Germans had started using gas as a weapon of war in April. The men got issued with gas masks. They quickly learned the routine of putting them on while continuing to fight. It was difficult as the small glass eyepieces could easily mist up obscuring vision.

"Christ," cursed Tommy Douglas on the second day of practice with the new masks. "This is bloody hopeless. We could end up killing each other."

"Have you something useful to add to the drill, Douglas?" Shouted 2nd Lt Robertson.

"No, sir."

"Good. Just get on with it."

"Yes, Sir." What Tommy said into his mask was unheard, which was just as well for him.

Getting on with it was a real problem. The fields that the men were training in were a sea of mud. It had been particularly wet, with almost ceaseless rain for much of the winter. Little did the men under training know that this would be good practice for what they would face in France. The anticyclone causing all this rain in the south of England stretched to the battlefields of France.

TWENTY-SEVEN

On Tuesday, 15 December 1915, the troops packed their kit bags and stripped their cots after breakfast. Rob posted his first letter to Lizzie on his way back to the huts. The letter gave little information about where he was or what he was doing. He talked about how he missed her and the five new friends he had made. Nothing to worry the censor.

The men paraded for a kit inspection. It was the prelude to them retracing their march back to the station in Winchester to board the train to Southampton. They completed the journey in the rain. The freezing needle-sharp raindrops hitting their very cold faces was painful. There would be grumbling among the ranks and a desire to get to France, where many thought there might be a warmer climate. They would get a hot reception in France, but it had nothing to do with climate change and everything to do with the Bosche army.

The train journey to Southampton docks was short. On the quayside, men milled around before being marched off to their ship. The port was full of cargo vessels. Standing before the SS Architect, some men wondered if this ship would get them to France. It was a relatively newly built cargo ship and certainly no pleasure liner. It was about 400 feet in length, but there seemed to be a lot of men to cram on board. Worse still, there were also some crates of supplies waiting to load.

On another ship along the dock, there were loading horses.

"No first-class cabin for the officers then," whispered John Christie.

"No cabin of any kind by the looks of it," said Rob. "I'm surprised they don't pack us in crates to load. We won't have much room to move."

"I hate the bloody sea." Grumbled Tommy Douglas. "If I'd wanted to go to sea, I'd have become a fucking sailor. Why can't they build a bridge to France? It's not all that far."

"No, it's not, but the water is deep," said John. "Can't get far enough down to sink pillars to support the structure."

"I should have learned to swim," grumbled Tommy. "You'd think to live by the sea, I'd have been able to do that."

"They'll have life jackets if we go down. They'll keep you afloat for a while," said Rob.

"That water looks bloody cold," complained Tommy.

"It is," said Joe. "It's winter, and the water will feel colder than the air around us. The water will make our uniforms wet and heavy. You will sink quickly. You might even freeze to death before you drown."

"Fuck," cursed Tommy. "There you go talking about death again. I'm sorry I brought the subject up."

"Right, you men," bellowed a seaman. "Get up the gangway and get yourselves a space for the voyage."

"Voyage," complained Tommy. "Makes it sound like a bloody cruise."

With that, the hordes of men shuffled towards the gangway and up onto the deck. On the deck, another sailor pushed them in the back.

"Move along now. We haven't got all day. We've got a tide to catch."

"How long will it take to get to France?" asked Tommy.

"Where you're going, about nine hours, so find somewhere to sit if you can."

The men shuffled towards a stairway and climbed down into the open hold. There was more space than they might have imagined from the dockside. They found space and laid their kit bags down. If it was going to be that long, then a short kip was probably in order. The bag would act as a pillow.

The engines sprang to life with a slow rhythmic thudding shaking the deck the men were either lying or sitting. Some men had stayed topside to watch the shop leaving. They would scamper below once they felt the cold wind blowing along the English Channel.

Passing the Isle of Wight, the engine noise increased as the ship gathered pace and reached full steam. The six men from Montrose had little interest in the sea. They had spent their lives living by it so. it held no great interest for them. Some on the ship had never seen the sea. They wanted to savor their trip.

The troops got hot soup around midday. There was also a small quantity of bread.

"What kind of soup is this?" asked John.

"Hot." was the monosyllabic answer from the sailor.

"Jesus," cursed Tommy. "It looks like a puddle of mud."

"Specialty of the day," mumbled the sailor.

"What happened to the Jolly Jack Tar we all hear about?"

"He's still at home in bed. I'm the miserable matelot."

"You should go on the Music Halls," muttered John as he shuffled down the rolling deck, trying not to spill too much of the soup.

Back at their space with their kit, the six sat and slurped their soup, dipping their bread into the soup. Drinking what remained was not easy, with the ship bouncing and swaying in the waves. All six wiped the spill from their greatcoats.

"At least we're not in with the horses," said Ian.

"That would not be so bad," said Rob. "Horses are docile animals and give off heat. It would be warmer with them than it is here."

"I should have joined the fucking cavalry," moaned Tommy. "I'm sure horses don't spend all their time talking about different ways to die."

"You're a right miserable bastard Tommy Douglas," said Joe. "It might have been better for us if you had chosen prison rather than the army."

"I'm beginning to think I made the wrong choice. Still, you're stuck with me now."

The group continued to finish off their mud-brown soup in silence. Terry wondered if his feeling of sickness was down to the soup or sea. Either way, he needed to get up on deck if he needed to throw up.

"I'll need to get up on deck. I might be sick."

"If you do throw up, remember to do it with the wind, not against it," said Ian. You'll know what rail to use as there will be others already there. Hold the rail tightly. You don't want to fall overboard. I doubt the ship will be able to stop and come back for you."

"Fuck, fuck, fuck," cursed Tommy. "There you go again."

Terry struggled through the mass of men towards the stair and vanished up onto the deck.

"I hope he's OK," said Joe. "Should one of us go with him?"

"No," said John. "There'll be plenty of people up there to help if he needs it. You've got enough of that soup down your uniform already. You don't want more, especially as it has come from someone's guts."

"You're disgusting," said Rob.

"That he is," said Joe. "Still, it makes sense. I'm staying put. Terry can do his worst on his own."

After cleaning up their mess tins, the men settled down and tried to get some sleep. Complaints about the hardness and rolling of the deck would pale into insignificance in the following days, weeks and months. This was almost luxury. Terry did not return to his pals until they started to approach the dock in Boulogne.

"If there's fish caught in the English Channel for supper tonight, don't eat it. I've seen what they eat, and it's not nice," he said.

"The thought of what you just said makes me want to throw up," said Joe as they all readied themselves to disembark.

Nine hours after leaving, the ship docked at the port of Boulogne in northwest France. It was dark, cold and very wet.

After the usual parade and roll call, the men were loaded onto trucks and headed off towards their positions at the front. His truck headed for an area between Roquetoire and Steenbecque some forty miles east.

Eight men from Edinburgh joined the group who had left from Montrose

The journey was bumpy and slow, taking over two hours. A full day in rough seas followed by a bumpy two-hour truck ride made for some world-class whining among the men. The distant sound of shellfire did nothing to lighten their mood, but nobody mentioned it.

They arrived at their battalion base tired, fed-up and hungry. First came the obligatory parade. The men were allocated their disposition to a company. Rob was in C company, as were Terry Greig and John Christie.

After a meal, they were all ordered their company billets. The three were surprised to see how few men were in the billets.

"Where are the rest of the men?" asked Terry.

"We are the rest," came the gruff reply.

"What happened?"

"Fucking war." That brought an end to that topic of conversation.

A corporal stuck his head into the room.

"I'm Corporal McLeish, your company NCOs. Get some rest. Stand to is at zero six hundred."

"And welcome to you too, corporal," muttered Rob.

"Did anybody say anything?"

"No, corporal."

After he had left, the man in the next cot to Rob spoke.

"I'm Jimmy. Jimmy Young."

"Rob Corsar."

"He's no so bad that yin. Some o' the others are real bastards. Still, we're being joined by whatever remains o' the 4th battalion in the next couple of days. We're ti build their huts."

"Why are they joining us then?"

"They're as bad beat up as us. Not much of either battalion left, so we're to become one."

"You mean that we're both so understrength that we have to combine to make a battalion?"

"Aye. That's what war does. Men die, go missing or get sent back home disabled, no able to fight. We're left ti get on wi it."

"Fuck."

"Aye. Best get some sleep because you'll be busy tomorrow. Night"

"Night." Rob lay back in his cot reflecting on the information he had just heard. I'll see you again, Lizzie, he promised himself.

TWENTY-EIGHT

Reveille on 16th December 1915 was at six o'clock as promised. The night had been a noisy one. There was much snoring and some men shouting during nightmares. As he started to get up from his cot, Rob asked Jimmy if the noise at night was normal.

"Aye lad, it is that. You'll see what this war does ti men. Best get going, or yon corporal will gee us hell."

The ablutions were some distance from the huts that the men slept. When Rob arrived, he could fully understand why this was so. The smell was ripe. The toilets were an open pit. The pit had sturdy wooden poles slung over it so that the soldiers sat and did their business.

As he sat and shit, Rob remembered his early life and thought that he must have had shit in worse places than this. On this cold, wet morning, he could not remember where that might have been. The smell made him feel sick. He got away as quickly as he could.

They washed and shaved in tin basins with cold water. Unknown to Rob at this moment, this was a luxury. Shaving and washing in water drawn from muddy puddles in the trenches were not uncommon.

Breakfast over, Rob and the rest of C Company were inspected. They went to build huts for men from the 4th Black Watch.

As a labourer in the Montrose docks, Rob worked with wood. He did not mind building huts. They were prefabricated buildings so, easy to slap together and nail in place, floor first. The walls were heaved up and nailed together. Each had openings for windows and a door. The roof was heaved into place and nailed. Finishing off the hut meant putting in windows and doors. Finishing touches were a stove, cots and cleaning equipment

Rob was anxious to find Lizzie's brother Willie. He spoke to his sergeant.

"My girlfriend's brother is in A Company, and I'd like to go see how he's doing and pass on messages from home."

"OK. They're over there." He pointed to a series of huts not far away. "Don't take long."

"No, sergeant. I'll be back quick."

Rob walked quickly to the area indicated by his sergeant. On arrival, he stopped to ask for directions.

"Is this A Company line?"

"It is. What do you want?"

"Where's Willie Ross?"

"Everywhere."

"What do you mean everywhere?"

"He's spread out all over no man's land. Took a direct hit from a shell a couple of days ago."

"He's dead?"

"That's what a direct hit from a shell will do to you. Why'd you want to know?"

"I'm walking out with his sister. We knew each other well."

"Well, he's gone now like all those others." He said it in such a matter of fact way that it caught Rob by surprise.

"Fuck. That's terrible. Lizzie will be beside herself. His mum and dad will be devastated."

"Lots of mums and dads are devastated now. There'll be plenty more before this war is over. Get used to it, lad."

"Thanks," said Rob absentmindedly as he walked towards his lines. He had no idea why he thanked the man for such terrible news. He wanted to scream his horror that his friend was spread-out all-over no-man's-land.

Of course, war killed men. Willie was the first dead soldier Rob had known. Willie was a good friend when he and Lizzie were first walking out. Rob felt a real deep sadness for possibly the first time in his life. He would sleep little that night. This news and the noise of men having nightmares would keep him awake. It was an occurrence that would become familiar. It would not take long before he would be so tired that he would mostly sleep through the din.

"Did you get what you were after?" asked his sergeant.

"He's dead. Blown to bits by a shell a few days ago."

"I'm sorry to hear it, lad. Best get on with your work to take your mind off it."

"Yes, sergeant." Rob went about his work as ordered. The weather was so bad that they cancelled the parade. Building the huts did not stop just because of rain.

After the evening meal, Rob returned to his cot. He was disturbed by the manner of Willie's death. He felt that he should write to Lizzie. He pulled out a piece of paper ready to write but did not know what to say. Sorry about the death of your brother seemed such a trite sentence. Rob had benefitted from compulsory education. Still, he did not know how to tackle this terrible task. He put the paper and his pencil down and lay on his cot.

"Is that you writing to your lassie?" asked Jimmy from his cot next to Rob.

"Yes. Her brother was in A Company, and I went to see him today, but he's dead. Killed in a direct hit from a shell."

"There's lots gone that way. At least they knew nothing about it. Bang, they're gone. Did you know him well?"

"His mother is a staunch catholic and used to send Willie out with Lizzie and me as a chaperone. He was good. He'd bring Lizzie to meet me, then stay mostly out of our way. I don't think his mum ever found out."

"He sounds like a good type."

"He was."

"Maybe best to leave it a couple of days before writing. There's an officer in our company called Glendinning He's good with words. He writes lots of letters to the families of dead men. He might be able to help."

"Aye. That's a good idea."

"Early stand too tomorrow. Best get some sleep while you can. There's no comfort in the trenches. Get your head down while you can. Good night."

"Thanks, Jimmy. Good night."

TWENTY-NINE

On 20th December 1915, Rob moved forward to the front-line trenches. It was not an easy journey. The communication trenches on the way were full of mud from the prolonged bad weather. Transit along them was difficult. It would be Rob's first close up experience of war in the trenches.

"I've seen peat bogs that were easier to cross than this," muttered Rob. He struggled to pull his boots from the mud that seemed to have hands trying to pull him down.

The front-line trenches themselves were every bit as bad. Looking around at them, Rob could see why Jimmy had warned him that there was no comfort in them. There was mud everywhere. He could even see the odd rat scurrying around.

Walking along duckboards, some of which were under mud and water, Rob looked at his home for the next few days.

The front trench wall had a fire step. There were sandbags in the wall up to a shelf holding ammunition boxes. Above that, there was an elbow rest with just enough room above for the parapet. The parapet was a solid wall of sandbags. Looking over the parapet, Rob could see the barbed wire rolls held in place by metal spikes driven well into the ground. It looked secure until he heard and felt the blast of a nearby exploding shell. He jumped at the sound.

Rob had only heard the noise of exploding shells from a distance so far. Up close, he heard and felt the explosions. The shelling was not intense, but a few exploded close to Rob's position. He jumped at each noise. He also felt the blast wave rattle his head when the shell exploded.

"That's just Fritz lobbing over a few shells to keep us on our toes," said Jimmy Young, who saw Rob's reaction to the noise. "Listen to ours going the other way. It'll make you feel better."

Rob did not know which noises signified allied or enemy shells.

"Don't worry, lad, when Fritz is serious about hitting you with his shells, you'll know."

Jimmy Young's casual demeanour helped Rob's fear a little, but not a huge amount. He was still remembering his friend Willie Ross. He remembered Willie sitting in the Traille Pavilion. He also had an unsettling image of Willie blown to bits.

Soldiers slept wherever they could find space. There were no beds or cots, just mud banks to rest on. In the front trenches, men dressed in kit ready for anything. They had their trenching tool slung over their back and their rifle to hand. Rob initially had difficulty sleeping. Mental and physical fatigue soon took care of that. Getting some rest was at a premium. He also did his turn on guard on the firing step. Even if it was quiet, there was still a need to be alert. Men slept with their kit handy ready for immediate action.

Every morning, an hour before dawn, there was a general stand-to in the trenches. Men were up and ready for a dawn attack by the Germans. There was a similar stand-too at dusk for the same reason.

After the first morning stand-to, the men stood ready for inspection. Looking at his kit, Rob wondered if he would pass muster. He was filthy, but his rifle was clean. That was the most crucial part of the inspection. The rest consisted of checking that he had all of the other bits and pieces he would need. The officer did not seem to notice his dirty state. He was no different from the rest of the men around him. After the inspection, he had a breakfast of bacon and bread and the daily tot of rum.

Soon after breakfast, they were all set to clean toilets, fill sandbags or repair duckboards.

"For any new men, here's the news. Over there are very accurate German snipers just waiting for a stupid Jock to put his head above the parapet," bellowed the sergeant pointing towards the enemy. "Keep your heads down, or you're just another dead soldier. None of us like dead soldiers because that means more work for the rest of us. Get to it then."

Rob's first task was to fill sandbags to shore up the trench defences. He was not afraid of hard work, but he was acutely conscious of the sergeant's warning.

"Where's the sand for the bags?" Rob asked Jimmy.

"You're standing in it, lad."

"So, I fill the sandbag with mud, not sand? How good is that at keeping us protected?"

"Not bad at all. Pack the bag hard enough with mud, and the Bosche bullets don't get through the solid dirt."

The explanation sounded good to Rob, so he got stuck into his task. It occurred to him that if he packed enough mud into the bag and put it on the parapet, there'd be less to walk around in.

Rob had written to Lizzie with the help of Second Lieutenant Glendinning, a man from Stirling. Still, it had not been an easy letter to write. He expressed his sorrow to her and her folks. He added a few words of reassurance supplied by the officer.

The rest was a report about the foul weather and conditions, especially the mud. It was a letter similar to many written before by other soldiers.

As he worked, he felt the thump and explosion from German shells. It did not take him long to determine the different types and the sort of damage they could do. The noise of them going the other way from allied guns helped even the score, he thought. They're getting some of what they're giving us.

On the second night, he got the job of repairing barbed wire in no-man's-land. It was dangerous work. German raiding parties might be out looking to kill or capture Allied troops. Then there were the snipers. Someone was always on guard for just such an event. Rob passed his first test unscathed physically. He had been acutely aware of the danger of working out in the open. All the time out there, Rob was on a constant lookout. The risk came from not watching what he was doing with the wire. He got caught up and spiked a couple of times because of inattention to his task. He remembered not to curse when he got spiked by the wire.

The following morning, a sharp nagging pain in his belly started to worry Rob. He wondered if he had caught some dreaded disease from the food or the conditions. He had already learned that stomach diseases were common in the trenches. Did he have one? The pain was getting much worse. He went to his Company Sergeant Major.

"Sir, I need to see the doctor."

"Why?"

"I have a stomach pain that's getting worse. I might have some disease or other."

There ensued a conversation that indicated that the CSM thought Rob might be malingering. Eventually, he relented.

"Right. Off you go, but be right back when you find out nothing's wrong."

"Yes, Sir."

Rob squelched his way along the communication trench to the first aid post where the M.O. was situated.

"What's your name and trouble, Private?"

"Private Corsar RS, Sir. I have a pain in my belly that won't go away."

"Point to the pain."

Rob pointed to the right side of his abdomen. "It's round here, Sir."

"Take your top clothes off and lie on that cot."

Rob obeyed, struggling out of his top and lying on the cot shivering in the cold.

"Here, you say?"

"Yes, Sir."

The doctor's hands felt about Rob's abdomen. He jumped when the doctor's cold hands touched his belly.

"Sore there?"

"No, Sir. Cold hands." The investigation continued with an occasional Umm from the doctor as he prodded and poked.

"Right, Private Corsar. Get dressed. Corporal Craig." The doctor shouted to the unseen corporal who came rushing in.

"This man needs to go to the base hospital for an operation. Get him there quickly."

"Yes, Sir."

"You have acute appendicitis. It needs to come out. You'll go to the base hospital for the operation. Any questions?"

"What's appendicitis, Sir?"

"It's inflammation of the appendix in your abdomen just about here." He put his hand on the right side of Rob's belly where he had the pain.

"What's an appendix, Sir? What's it do?"

"Good question, Private. No one knows what it does. It might be a useless organ, leftover when humans scratched about in caves or swung about in trees. What we do know is that it can be dangerous if not treated, and the only treatment is to cut it out."

"It's not something that I might need later on, is it?"

"No, you're better off without it. Once out, it won't trouble you ever again."

"This way, Private." Ordered Corporal Craig. "Transport's out here."

Rob was loaded onto a cart and driven off to the field hospital about a mile further back from the front.

At the tented hospital, Rob underwent a similar examination.

"Your M.O. got it right, Private Corsar. You have appendicitis. We'll have it out in no time." The decision was made by a Major who had introduced himself as Carlton-Smith. "Put him on a bed. No food or water, and we'll have him on the table as soon as one becomes free."

Later that night, a male orderly approached Rob with a shaving kit.

"I'm here to shave you. It's my Christmas present to you."

"I can shave."

"I'm sure you can shave your face, but I'm shaving your bollocks. That's where we operate. It needs to be as smooth as a baby's bum."

"Oh. Fair enough. Is it Christmas day then?"

"It is. Merry Christmas."

"And to you. Be bloody careful with that razor."

"Don't distract me. I've not had an accident doing this...yet."

The orderly had done it many times before.

"Right. Just wait for the operating table to be free, and you're off."

About an hour later, Rob went to the theatre. There were a couple of men in white coats and a nurse waiting. He recognised Carlton-Smith, who stood over him as he lay on the table.

"This is Doctor Taylor. He'll put you to sleep while we operate."

The shorter man stepped forward and explained the process.

"I'm going to put this mask above your nose and mouth." He showed Rob the steel instrument covered with gauze. "I'll put a few drops of liquid onto the mask, and you should breathe as normal. It'll seem strange, but don't fight it. Just breathe slowly and deeply, and you'll nod off to sleep. When you wake up, it'll be all over. OK?"

Rob just nodded. The mask stopped just above his nose and mouth. He just saw Taylor's other hand tilt a small bottle and soon started to feel drowsy.

"That's right. Breathe deeply," were the last words Rob heard. His eyes got heavier and slowly closed as he dropped off to sleep.

Rob eventually woke up in a bed in broad daylight. The curtain over his eyes was drawing back slowly. Soon, the tent roof started to come into focus. There was a soft female voice nearby.

"Hello. I'm Sister Gough. Everything's fine."

"Uh."

"You're in the ward now."

"It's done then?"

"Yes."

"It didn't take long. I was only out for a minute."

"It was a bit longer than that."

"How long then?"

"About an hour."

"It seemed shorter."

"The dressing is fine. There's no leaking from the wound, but you'll have to take it easy for a while until the stitches come out. Do you have any pain?"

"My belly feels like it's been kicked by a horse."

"I'll get you something for the pain. Here, sip this water."

Rob felt a tin spout on his lips. Tepid water flowed into his dry mouth.

"Not too much. Little and often for a while yet. Once we're sure everything is settling, we'll give you some tea and a little food."

"Thanks."

"Lie back and rest now. I'll be back soon with some pain relief."

Rob did as he was told. Despite having been asleep, he felt tired. The sister returned soon with pain relief and a little more water. Rob fell asleep almost as soon as she left.

Rob spent a couple of weeks in and around the hospital. When the surgeon was happy that the wound had healed, he returned to his unit. He also spent some time with a physical training instructor helping him regain muscle strength and mobility. Getting men back to the front as quickly as possible was the order of the day.

After a couple of weeks, the doctor took the stitches out and got sister Gough to redress the wound.

"You've done very well, Private Corsar. Your wound is healing nicely, and your mobility is good. You're going back to your unit, but I've ordered another week of light duties. Not too much strenuous exercise, or you'll split that wound in your belly. After that, it'll be up to your unit M.O. to decide what's best. We don't want you putting too much strain on your abdomen just yet. Don't want to undo our good work with a stupid heroic effort."

Rob picked up his kit bag and headed for the transport that would take him back to his unit.

THIRTY

The Company Sergeant-Major met Rob when his transport stopped at the orderly tent. He snatched and read the report that Rob handed him. He was not best pleased with what he read.

"Right, Corsar, stow your gear in that hut and report to the unit M.O. immediately."

"Yes, Sir." Rob marched back to the hut and lobbed his kitbag onto an empty cot. The billets were empty.

He stopped at the entrance of the medical tent and waited. His abdomen was still a bit sore.

"What's your problem, soldier?" asked a small gruff man in a dirty white coat.

"I'm reporting as ordered, Sir. I've just returned from the hospital. Here's the report the hospital sent with me."

The doctor took the envelope, pulled out the report and read it. He occasionally looked up at his patient assessing whether he was swinging the lead.

"Right, Private Corsar, let's have a look at this wound of yours. Take your top off and lie over there." He pointed to a small table.

Rob got out of his uniform and climbed onto the table. The doctor saw the dressing on his abdomen. He peeled it back and took a look.

"Yes. Not bad. They've done a decent job at the hospital. Still a bit early for full duties, Private. Don't want the wound opening up under heavy exercise. I'll keep you on light duties for a couple of weeks."

"Thank you, Sir."

"Don't be in a hurry to thank me, lad. It's my job to get you back into the trenches as quickly as possible. When I do, I don't want that wound opening up, and putting you out of action without a fight. I doubt you're in a hurry to get back there."

"No, Sir."

"No, indeed. It's a bloody mess out there. I'll dress the wound again. Need to keep it clean and free from infection. Ramage, my orderly, will redress the wound as needed. I'll get him to contact you later today. Here's your chitty for light duties."

"Thank you, Sir."

As they spoke, the doctor redressed his abdomen.

"Put your uniform back on. Keep it clean for another couple of weeks, and it should be fine. Off you go then."

"Thank you, Sir." With that, Rob marched off back to his company office to hand in his chitty. The Company Sergeant Major was unhappy seeing the one-week light duties report from the hospital being added to by the unit M.O.

"Is that doctor a relative of yours, Corsar?"

"No, Sir."

"Two bloody weeks of light duties. Right Corsar." Said the unhappy CSM. "We'll have you working in the orderly room, the kitchen, the stores and as a general runner. That should keep you occupied and out of mischief."

"I have to meet an RAMC medic called Ramage to have my wound looked at and dressed every couple of days. He needs to make sure it won't open up or get infected, Sir."

"Fine. There's Ramage over there. Ramage." The loud shout startled Rob and Ramage.

"Sir." Ramage's head swivelled as he recognised the CSM's roar. Feigning deafness was not an option. Such a bellow usually meant trouble.

"Here now, at the double."

Ramage trotted very quickly towards the two men and stood at attention.

"At ease, Ramage. This is Private Corsar. You are to dress his wound and get him fighting fit."

"Yes, Sir. The M.O. told me to find him."

"If I catch either of you malingering, you'll wish you were dead. Start tomorrow after breakfast. I'll be watching you. Dismissed Ramage." Gordon Ramage snapped to attention, about turned and marched away.

"Right, Corsar, we'll start you in the store today. We're checking equipment stocks. You can count, can't you?"

"Yes, Sir."

"Right. Report to the quartermaster. He'll know what to do with you." Rob snapped to attention, about turned and marched off to the supply store.

The duties assigned to Rob that day were not arduous. It was a relief. After the evening meal, Rob found a letter for him on his cot. It was from Lizzie. It lifted his spirits as he opened and read it.

My Dearest Rob,

Your letter came today, and it was so good to hear from you. It has been hard here since Willie was killed. Mum spends most of her time crying, and Dad walks around muttering to himself. I can't hear what he is saying, but it sounds like he is in a temper.

Christmas was so sad for us. We did not celebrate because we were all upset at the news. Mum goes to the chapel a lot. She gets comfort from the priest. He tells her that Willie's in a better place now. I can't bring myself to go with her. I'd likely ask the priest where was God when Willie needed him. I'm sure the priest would not like that.

I answered the door when the telegram came. As soon as I saw the postie, I knew what it was. I didn't want to take it. The postie was also upset at having to hand these things out. I nearly fainted when Dad read it out. I'm angry at God for what he let happen to Willie.

I took the day off work. When I went back, old man McArdle was angry at me. Rose gave him a tongue lashing reminding him of his son at the front. He did apologise.

I hope you are OK and keeping safe. I miss you so much and long for you to come home to me. I think of you often, and I kiss your little brass engagement ring for you every day.

I have heard that soldiers at the front get leave to come home. Do you know if you will get any? I'm so desperate to see you again.

I wish this war was over, and you could come home safe to me.

I Love You

Lizzie

The letter boosted his morale, but he realised he might have to write to Lizzie and tell her he had been in hospital. Still, it was not for a proper war wound, just an inflamed appendix. Not so bad.

My Dearest Lizzie

I am sad to hear of your folks' troubles. I've no idea how it must feel to lose a child. I hope that time will heal.

I was in the hospital over Christmas. I had a bellyache that turned out to be appendicitis. They said it needed taking out, so they put me to sleep and cut it away. It seems an appendix has no function in the body except to cause trouble. I'm still a bit sore. It kept me away from the front, and I've got light duties until I'm well enough to go back to full duties.

The weather here is terrible. The rain never seems to stop, and we spend our time wading through deep mud. Not pleasant when you can't wash properly in the trenches. We all smell a bit. Since we all smell, it's not that bad.

The chaps are spending a lot of time training at the moment. We've had a lot of new lads join us, and we're trying to fit together. Many are lads from the Dundee area, so no problem understanding each other. The English lads in the battalion have real difficulty understanding our accents. Things coming along fine.

The fighting goes on as usual. We lob shells at Fritz, and he lobs shells at us. Strange how quickly you get used to the noise followed by an eerie silence. Still, the brass keeps us active with lots of training, building and repairs to equipment, huts and trenches.

I miss you. My love to you and give my best wishes to your folks.

Rob

At the end of his two weeks of light duties, Rob was pronounced fit by the Medical Officer.

"Sorry old chap, but it's up to the front for you now."

As he thanked him, Rob realised that this was an automatic response.

His thanks to the doctor were not sincere. They would have been if he had sent him back to Scotland, out of the war. Still, he'd had a few weeks away from the hell of the trenches. Being grateful for small mercies was how he looked on it.

"Well, Corsar, you're back in this war," said Company Sergeants Major Fowler. "The Bosche will be shaking in his boots."

"I'm sure they will, Sir."

"Back to C Company for you. Report to Captain Hoyle first, he'll sort you out."

"Yes, Sir." Rob snapped to attention, about turned and headed for his company Commanding Officer, a man he did not know.

"Private Corsar, fit and ready for duty, it says. You're to report to your platoon commander, Lt. Duke down there."

"Yes, Sir." Rob walked off down the trench to find his platoon commander and re-join the war. He did not think for one moment that Fritz would be shaking in his boots.

THIRTY-ONE

Since the start of the war a year earlier, the 5th Battalion Black Watch had suffered heavy losses. The unit was under strength, despite a regular trickle of recruits. It was now well below half strength. That much was apparent to Rob.

The 4th Battalion Black Watch was in a similar position. The two half-strength battalions in the same regiment joined into the new nearly full-strength 4/5 Battalion Black Watch. There would be as much paperwork created about the name and dispositions of officers and men of the new battalion as there would be in a battle report.

As he rejoined the war, the officers and men of the two battalions were busy sorting out their dispositions. The compositions of each company and platoon also required skilful management. There was lots of chatter and administration between officers and NCOs to ensure an even spread of appropriate skills in all parts of the new battalion.

It did not take long for Rob to fall into the routine of the war. It may seem odd to suggest that a supposedly chaotic war could be routine, but it was. It had its rhythm. As a result, each man fell into the pattern that the army wanted and needed from its front-line troops.

Each man spent about eight days in the front-line trenches, about eight days in the reserve trenches and about eight days at rest behind the lines. The plan was an eight-day rotation, just like a factory shift pattern, only measured in days, not hours. Naturally, this routine only applied if it suited the army and the situation at the front. In war, everything is in a constant state of change. As such, change itself becomes routine for ordinary foot-soldier. It produced a lot of ammunition for them to grouse and moan.

At rest, behind the lines, was hardly an accurate description. One of the first jobs was to be de-loused. There might even be a hot bath to wash out the dirt and mud from every part of a human body. It would be a communal bath in a giant wooden tub.

The clean man now had to do the same for his uniform and equipment. Getting the lice out from the pleats in a kilt was no simple task. There were frequent kit inspections. Woe betide any man not found up to scratch, which seems an odd phrase for men who had just been de-loused.

There was a shortage of labourers in France to build roads, railways, and all the paraphernalia of a wartime army. Troops supposedly resting behind the lines were co-opted into those tasks. Rest was a relative term, meaning less exposure to shell-fire and machine guns.

All men in a platoon or company were to behave as a team. The introduction of so many new men made this challenging. The army reverted to the tried and tested ways of ensuring teamwork. Teamwork was another name for prolonged close order drilling. The sight and sound of groups of soldiers marching, turning and halting as one was satisfying to most NCOs. Those NCOs with an evil streak were never content.

There were physical exercises to keep the men fighting fit. They also underwent exercises in hand-to-hand combat and bayonet skills to make them effective killers. There were also training exercises on how to throw grenades. Gas mask drills increased. It had become a more frequent form of attack.

The most regular lectures were those describing proper personal hygiene. Personal hygiene also required discussion about venereal disease when close to local towns. In almost every war, sex-trade flourishes close to the battle zone. There were even occasional silent films screened.

During the Boer War, the British army lost around twenty-two thousand men from an army of half a million men. More than half of these succumbed to diseases, like typhoid, dysentery and other intestinal disorders. Had there been proper regard for the personal hygiene of the ordinary soldier, fewer deaths may have occurred. During this war, the army decided to avoid the same mistake. Given the conditions in the field for the men, this was an uphill battle.

It is a myth that life in the trenches was day-long chaos and carnage. The truth was that life in the front-line trenches was long periods of boredom interspersed with relatively short periods of terror and carnage.

Rob's day started with the stand-to an hour before dawn. All men in the trenches stood ready to repel an enemy dawn attack. The enemy also started the day with a stand-to. Most attacks happened at dawn, so both sides had learned by experience.

After stand-to, there was breakfast and ablutions. Shaving in dirty puddle water was usual. The army required its men to be clean-shaven at all times. They spent the remainder of the day repairing or shoring up the trench if needed. They also took turns on the fire step on guard duty. All of this was done with their heads down for fear of German snipers. Then there was chatting. While there was talking, it was an exercise in personal hygiene. The men spent time finding and killing lice in their uniforms and bodies. They killed lice by crushing them between thumb and forefinger. It was an unequal struggle. Sometimes small groups of men would sit together, grooming the hair of their fellow soldiers. Seeing this display, one might think that homo sapiens had not evolved very far from their ape ancestors.

Cards and gambling were also everyday pursuits. Rob learned card games he had never heard of or seen. He tried a couple, but rapidly dwindling cash in his pocket soon stopped that. Rob's inexperience was easy prey for the hardened gamblers in the battalion.

Occasional music from someone who had an instrument such as a mouth organ helped break the monotony. Scottish Regiments had their pipers. They were a brave, hardy bunch. They would sit in the trenches and dug-outs playing during long periods of inactivity. They were also there to lead men into battle. Rob had seen them clamber over the wall, fill their bagpipes with air and play as they marched towards the enemy guns. They carried no weapons, and many were killed or seriously wounded. Rob was glad he wasn't musical. Still, Rob found it was easy to march behind them as he and his mates left the trenches and wandered about France. Sometimes they could hear music coming from the German trenches.

They did work outside the trench under cover of darkness. Darkness could be made bright by enemy star shells bursting overhead. Facedown in the mud was the best protection from this situation.

Two other activities usually took place at night. Parties returned to the supply depot for ammunition, food and water. Changing of the troops in the trenches also took place at night. There was little chance for detection from German spotter aircraft.

Sitting in the trench idling his time cleaning his equipment or chatting, Rob was only too aware that terror could descend at any moment. When he heard the scream of incoming shells, Rob could now determine if they would land close to his position or not. A sudden dive for cover was often required. Rob had seen what was left of men who were not quick enough.

Except during an attack, enemy shelling was sporadic and random. The lull between incoming rounds gave Rob some respite, but he was in a constant state of readiness. He often left the trenches after what was described as a quiet period, very tired. He thought it was just sleeping in fits and starts in uncomfortable positions. Nervous exhaustion was not a phrase known to Rob or any of his pals.

Jimmy Young's words often came to Rob in the front-line trenches. "We lob shells at them, Rob, and they lob shells at us. Neither side knows if a real attack is coming or just some artilleryman needing aiming practice. Ours need all the practice they can get. They have killed enough of us. Blind bastards."

It did not take Rob or any new man to the trenches to know when an enemy attack was coming their way. Their barrage fell in front of the Black Watch trenches. It was to cut the barbed wire. It was an announcement of an impending attack. Rob did not need telling what was about to happen. Allied attacks started in the same way.

Rob had learned that there was a subtle difference. The German trenches were much better fortified. As soon as the Allied shelling stopped, the Germans clambered out of their holes to prepare their machine guns. As the Boers learned, rows of men marching slowly towards them were easy targets for guns.

The only silent attacker was gas. Weather and wind conditions dictated when these attacks took place. Canisters of gas were placed in front of the trenches, and their valves opened when the wind was right. The gas drifted silently towards the unsuspecting enemy on the prevailing wind. Shouts of Gas, Gas, Gas, accompanied by the clanking of metal on an old shell case from the defending troops spread panic. Gas was not a very effective killer of men but did have a psychological benefit.

All soldiers in the front-line trench had two jobs. In an attack, he was the first over the top to face deadly accurate German machine gunfire. If the enemy attacked, his second task was to be the first line of defence. He had to stand and hold the enemy advance at any cost to himself.

Soldiers in the reserve trench would constitute the second wave of an advance. Rob stood in the reserve trenches hoping that the first wave would do everything needed and he would not have to follow into the murderous machine gunfire.

Rob and the rest of the men knew what they had to do in any attack. It was all written down in detail like a plan for a parade. The number of paces apart, start time, march line abreast keeping good dressing, take the objective. As soon as Rob and his pals moved forward, they all knew the plan would fall apart. There had been a case where the second line of advancing troops fired on troops coming the other way only to find their first line retreating. That was not in the plan.

If the attack had not gone to plan, junior officers often waited until they got instruction from their senior officers. Meanwhile, Rob and the rest of the men headed for cover. They also waited to be told what to do next. Self-preservation took over. The chain of command had to be observed.

Despite combining the two half battalions and a steady trickle of new volunteers from home, the balance of the battalion's manpower establishment was still in a slow, steady decline.

THIRTY-TWO

Throughout February and March 1916, the two sets of men and officers set about making a cohesive unit of the new composite 4/5 Battalion of the Black Watch.

The new composite unit was to be called the 4/5 Black Watch. It got its name on 15 March. It took the army almost three months to come up with that name. The Battalion was under the command of Lt. Col. Sceales. His new company Officer Commanding was to be Major Cruickshank.

On Sunday 19 March 1916, Rob went to see his Company Sergeant-Major, Steele. He was Steele by name and steel by nature.

"Sir, can I be excused from the church parade?"

"Why? Are you sick?"

"No, Sir, I don't believe in God. I'm an atheist."

This information took CSM Steele by surprise, and it took him a few seconds to gather his wits for a reply.

"A what?"

"An atheist, Sir."

"No, you're fucking not Corsar. You are in Gods army, and you are a fucking Christian. What's more, you are a Church of Scotland Christian."

"It says on my papers that I'm an atheist, Sir."

"I don't care what it says on a fucking piece of paper. There are no heathen atheists in my company. Got that Corsar?" The CSMs voice carried far and wide as if he wanted God Himself to hear what he was saying.

"Yes, Sir. I'd still like to be excused church parade." The Sergeant Major thought for a moment before he spoke again.

"OK, Corsar, you are excused church parade." Rob's smile of triumph was short-lived. "Church of Scotland Christians attend church parade. Heathen atheists run around the parade square in the full kit until the church parade is over. So, Corsar. Christian or atheists?"

It took Rob no time at all to make that decision.

"I'm Church of Scotland Christian, Sir."

"I thought you might be. Get fell in with the rest of the Christians. Don't let me hear any more heathen shite in my company again."

"No, Sir. Thank you, Sir." Rob about-faced and marched off towards the other troops assembling for the church parade. It was worth a try, he thought. Rob thought it a pity that he was not off sick, along with about 150 other men who all had scabies. "They are not going to church today," Rob muttered to himself.

The Reverend Hagan's service was every bit as dull, dreary and uninspiring as the weather.

On 23rd March, The Battalion marched from their base at La Belle Hotesse to Hazebrouk, some five miles away. The weather had changed from a burst of brief spring sunshine to wet and snowy making it a difficult journey. At Hazebrouk, they jumped on a train and headed to Etaples, or Eat Apples as the troops called it, south of Boulogne.

The following day the men paraded for a medical inspection as there had been another mass outbreak of scabies. There was another full kit inspection.

On 25th March, they moved to the 39th Infantry Brigade Base Depot. They all underwent complete disinfection that included a complete change of equipment and underclothes.

The process of ridding soldiers of the contagious scabies was treatment over several days. First, they were rubbed all over with soft soap. They then lay for twenty minutes in a warm bath. The last five minutes of the bath, they scrubbed each other's infected sites with a soft brush. They dried themselves and were then liberally covered with sulphur ointment.

"Pay special attention to hands, feet and cocks," shouted an RAMC doctor. "A gentle scrubbing of your cocks is all I want to see. Anything else, and you are on a charge. See you tomorrow for a repeat."

After four days of treatment, Rob got a new set of everything he wore. Everything that he used had to be disinfected, including the string of his identity discs.

"That's one pile of uniform we won't need to hunt for lice in." Rob, like several others, was standing naked, waiting for his new underwear. "It's bloody cold standing like this."

"I can see that," said Jimmy Walker, who was looking down at Rob's genitals.

"Very funny, Jimmy."

The following day, more reinforcements arrived. His company received thirty-four new men. It was helpful, as the next day they were all employed digging trenches as a training exercise. Who knew that there was a right and wrong way to dig a hole in the ground, thought Rob?

By 1st April, the unit had marched the seven and a half miles from Caudescue to Riez Bailleul. Four days later, they relieved the 1/6 Cheshires. They were south of La Gourge at Ebenezer farm. It was a quiet section of the line. Nevertheless, three men were seriously wounded.

There was a general issue of the new Khaki Tam O'Shanters to all other ranks when relieved on the 8th of April. Better still, back at the depot, the men could have a bath, and more clean clothing was also issued. Rob looked at the neat piles of clean clothing on tables and the piles of dirty clothing on the floor. Maybe the mills back in Montrose are getting good work out of this, he thought.

This resupply was a prelude to ceremonial inspection by the XI Army Corps Commander, Lt General, Sir R.C.B Harding. It was not a regular inspection or parade. It was a ceremonial parade, with the pipe band, befitting the top brass. Any cock-ups or failures on this parade had dire consequences. None happened. The unit was congratulated on its skill, especially since it was a new composite battalion. The routine continued as before, with the unit moving forwards and backwards as ordered.

Late in April, the Battalion was at rest in La Pannerie. There were sports competitions between companies. The men enjoyed the weather that was good enough to take daily baths in the nearby canal. Having swum in the North Sea, which was cold, even in summer, swimming in a French Canal in Spring was bliss by comparison. Rob enjoyed the light relief afforded by these swimming days. He was not a good swimmer, but splashing about in a canal was good fun.

April was a good month. Only seventeen men were wounded and one killed. May was a similarly quiet month with one man killed and twenty-one wounded.

Sitting in the trench cleaning his uniform on a quiet day in May, Rob absentmindedly looked up. His eyes traversed up the dark trench wall, and in the gap between the front and back parapets, he saw a mostly blue sky with occasional white clouds. He was transported back to his youth. The view reminded him of one day in particular. He thought he would be about six or seven years old. He had no work on the farm, so he took himself off to his favourite place about a mile from his family cottage. He did not know it's real name, so he called the Wee Glen. In truth, it was not much of a glen. It was only about one hundred and fifty feet deep and less than a hundred yards edge to edge. It had been carved out over centuries by the wee burn that ran down from the nearby hills.

On the slopes of the glen, there were a variety of trees. As a country boy, he had learned to identify sycamore, silver birch, oak, chestnut, rowan and beech trees, all of which inhabited the slopes and rim of the glen. Under the trees was a blanket of ferns about the height of a small boy. All over both slopes were small glades, with patches of sunlight streaming through the trees onto the ferns below.

As he sat in the trench, Rob remembered walking into the ferns and finding a small clearing in the trees. He flattened some ferns to make a den and lay down on his back in the dappled shade. Rob stared up through the clearing at the light blue sky. He remembered a white cloud meandering across the clearing onto his blue canvas. At first, it looked like a tree with a bushy head and small trunk. As it moved on, the wind changed its shape. It became a man with a long nose before sliding out of view behind the canopy. Other clouds followed, and he remembered trying to identify their shapes.

As he lay there, he remembered hearing the pee-wit and burbling sounds of the Lapwings and Curlew from the moor on the other side of the glen. There was even the occasional cooing of a Wood Pidgeon, lowing of a cow or bleating of a sheep. The leaves of the trees gave a faint rustle in the gentle summer breeze. Lying on his back, looking up and enjoying the day, he saw a tiny brown speck fluttering high above him. He heard the unmistakable trilling of a skylark. He had heard one before, but this was the first time he had seen and heard one in flight.

Rob loved the countryside as a child. It was wide open and offered him so much freedom to roam and play. Despite appearing empty, it was full of life in the form of animals, birds and fish in the rivers. He also liked the landscape that changed colours with the seasons. He enjoyed time with other children. He also enjoyed his own company.

The Wee Glen was a place full of adventure, he remembered. He could not remember how many battles he had fought here alongside Robert the Bruce when he and his trusty wooden claymore had slain many English invaders. The burn had flowed red with their blood. He'd also taught the thieving MacDuffs a lesson for stealing his clan's cattle. On this day, there would be no battles against the English. The clans were also at peace. Remembering where he was and why he wondered if this relative peace would last.

He stood up and looked through the holes in the parapet at the land before him. It must have been countryside at some time, given the names of farms or woods that they spent time marching past. It was not the countryside now. It was a thin desolate, pockmarked strip of foul-smelling waste ground devoid of vegetation, There were no trees or bushes for the birds to roost or nest, only shattered stumps, between two warring armies stretching as far as the eye could see in both directions.

It was the area known as No-Man's-Land. The suggestion that no man resided here was wrong. The ground was full of the decomposing bodies of young men from all corners of the globe, buried in this thin strip of foul-smelling desolation.

And yet, the area was also full of living creatures. There were thousands of rats and countless millions of bloody lice. This last thought made Rob scratch his head.

"If this war ever ends, I wonder if this place will return to being countryside once again?"

"What's that you're sayin, Rob?"

Startled out of his daydream, Rob turned to see Dougie Henderson. "Sorry, Dougie. I was talking to myself."

"Bad habit Rob. You were asking if this war would ever end, weren't you?"

"Aye, I suppose I was."

"This war will end someday, Rob. At the rate we're killing each other, one side will run out of men to fight, and the war will be over."

"That's a cheery thought and no mistake, Dougie."

"Maybe so, Rob. Maybe so."

His daydream shattered Rob sat back down and got on with the mindless task of cleaning his equipment and killing lice. This last task was an unequal battle. Killing lice between thumb and forefinger made a squelching noise. No matter how many lice he killed, he knew that this was one foe that never seemed to run out of troops

On the 10th of June, a Captain Watt Commanding of B Company was in temporary command of Rob's C Company. There was a sustained barrage of rifle grenades on Rob's position. The Captain got hit on his thigh and evacuated to the CCS. All around him, Rob saw men hit by shrapnel from Bosche grenades. Lying and bleeding from their wounds, Rob and his uninjured comrades quickly dashed to help.

Robs first effort was on Archie Duke, who had wounds to his legs and thighs. Rob grabbed Archie's webbing belt and tied it tightly around the top of Archie's thigh. Rob could not see if that helped. Stretcher-bearers arrived and pushed him out of the way.

"Out of the way," one ordered. "We'll get him to the Clearing Station. He needs a doctor."

There were not many stretcher-bearers, so Rob moved to the next man, Lachlan McKay. His wounds were superficial as far as Rob could tell.

"Stick your field dressing on it. You'll be OK," said Rob.

There was not much that Rob could do except try to stem any bleeding before being carried away to the CCS. Rob watched some of the men he had befriended and many he did not know, being carried away wounded. The unrelenting carnage was getting to him.

Rob had become upset when he heard of Willie Ross's death in December. Now, some of the dead and wounded were his pals. He had bunked down beside them. He had chatted with them and played the occasional game of cards, sometimes winning money and sometimes losing. His night-time dreams, full of shattered bodies, bloody wounds and the screams of dying men he had known, were becoming more frequent. He often woke, mid-dream, with a jolt and shout.

On the 16th of June, Rob got a 19th birthday gift of sorts. One of the Bosche rifle grenades exploded in his trench only a few yards away. The man between Rob and the grenade took the brunt of the blast and died. Rob got away Scot free. Not that Rob had any chance to celebrate his birthday, he was too busy helping the wounded, cleaning up and dodging grenades.

On the 24th of June 1916, Rob and his pals got disturbing news. They learned that everything was to be made ready for the Great Western Offensive.

"I suppose this quiet could not last," said Rob to Jimmy Young.

"No. The brass always has some hair-brained scheme to get us all killed. Better start wring letters home, Rob. Who knows what we're in for. The bastards had me on that black-hand-gang on the 16th. Shite, it was hairy. The Bosche will get me one day."

"Good idea about the letters. Don't know why you're grumbling since you got back safe. Those miners did a good job distracting Fritz."

"They did. It wasn't a big mine but enough to worry Fritz. Helped us sneak in before they knew we were there. We killed a few and took a couple of prisoners. Some of our guys were wounded. We were lucky that none got killed."

"I heard you only captured one Bosche? Is that wrong?"

"Yes. The second one created such a commotion that somebody said, I will name no names, shoot the bastard. Put him out of his misery. So, he was shot and left. One more tick in the killed column."

"That's a bit harsh. Was he that much trouble?"

"You've no idea. He was shouting and carrying on like a lunatic. The best thing for him I think."

"One less to worry about when we go over the top for the big push."

"True, but he's got thousands of pals who are all still alive."

"Maybe this will end the war, this big push."

"Aye, maybe so. If it's like the other big pushes, it'll get lots of us killed, and the war will go on."

"Do you think so?"

"I've no idea, lad. The brass has had similar plans in the past. None helped us win the war then. Still, it gave us lots of practice at burying bodies."

"You're a cheery bastard and no mistake."

"Best get your letters written. Who knows when we'll get the off."

As he wrote his letter to Lizzie, Rob was a bit worried. The letters from Lizzie had not been regular for a while. They were also not quite so warm as they had been at first. He wondered if it was just the fact that he was permanently on the move. Still, others were getting their letters. Maybe something had happened to her on the farm. She could have been injured or something like that. Even with that thought in his mind, he sat down and wrote his letters. He did one for Lizzie and one for his folks. He did not get much in the way of response from his folks. A couple of letters from his sisters, nothing more. They usually arrived in the same envelope, each sister writing a single page.

THIRTY-THREE

Far from July being the big push for the men of the 4/5 Battalion Black Watch, most of the month, and a portion of August, was spent marching. They started at Festubert, and by late August, they were at Englebelmer some fifty miles away. If there was a big push, it was happening elsewhere. Mind you, with a seventy-pound pack, the march was quite a push on its own.

On the first day of the march from Festubert, the troops set the tone for the following days.

"What about a song, lads?" shouted Duncan Kennedy on the first day.

Within a few seconds, a voice in the ranks started singing, We're Here Because We're Here. Men around him joined in, and soon the wave of noise spread throughout the troops. The tune was Auld Lang Sine, but those were not the words sung. The words were "We're Here Because We're Here Because." It would not be seemly for officers to join in such singing. Had one been close enough to Captain Rettie marching at the head of the company, they would have heard him humming the tune. He also had a slight grin.

There was a wide repertoire of songs heard during the next few days. It's a Long Way to Tipperary, Bombed Last Night, Two German Officers Crossed the Line, Pack Up Your Troubles, and many more sung on these days.

The one song that senior officers objected to was 'Hanging On The Old Barbed Wire'. Different Regiments had different versions of the words.

Rob and the other soldiers could not tell higher ranking soldiers what they thought of them face to face. They put their views into a song.

It helped their morale while poking fun at the distant location of senior ranks. It allowed them to voice opinions they could not speak openly. Senior Officers especially came in for some disrespect in the song.

The title tells you the position of private soldiers. They were all hanging on the old barbed wire.

They marched about eight miles a day in the searing heat. Rob spent much of his time wiping the sweat from his face with the sleeve of his tunic. The redness of his face was partly due to rubbing it with his coarse tunic and partly down to sunburn.

There were occasional rest days on the march, but they often involved kit inspections. Then there were the parades. As they moved from one Commanders area to the next, the new man wanted a parade and march past.

"Who the fuck is inspecting us today?" Grumbled Rob.

"Fucked if I know," said Davey Roberts. "Just another high up yin wanting to show who is boss. Let's get fell in before the CSM comes and looks for us."

They spent much of their time marching. When not marching, the troops endured parades and march pasts for various Generals. There were frequent kit inspections and training. All the while they sweated in the searing heat.

"I suppose marching, even in this heat, is better than getting shelled and shot at in the trenches." Rob was speaking to the man next to him in the column. It was a recruit that Rob had not met before.

"I've no idea what it's like in the trenches, I'm new out here."

"Why'd you enlist?"

"No choice. I got conscripted."

"Shite. What were you doing to get conscripted?"

"Nothing. My name just came up, and away I had to go. Any idea where we're going?"

"Not a clue. We usually only find out when we arrive. We heard a few weeks ago that we were to be ready for the big push. I suppose we are being sent somewhere dangerous."

"Isn't everywhere dangerous in a war?"

"True, but some places are more dangerous than others. By the way, I'm Rob, Rob Corsar from Montrose."

"Arthur Herschell from Dundee."

The pair carried on marching to an as yet unknown destination. Unknown to the two, in 1935, Arthurs niece, Gertie, would marry Robs younger brother, Frank.

"Are there any more of your family here?" asked Arthur.

"No. Just me. My oldest brother was at sea at the start, but he jumped ship in America."

"Safe there, at least."

"What about you? Any of your family here?"

"Aye. My eldest brother has been out here since December last year."

"Is he somewhere in the Black Watch?"

"No. He's with the Field Artillery somewhere behind us."

"If you are going to use a gun, best make it a big one that you can fire from a distance. We call it long-range snipers."

"Good thought. Had his fill of carrying a rifle in the Boer War."

"That was a bloody affair I heard from an old pal of mine in the Montrose shipyard. I suppose he got his fill of marching about in a bright red uniform. It made a great target for the Boers."

"He was a horseman in some unit of guides. Not sure what he did. He doesn't talk much about it. Came back a changed man."

"How so?"

"He was bad-tempered and a bit too handy with his fists. He used to be good company, but that all changed after the war."

"No family then?"

"He has. He's got seven kids, and they live in Montrose. You might have met him around. His name's Allan Herschell."

"Met plenty like him, but I don't remember the name."

"He's a good bit older than you. Ten years older than me, mid-thirties now."

"Well, I hope he can aim straight with that big gun. A few of our men have been killed by our guns. Bad enough if Fritz gets you, at least they aim at you."

"Looks like we're getting ready to call a halt for the day. I'm glad as my feet are sore. I'm not used to all this route marching yet."

"It's what we do, Arthur. We're infantry foot soldiers. Best get used to it."

THIRTY-FOUR

By the 1st of September, the battalion was in billets in Englebelmer. Now, they were being made ready for their part in a big push on Beaumont-Hamel and the surrounding area. On the 3rd of September, the battalion went into action along the valley of the river Ancre east of Beaumont-Hamel.

"Must be serious," said Rob to Jimmy Young. "Look at all that fucking kit they're having us carry."

"Can't be anything good, that's for sure."

"Well, best get ready for the off."

"A Company is to lead, it seems. We're behind. There they go."

With that, the men of A Company marched out of their narrow starting point. It would have been a problem in daylight, but it was night.

"Move up." The order was shouted, by the Company Commander.

Rob and Jimmy marched forward to the point where A Company had just left.

"Nothing happening from the Bosche," said Rob. "Maybe we've caught them asleep."

"No fear of that, Rob. They've got men watching just like we have. They probably can't see us in the dark."

"Right men, off we go. Keep your dressing."

Just as he heard the order, all hell broke loose on A Company. The enemy was not asleep.

C Company moved forward, rifles at the ready. Rob was terrified. He remembered Eric Wilson's comments about hearing and smelling war without seeing much of it. There was the crash of the German trench mortars and rifle grenades. There was also the unmistakable crack of rifle and rat-tat-tat of the machine guns all pointing at him, or so Rob thought. He heard the sickening noise of bullets entering flesh all around him, the screams and cries of wounded and dying men. Then there was the bee-like buzzing sound as bullets rushed close by without hitting him. There was also a terrible smell of cordite and rotting, decomposing flesh from previous attacks. As shells exploded, they threw up mud and decomposed body parts. He got covered in detritus. Any minute now, he thought. Not long afterwards, Rob saw some men heading towards him.

"There's Bosche coming at us," yelled Rob.

"No. It's A Company. They've got kilts on." That was the voice of the Company Commander. "They must be being pushed back."

Sure enough, men of A Company started to arrive in haste and confusion.

"Hold there, you men," shouted the Company Sergeant Major. "What happened?"

"We got to our objective fine, and then they shelled, bombed and machine-gunned us. We were outnumbered and outgunned. Men were falling everywhere." It was the voice of corporal of A Company. He was distressed at what had happened.

"Right," said Captain Wilson. "You men stay here and wait for orders. Where are your officers?"

"There's only Lieutenant Edwards left. All the rest are dead."

"Where is Lieutenant Edwards?"

"He's coming up behind us somewhere."

"Find him and bring him to me, corporal."

"Yes, Sir."

The corporal rushed off to look for his officer. In the dark, what remained of the men were reorganised.

Battalion HQ gave orders to advance. The surviving men of A and C Companies moved forward again. This move resulted in even more casualties.

"Fuck." Rob swore as he moved forward. It was an expression of fear for his life. "Make it clean and quick," he muttered quietly to himself so as not to alert his comrades to his terror.

The remaining men halted short of their objectives and dug in. They were unable to advance as they had already lost too many men. They had not received orders to retire, so they hunkered down, kept their heads down and hoped.

During the day, the Germans used trench mortars and rifle grenades on the Black Watch positions inflicting even more casualties.

An officer appeared and started to take stock of the situation. He ordered a Lewis gun onto a nearby bluff to give them cover. It proved a sound move. Orders came back and forth with Rob and the rest of the soldiers no wiser as to what might happen next.

"We're going forward. The Sussex regiment on our right is advancing. We are to keep up on their flank."

The officer shouted so that the men could hear over the din of gunfire. "Keep your heads down, men. Advance."

The forward momentum did not last long. The enemy gunfire was too precise, and casualties were mounting. Men were falling all around Rob. Looking around at the wounded, he was sure he would die. He wondered what death would be like when it came.

In the daylight, the situation was clear, even to the ordinary soldier. Their position was hopeless. Still, the men kept up their efforts to consolidate as best they could. Rob and two other men were sheltering in a shell hole, giving fire when they could. Bullets came at them from the front and both sides. Rob had no idea if any of his shots hit a German.

Close to his position, there was a tremendous blast. The percussion and clouds of earth were dreadful. Some of the dirt fell into Rob's hole.

"There's men buried under that earth." A voice called from somewhere between Rob and the point of the blast. "We need help to dig them out. Anyone near enough to help?"

Rob thought about it for a moment. He was not keen to launch himself into open ground. He realised that if he were in that position, he would want others to help.

"I'm off to help," said Rob to the other two. "Come or stay. It's no matter to me."

"I'll come said one."

"No bloody fear," said the other. "I'm staying."

The two men peered over the edge of their shell hole. A hole nearby allowed them to advance safely. They sprinted into it. Using the same technique, they made their way to the buried men. They got their shovels and trenching tools out and started digging from a lying position.

They rescued ten men. Some were wounded, but all were alive. They identified four more men who were dead. They left them buried in no-man's-land. They headed back to shelter under heavy fire.

By noon, the situation was deemed hopeless. The troops got the order to retire. Badly beaten up, the Black Watch and all other Allied Battalions retreated. The casualty list was long.

Private Robert Corsar survived the carnage physically unhurt, but his mental state had taken a battering. He knew that men got blown to bits, but this was the first time he had been close enough to feel and see it. He had heard the terrified cries of wounded and dying men. The terror on the faces of the buried men he had helped to rescue. The noise and smell of the battle were in his ears and nose. Worse still, many men had died, were wounded, and the battalion had gained nothing. The carnage would go on. Rob looked at his ammunition pouches and noted with dismay that he had not fired as many shots as he thought. Those that he had fired could have gone anywhere. Rob had no idea if he'd shot a Bosche. He was sure he aimed at Germans, but in the chaos and confusion, he could have hit anything or nothing. His bullets might be in sandbags or the ground.

"What the fuck was that all about?" Rob muttered to no one in particular.

"What's that, Rob?" Asked Archie Russell, sitting next to him.

"I've got lots of ammo left. Why the fuck did I not shoot more?"

"I've got a fair few rounds left myself. I couldn't see what to shoot at. It was all dark, flashes and smoke. I tripped up twice in the dark."

"I spent time digging men out from under the dirt. They got covered in dirt when a big shell went off."

"Were they alive?"

"Most were, but some were beyond help. We left them buried there."

"They won't be the last dead men left in no-man's-land."

"No. I guess not. I'm sure the brass have plans for that."

In the chaos, Rob could not find his friend Jimmy Young. He hoped he was somewhere safe. No one seemed to know what to do.

Jimmy Young was not as fortunate as Rob. Jimmy had not gotten very far before he was seriously wounded, in his left leg and abdomen. He had been dragged back and was in the dressing station when Rob and the rest of the men returned. Rob learned of Jimmy's situation. The opinion expressed was that he would be fine. Back in the trenches soon.

"Poor bastard. Send him home, he has done enough," Rob muttered to himself. Fortunately, no one senior heard him. It was defeatist, mutinous talk.

Looking around, those men who survived the battle could see the damage to their comrades.

Many of the battalion officers were not present. They had either been killed, wounded or were missing. There were also gaps in the ranks of the ordinary soldiers. Looking around at those left standing, Rob could see how badly the battalion had fared. The day had not gone well for the 'Jocks'.

A few days after the attack, Rob met Terry Greig in the cookhouse. He was in A Company.

"Terry. How are things with you?"

"Still here, Rob. And you?"

"Like you, trying to survive."

"Never imagined anything like this when we came out."

"No. Who could have imagined this, even in their worst nightmares?"

"Remember Ian?"

"Yes. He came out with us."

"He did. Killed in that last attack."

"He was about the same age as me, eighteen. Quiet lad as I remember."

"He's certainly quiet now."

"My girl's brother got hit by a shell just as we came out here. Blown to bits."

"Ian took several bullets from machine guns. He was not far from me when he went down. He stood no chance. As you can see, I got out Scot free."

"Let's hope your luck continues, Terry."

"And yours, Rob."

Despite the setback, the Black Watch had acquitted themselves well in the battle. It was to have significant repercussions for the rest of the war.

THIRTY-FIVE

Jimmy Wilson returned to duty by the 8th October 1916 and joined the 4/5 Black Watch in old German trenches in Thiepval. The battalion's next task was to attack the heavily fortified Schwaben Redoubt. Previous attacks over several months had captured much of it. A substantial area was still in German hands.

"Are you OK, Jimmy?"

"Not bad, Rob. Nice rest in the hospital with all those lovely nurses fussing over me. I could have done with a bit more of that."

"Are you fit enough to be here now?"

"Doc says I am, so that's the only voice that counts around here for the wounded."

"We've got a job coming up along here somewhere," said Rob in a low voice.

"No doubt we'll hear about it afore we go over the top again."

"More letter writing to home, is it then Jimmy?"

"Aye, lad."

By this time, letters from Lizzie had become few and far between. He also sensed a different tone. They seemed less loving and more matter-of-fact. He was worried.

On paper, the plan of attack against the Schwaben Redoubt looked remarkably similar to the one against Hamel a month earlier. This time the Cambridgeshire regiment would accompany the 4/5 Black Watch.

The attack plan almost described a parade. It was so formal. They placed tape on the ground to ensure troops kept the correct distance apart. There would be a rolling barrage by the artillery.

Ready for the attack on the 13th of October, Rob and Jimmy sat quietly, contemplating what was before them. They handed their letters to the officers in the HQ tent.

Assaults to finally take the remainder of the Redoubt had been failing for several months. Some sections of its defences had held firm. It had cost a great many Allied lives so far. Prepared and ready to go, the attack got postponed until the following day.

"Typical fucking army," moaned Jimmy. "Can't make up their mind."

"Who knows, Jimmy, we might not be going."

"Not a chance Rob. We'll be off soon enough you wait and see."

"That looks a strong position the Bosche are in over there."

"Aye, it does."

"Bugger, fuck, bugger." cursed Rob, who was showing his fear. He was shaking already.

"And you can add a double shite for me to that."

On the 14th, The Black Watch lined up at the southern end of Authuille village. At 11:45, the men marched off by platoons at 100-yard intervals. Zero hour was 15:17. The 4/5 were to attack the north face of the Redoubt. Typically for the army, things changed yet again. Zero hour moved forward to 14:47. Not that Rob or almost every other ordinary soldier cared about the time. Most did not have watches, so the starting off time was a matter of indifference. They went when ordered.

The men were all told to lie on the ground, ready for the assault. At zero hour, the artillery opened up on time. The men rose and started forward behind the creeping barrage.

Rob was in platoon ten. It placed him behind platoon nine during the advance. As the barrage started, all men stood up, with the first wave moving off behind it. Rob's second wave platoon gave them a start of several paces as laid down in the plan.

It did not take long for Rob's platoon to become the front rank. It was due to heavy casualties. Some were from German fire, but some were killed and wounded by allied guns. This much was clear to the men at the forefront of the advance.

Rob could hear some young officer shouting curses at the artillery for falling short and killing his men. A runner went back to alert the battalion HQ what was happening.

A short while later, the runner returned. Rob could see him frantically looking for the officer. He grabbed a Sergeant near Rob and shouted.

"The lines are down, so they're sending a Pidgeon to the artillery to lift their fire. I can't find Lieutenant James."

"He's dead, son. Get back into position and advance."

No one in the artillery knew what batteries were supposed to be falling short. They did not adjust their plan. The carnage continued.

The Cambridgeshire Regiment was advancing under the same rolling barrage. Exuberance new young Black Watch officers had moved forward too quickly, directly into the range of allied guns. The cut-up ground was not bad enough to slow an eager young officer's advance.

"Fucking Herschel's brother needs his eyes tested," muttered Rob. No one heard him in the commotion.

Rob got covered in mud and body parts from at least one of his comrades. He saw dirt flying everywhere, and his closeness to the blasts made his head and body shake. Rob stumbled over the outstretched leg of a dead man. Looking down, Rob could not say who he was because of the extent of the injuries to his head. All that remained of the man's head were bits of bone, brain and a single loose eye. Rob felt physically sick. He pressed on, knowing that to turn back could get him shot by his side as a deserter.

It did not take long for the company's attack to flounder. Rob was in the centre of the assault. The wire in front of them was not cut enough to make an easy passage. Many men got hung up on the wire and were easy targets for German guns. They hung there like limp scarecrows dancing as each bullet ripped into their bodies. Casualties mounted. All of the officers of C Company were lost, killed or wounded.

Rob had not reached the wire when he felt a tremendous thud and pain in his back. It knocked him off his feet and threw him into the mud, face down. He let out a scream from the pain that suddenly washed over him. He was wounded by shrapnel from an Allied shell that fell some way behind him. The pain he felt made him dizzy, and he thought he might pass out or die.

"Fuck," he yelled. "Stretcher-bearers. Help, help. I'm hit."

It took some time for help to arrive, given the number of casualties and relays for more field dressings. Two men with a wooden stretcher eventually found him.

He had a sharp, searing pain in his back. He tried to stand but fell back on the ground. The pain continued to wash over him. He thought he might pass out, but a voice from one of the stretcher-bearers jolted him.

"We've no morphine left," said one voice. "We'll get you back, and the doc can have a look at that wound."

"Lie still," said the second voice. "This looks a nasty wound. It'll need to be covered." He proceeded to wrap the dressing around Rob's shoulder. "There's a bit of metal sticking out of the hole. Don't move. We need to keep it in place and let the doc take it out in case it bleeds too much."

"Aaah. Fuck." shouted Rob, as he was dragged and then lifted onto the stretcher on his side. He shouted, cursed and swore many times as he bounced his way back to the Black Watch first-aid post.

THIRTY-SIX

The stretcher-bearers had little time for small talk or niceties as they struggled to navigate the muddy trenches. Worse still, there was a line of men on stretchers. They were all heading in the same direction through the mud.

"Put him there." It was an English voice belonging to someone in a dirty white coat covered in blood. "He won't bleed to death, so I'll get to him after I deal with this man. Get him ready."

A man with RAMC flashes rolled Rob over onto his front. Rob let out a scream of pain.

"Sorry," said the man, "but it's necessary to get at the wound."

The apology hardly helped Rob cope with the pain. His foul language made that abundantly clear.

"I'll give you some morphine to help."

That sounded better, and the sharp jab of the needle was hardly noticed, among the other pains that he had. Rob heard the snip of scissors cutting away his uniform, such as it was. The drug was slowly beginning to take effect, but Rob was still in pain.

Rob could see many wounded men in the Casualty Clearing Station. He knew the attack had not gone well.

Sometime later, the doctor reappeared and started working on him. The morphine was helping, but he still sharp felt pain in his back.

"That's the best we can do here. Get him to the ADS. They'll be able to do more for him,"

Two men picked his stretcher up. They carried him into the cold, dark, wet night. He had also been covered by a groundsheet, to keep the worst of the rain off.

The journey to the Advanced Dressing Station was only about four hundred yards, but the terrain was rough and rutted. Rob bounced about on his stretcher. Still, the painkillers were taking effect, so he did not feel so bad. He could still feel the pain in his back, but it was less sharp and more of an ache. Even the frequent bumps along the way did not make the pain any worse. Rob had no idea how bad his wound was, but he now knew that morphine was good.

His stay in the ADS was short.

"There's metal and cloth in that wound that needs digging out. He'll get it infected if it's left" The voice was calm and cultured. "Put another dressing on and get him to the Field Ambulance."

"Yes Sir," was all Rob heard. The morphine was making him drowsy, which was just as well for the next stage of his transit.

His stretcher got loaded onto a two-wheeled trolley, and he was driven off behind a horse to the Field Ambulance about one mile away. In his doped drowsy state, his mind wandered. I wonder if this is death. If it is, it is not so bad.

At 132 Field Ambulance, Rob did not hear much of what was said. He did not understand what was happening. He was still in pain, but the morphine was still working. He heard a comment that he needed to go to the base hospital where they had an x-ray machine. Rob had no idea what an x-ray machine was. Before being loaded into the ambulance, he got another shot of morphine. The ambulance driven by a woman volunteer bounced about as it tried to avoid the ruts in the track. Rob was glad of the morphine.

At the hospital, Rob got placed under the x-ray before being whisked off to a bed. He was so full of morphine that he cared not a jot what was going on. Eventually, a doctor appeared at his side.

"Private Corsar, we've had a look at the x-ray, and we need to cut some small fragments of shrapnel from your back."

Rob just nodded.

"We'll operate as soon as a table is free."

Rob just nodded again.

Eventually, Rob got carried to the operating table. He had no idea of how long he had waited. Under a bright lamp, a voice told him what was about to happen.

"I'm Captain Stewart. I'll put a small mask over your face and drop some anaesthetic into it. Don't worry. Just breathe deeply, and in no time, you'll be asleep. Ready? That's it. Just breathe deeply. Don't fight it."

Rob just nodded. The mask descended, and he breathed in the fumes. The bright light dimmed as the curtain of darkness slowly covered his eyes. He remembered that he had been here before.

It seemed like less than a minute later that Rob woke. The curtain over his eyes slowly opened to reveal the hospital roof.

"Private Corsar, your back with us now." A short man in his mid-thirties stood before him wearing a white coat. "I'm Major James, and I operated on your back."

"Thanks," croaked Rob.

"Not at all, old chap. All part of the service."

"What happened?"

"You took some shrapnel in your back from a shell. I removed the metal and scraped out the material from your uniform that was embedded. Everything is clean, and you should be right as rain in no time. The nurses will take care of you until you can take care of yourself. Anything you want to ask?"

"It hurts like hell. Can I get something for the pain?"

"Yes. I've written you up for some pain medication. That should help."

"Will I be OK, or will I be sent home disabled?"

"Afraid not, old chap. You'll be fine in a few days. Once the stitches are out and we get you mobilised, you'll be back with your regiment in no time."

"Thanks." That's not really what Rob meant, but he said it as a matter of politeness. I must stop thanking people for shite news, he thought. He had been in France for nearly a year. He had seen and heard some terrible things in that time, and he was not overly anxious to stay. He lay for a few minutes when a nurse in a white uniform, cap and red cape arrived with a small bowl.

"Private Corsar."

"Yes."

"My name is Mary Blair. I'm an army nurse. Robert, isn't it?"

"Yes, but I get called Rob."

"Do you mind if I call you Rob?"

"Not if I can call you Mary."

"That's fine then. Some nurses don't like to be overly familiar and insist on proper titles. You'll need to find out as you go. Here is the medicine the doctor ordered. It'll help with your pain."

Rob swallowed the medicine with a gulp of water from a cup.

"Now, Rob, can you roll over for me, please?"

Rob struggled with the pain, so she gave him a hand. She looked around his torso and checked his bandages.

"That looks fine. We'll keep the wound clean and change your dressings regularly. Don't do too much at first, so you don't disturb the stitches in your back. Give your skin time to knit and heal."

"What did they do to me?"

"Didn't the surgeon tell you?"

"Yes. That's right. He said he'd taken some stuff out of my back."

"That's correct. You will have a shallow dent on your back.

"Why?"

"He had to take some flesh out to get to the metal and cloth in the wound. It'll be alright, and you should have a full recovery in no time."

"What day is it, please?"

"It's Tuesday, 17th of October 1916."

"I was out of it for a bit then."

"Yes. Anaesthetic and morphine will do that to you."

"Can you give me enough to see me through this war? Send me back to my lassie."

"No. I'd like to be able to send you back because that means we would all go home, but we can't just yet."

"I've only been here for a few months. The day I arrived, I heard my girlfriends' brother was dead. My best mate got wounded. Men got blown to bits all around me. Then there's the gas. Who knows what will happen if it drags on much longer. I'm sick of it and the mud."

"You're not the first that's said that to me, Rob. No one knows what will happen. We will just have to trust God."

"I'm not a believer, never have been. I'll trust my pals and my rifle."

"Not a believer then. What does your girlfriend think of that?"

"Not much. She's a catholic, and her mother is staunch. Lizzie was wavering before I came out here. I expect the news of her brother's death will have changed that for good or ill. Perhaps ill."

"Death of a loved one affects everyone differently. Now, Rob, there'll be some soup along soon, so get some rest. You'll need it because as soon as you are fit enough, you'll be up and exercising to build up your muscles."

Rob looked around, and his eyes came to rest on a pile of something he did not recognise.

"What's that over there?"

"Don't dwell on that. It's the amputated limbs from the theatre. We will get rid of them as soon as we get time."

"Oh." Rob was horrified. Of course, men lost limbs in war, but to see the pile made him squirm. "I've got all mine, haven't I?"

"Yes, you have. That's from the latest battle that I suppose you were in."

"I was. It was chaos, just like the rest."

"War's a messy business. Still, you wouldn't want to be ruled by the German Kaiser, would you? You fight for King and country."

"Our King's German, if my schooling is correct. So, changing one German for another is not much of interest to me."

"What about our British way of life. Is that not worth fighting for?"

"My family's been fighting for that to change for years."

"How so?"

"My mum and dad were founding members of the Scottish Labour Party. They were also involved in setting up Trades Unions. That's the change we want."

"Your family's socialist then?"

"If that's your take on it, yes. We only want better conditions for the working people. A fair share for all."

"That sounds reasonable when you say it like that. What about us women?"

"My dad's at home agitating for votes for women. He's been doing that for years."

"Oh." There was a pause. Nurse Mary Blair had not expected that "Thank him for me when you next speak to him." With that, she moved away. "I'll bring you some water and soup later."

"Thanks." Rob lay back and drifted off to sleep. He had no idea how long his eyes had been closed, but he woke shouting.

He had had a terrible nightmare. He was reliving the battle. He saw the shattered face of the man he tripped over, showing his brains and a disconnected eye that slowly closed as he watched. He heard the shells and a voice from the shattered head saying, "You're turn soon, Rob." Rob started to fall into a dark nothingness when he suddenly woke shouting.

THIRTY-SEVEN

It did not take long for the nurses and doctors to get Rob moving. His dressing was checked and changed as regularly as was needed. He started exercising his shoulder as soon as the doctor thought everything would hold together.

Rob had a look at the wound in a couple of mirrors that one of the nurses had brought him. He could see the stitches and the hole in his back. Having seen the pile of amputated limbs a few days earlier, Rob considered himself lucky. He had written to Lizzie to tell her what had happened.

After they removed the stitches, Rob spent a few days under the care of a man who gave him lots of physical therapy for his back and shoulder.

"You could have been a torturer in Edinburgh castle in a former time," grumbled Rob after yelping with pain.

The man, named Derek Proudfoot, said something that Rob could not understand.

"What'd you say? I don't understand your accent. Where's it from?"

"I'm from the black country in England. I suppose it's appropriate that I'm treating the Black Watch today."

"Very droll."

"I said, you need to try harder to complete the exercises. We might think you don't want to go back."

"Then you'd be right. Nobody in their right fucking mind wants to go back to the trenches."

"I understand that. We RAMC types also serve in dressing and first aid stations, sometimes as stretcher-bearers in no-man's-land. I know what sort of hell we all go through. It's a relief to get back here sometimes. Now get on with the exercise."

"Private Corsar, we're going to give you four days leave back home." Major Stewart gave Rob the news. You've had a rough time a bit of family time will do you good."

Three days later, Rob boarded the boat at Boulogne harbour. He was bound for Southampton. He had his leave pass and his railway warrant for travel to Montrose.

The journey by boat and train took a whole day to complete. It was slow and tiring. He occasionally drifted off to sleep but woke each time with a jolt after another nightmare. He had to apologise to the other occupants of his carriage for shouting.

By the time he arrived in Montrose, he could spend just under two days at home before he had to make the journey back. Still, he would get to see Lizzie.

He had had a few replies from her to his letters, but not as many as he had hoped. He assumed that was because she was busy working long hours on

McArdle's farm, but he was worried by the tone of her letters.

His first port of call was his parent's home in Market Street. His mother looked up from her seat as he walked in the door.

"It's yersel. You'll be wanting yer tea then." It was almost as if the lodger, who walked out of the house in December 1915, had returned. Rob expected no more.

Mary put the kettle on the fire, and the kids all sat round to hear what he had to say. The more morbid wanted to see his wound. That would be a talking point at school for days.

When his father arrived from work, he shook Rob's hand.

"Glad you're safe, boy."

"I got leave because I got a wound in my back."

"War's a dangerous business." Sandy did not need to remind Rob of his outburst in 1914 when he first saw his son in uniform. Rob was only too aware of his father's misgivings and warnings. Neither needed reminding of the old conversation.

His siblings were more enthusiastic about his arrival than his parents. Mary and Jess hugged him, and Mary went to make the tea.

"How long have you got?" Asked Mary.

"The rest of today and tomorrow. I'm due back after that."

"That's no time at all." The unexpected voice was his mother's.

"No, it's not, but that's all I get."

After tea, Rob left to meet Lizzie.

He got to her house to be greeted by her mother. "She's not here."

"Is she at work on the farm?"

"She's at the farm alright. You best go and speak to her."

Before he left, Mrs Ross had been very civil to Rob, but her tone was less so now.

"I'll walk up there now."

"Goodbye."

At the farm, Rob passed Rose working in the farmyard.

"Hello, Rob. It's good to see you. Lizzie's in the big house." Rose gave Rob a quick hug. He was making his way to the front door of the farmhouse.

"What's she doing there then?"

"You best go and find out for yourself, Rob."

Rob strode off to the big house front door and knocked. Mrs McArdle answered the knock.

"Yes?"

"I'm Robert Corsar, and I've come to see Lizzie."

"Stay where you are. I'll send her out." She shut the door in Rob's face. Rob heard her call Lizzie and tell her a soldier wanted to see her.

Rob stood for a few moments, and the door opened. It was Lizzie, and she was crying. He went to hug her, but she stepped back.

"What's up?"

There was a long pause before she answered.

"Things have changed for me, Rob. We can't see each other again."

"Why not?"

"I'm living here now."

"Why? Have you fallen out with your folks?"

"Yes."

"What happened? Was it Willie's death?"

"Perhaps."

"What do you mean perhaps?" Rob's voice was becoming louder and angrier.

"Things were bad in the house. I was upset at Willie's death. I went astray."

"What do you mean you went astray?"

"The thing is, Rob, I'm carrying Stuart McArdle's baby."

Rob had seen and heard many traumatic things, but this hit him worse than the shrapnel had in his back. He was stunned. It took him a few moments to realise that this was the reason for the changed tone of her letters. He had not noticed the lump on her belly. Now he looked and did.

"What are you saying, Lizzie?"

"I did some stupid things. I started drinking a lot. Stuart came home on leave in May. He'd had a rough time, and I comforted him. It got out of hand... and well... I let him have his way with me."

Rob was lost for words. His blood boiled, and he wanted to slap her, but he just shouted.

"You swear that you'll wait for me and carry my ring. Then you lay down with the farmer's son, and now you're carrying his child. Stuart's had a rough time, has he?" Rob's voice was rising as he shouted at her. "Well, I'm on leave because I've just got out of hospital after being badly wounded in my back. I've been gassed, starved and eaten alive by lice and rats. I've had a fucking rough time myself. All the while, I thought I was coming home to you, and you've let the farmer's son tup you.

Lizzie was now sobbing almost hysterically.

"I'm s-s-s-orry."

"So, I see. You're now living in the farmer's big house. Is he there too?"

"No, he went back to the war."

"I hope he gets fucking killed, you whore."

Mrs McArdle appeared at the door shouting.

"How dare you say that about my son."

"Missus," Rob shouted back loud enough so that Rosie and the other Land Girls could hear, "I'm going back tomorrow. It's hell over there. Your son's got as much chance of coming back alive as I have, and that's not fucking much. We're all going to die face down in the mud and be eaten by the rats. We'll be just like her brother." Rob jabbed his finger towards Lizzie. "He was blown to bits by a shell and spread all over no-man's-land. Not enough of him left to find and bury."

"Oh, no," Lizzie shrieked.

"You." Rob was again jabbing and pointed at Lizzie. "The war disgusts me, but your whoring disgusts me even more. Fucking good riddance." With that, Rob turned and strode off seething. He did not want to stay any longer to stop himself from doing something stupid. Rose caught up with him as he walked.

"I'm awful sorry, Rob. I'm not speaking to her because of what she did. None of us girls wants to know her. She said she loved you and did this to you. That's unforgivable."

"Thanks, Rose, but I need to get away, or I'll throttle her."

"I'm sorry, Rob. Come back safe."

"Thanks, Rose. We're all doing our best to stay alive out there."

Rob strode off, kicking stones and tufts of grass as he went. His intemperate language was as ripe as the nearby oats and foul as the Flanders mud. The black images of the war joined the even blacker ones of Lizzie and some man he'd never met. Relaxation this was not.

His siblings were sympathetic and gave him as much love as they could when they heard his story. If his parents felt the same, they did not show it.

"If that's what she's like, you're best out of it, lad," was his mother's only comment.

The following day, Rob headed back to the war. His mood was foul. He had been fighting to stay alive and come back to his sweetheart, and she had betrayed him. He wondered if Will had done the best thing and got out of the country and the war. Desertion slipped across his mind but quickly faded. He did not care what happened to himself now. "What the fuck's it all for?" he thought.

THIRTY-EIGHT

When Rob returned to his battalion on the 12th of October 1916, he was just in time for more heavy fighting. He also learned he could wear a wound stripe on his left sleeve. It was a two-inch piece of brass. It showed he had got his wound in battle. It was a sort of badge of distinction, showing that he had survived. At least it is not a headstone, thought Rob, just something more to keep clean.

Rob was angry at the war at Lizzie. He wanted revenge for both. He was going to take his anger out on some Germans. It was all their fault that this war had happened. If it not for them, he would be back home with his lassie, and none of this shite would have happened. So, he was going to make them pay. He polished his equipment and sharpened his bayonet. He went about training with new vigour.

There were Bosche positions along the Ancre river that they were to assault. There was hardly any need to distribute a battle plan as it was very similar to the many that had gone before: Line up in rows and march towards the enemy machine guns.

Looking around at his battalion on parade, Rob could see that they were understrength again. His own company was probably about half strength, and the others fared no better.

The attack on the twelfth got postponed because of bad weather. Unluckily, it would take place on the thirteenth at 05:45.

Rob found his company in the third wave of the attack. He did not doubt that the going would be hard for two reasons. The ground was a watery mess after months of shellfire on already marshy ground. At 05:45, it was dark, which was a bonus. The difficulty was that there was a heavy fog. Visibility was only about fifteen to twenty yards. Not only could he not see his target objective, but he could also hardly see the platoons in front of him in the second wave.

Rob waited with his platoon to march off twenty paces behind the first platoon of the second wave. His anger at Lizzie was still vivid. It bothered him that he had been so vile and blamed it on the war. He could not forgive her for what she had done, but he would try to forget. He'd show her. What he could show her never crossed his mind.

As he moved off and struggled as quickly as he could through the marshy ground, Rob thought about firing his rifle. His dander was up, and he wanted revenge on any German. If not for them, he would not be in this position. He would not have come out here, and he could be at home with his girl. He considered blasting off with his rifle in the general direction of where he thought the Bosche were. He was marching towards them, so they were somewhere in front of him. Rob stopped, remembering that his men were also somewhere in front of him in the dark and fog. Mind you, if it had been Stuart McArdle in front, he would have aimed and fired. Unfortunately for Rob, McArdle was in a different regiment.

Rob had started his advance with his head up, looking forward. Almost as soon as he started forward, he slipped and almost fell down a shell hole. Rob looked around, and it was clear that there was little ground safe enough to walk on. He kept his head down, watching where he was stepping. He was not watching where he was going. Neither were many of his comrades. They were all heading in different directions and were essentially lost. The muddy, dark ground was not a parade ground where men could keep their dressing and straight marching lines. Falling into a deep sodden shell hole with the prospect of drowning in mud was terrifying to every soldier. Head bent, he dodged holes as best he could.

The only advantage of these terrible conditions was that the enemy could not see Rob and his pals coming. Their rifle and machine-gun fire was inaccurate except when the advancing troops were closer.

At about 9 am, his platoon had come together and fallen upon a trench full of German soldiers. The red mist got the better of him, and he fired wildly into them. A German soldier came around the corner of the trench with his rifle raised in the ready position. His training took over. He evaded the Bosche bayonet and thrust his into his chest. The German dropped his rifle, shouted something as his hands flew to his chest, where blood was already oozing. He was trying to pull the bayonet out, but all he did was cut his hand on Robs recently sharpened weapon.

The force of Robs thrust pushed the German back against the trench wall. Rod withdrew his bayonet, and the German slid down the muddy wall howling but still alive.

"Finish him, Corsar." The order came from his CSM Bruce standing behind him.

Again, Rob training came to the fore. Private soldiers did as ordered, and it is what Rob did. He raised his rifle and shot the German in the head. As he did, he looked at his enemy. A boy of about fifteen or sixteen. He should be in school learning, not in a trench dying.

The thud of his rifle barrel hitting the German chest with the man screams and dying gasps brought Rob back to his senses. The feeling of the bayonet scraping the ribs and the agonising cry of his enemy sent shivers down his spine. He had never done anything like this except to a sack of straw. It was different. Pushing the bayonet into a live body covered in clothing was harder. The man's momentum had rocked him back on his heels a bit. Bags of straw never did that. He had to push the man back with his rifle to be able to get his bayonet out of his body. There was Bosche blood dripping from the end of his bayonet. That could be me one day, he thought. It made him feel physically sick. He paused for a moment.

"Come on, lad, he's done for." It was the voice of his CSM. "Watch out for any of his friends."

Rob jolted back to reality, and he set himself ready to defend if other Germans came for him.

The assault was now over. The remaining men left standing rounded up a few prisoners. They pushed them out of the dug-out and sent them down the line.

Having achieved their objective on the riverbank, the men slipped into the German dug-outs, ready for the anticipated German response. They hurriedly set about shoring up their defences.

The German response took a couple of hours to come. They shelled their old positions heavily, and casualties continued to mount for the 4/5. Rob, and the remaining men he sheltered with, kept their heads down and tried to stay alive. There was no thought of firing back. The shells came from many hundreds of yards away. They were well out of sight or range of a Lee Enfield Rifle. No one took any opportunity to stick their head over the parapet to see what was there. They all knew that German snipers were very accurate, so they huddled in their holes, shaking with fear and cold.

"Another fucking shambles." The comment came from someone a few yards from Rob and was barely audible between the blasts of falling shells.

"What do we do now?" said another. "All the officers are dead."

"We stay here until someone says different." It was the voice of Corporal Beith. "Anybody who goes out there will be killed. Stay here and keep your head down."

It was advice that everyone who heard was willing to take. Eventually, at about midnight, the shelling had abated. The battalion was relieved and sent to the rear.

After midday, Rob and his pals got the order to move to another position, about a thousand yards away. There was confusion all around him. Officers who should have commanded were wounded or dead. Supplies for the men were behind their current position and nowhere near their new objective. The well-ordered structure of the battalion and its companies had become a mess. Rob got mixed with men from different companies and different units. It was a situation that was fertile ground for grousing.

"What a bloody mess," said Rob, who was sitting among a group of men he did not know.

"Are you one of them Jocks that was fighting with us?" said a man nearby.

"Aye, I am. What lot are you from?"

"First Sussex."

"Cambridgeshire." Said another man.

"We lost a lot in that fight, what about you?" said Rob

"Same," said the other two men.

"Well, I'll just rest here until I get fresh orders." Rob lay back on the ground and tried to sleep, but the image of the young German boy he'd killed haunted him.

Officers scurried about trying to find the other units in the attack. They spent much of the afternoon doing this. Finally, the men were pushed forward to a more sensible position. Rob and the mishmash of men eventually reached their new destination at about 20:00 on the fourteenth.

The enemy artillery soon got their range. They started heavily shelling the new position. At about midnight, what remained of the battalion was relieved. They eventually marched down the Hansa Road to billets in the Martinsart Wood.

These billets consisted of unfloored huts built of tarred felt and surrounded by mud only slightly better than in the trenches. The lights and noise made by the men arriving scared the rats, which infested the camp.

That night Rob had another nightmare. It woke him screaming again. When awake, he could not remember what he was dreaming, but in there somewhere were pictures of Lizzie Ross being stabbed and eaten by rats.

The battalion was moved further to the rear and reequipped. There was much talk in the ranks about where they were going next. Any number of possibilities were advanced because no one knew. Grumbling and speculation were what foot soldiers were very good at when they were relatively idle.

From here, the battalion moved on foot to Warloy-Baillon, about nine miles away. Back on their feet the following day, they moved to Amnplier some twelve miles further on. Then another six miles to a place called Candas. Then relief, as they boarded a train that took them to Wormhoudt, not far from Dunkirk.

THIRTY-NINE

Christmas day 1916 saw the battalion in reserve trenches yet again. This time they were on the Yser canal near Ypres. It was not a joyous Christmas day as the dug-outs were waterlogged.

Waking up from his disturbed sleep on Christmas morning, Rob found no stocking filled with goodies. Santa had not been, but the rain had. There were a few half-hearted Merry Christmases. There followed several lewd suggestions as to what you could do with the greeting.

"This is the third Christmas, and this fucking war is still not over," someone complained loudly. The observation needed no comment.

Rob's company was moved to the front-line trenches on 29 December and would spend New Year's day 1917 there.

"We've had intelligence that the Bosche are going to launch a raid on our position tonight," announced Captain Stewart, the Officer Commanding C Company. "We're going to stand too at 18:30. When their barrage starts, we retreat into shell holes behind the trench and wait for them to enter the trench. When they do, we rise and kill any that get into our position. We'll have a tot of rum when it's over. Good luck and a Happy New Year, Lads."

The men all stood to at 18:30 as ordered. As he stood there, Rob's mind could not help but hark back to how he had entered German trenches and bayonetted their men. He remembered the feel of his bayonet entering their bodies and the horrified look on their faces. He had no desire to be on the receiving end of a Bosche bayonet. The thought terrified him, and he stood there shaking as he waited. He was not alone. Others were shaking, and a couple were praying.

The heavy shelling started at 22:40 all along the front. The German bombardment began with trench mortars and artillery. The Allied artillery responded by putting up a barrage into no-man's-land to deter the German attack. The hope was that this would kill or discourage the enemy.

As soon as the enemy barrage started, Rob and his pals climbed the back wall of the trench and scuttled back towards any shell holes that they could find. There they waited for the barrage to stop and the Bosche to advance. It was cold and wet in their shell holes, but they were not the principal target of the German artillery. That was a bonus. Nevertheless, the odd shell overshot its mark and landed beside the Black Watch. Some men were wounded.

Fifteen minutes after it started, the German barrage lifted. "Here they come." said the Captain. "Get ready." The message passed from one shell hole to another.

Lying in his shell hole behind the trench, Rob got blinded by German Very Lights. He could not see what was coming at him, which was the whole point.

Unfortunately for the Germans, allied units on either side of the 4/5 defensive position could see the Germans quite clearly in the bright light. Their Lewis guns had a field day. Rob could hear the Allied machine guns on either side of his position.

"That's it. Give the bastards hell." Rob muttered.

"That's the lads from Liverpool and Cambridge having a right good time," said Archie Phillips, who was also in the shell hole. "Thanks, lads."

The machine gun barrage from the left and right of their position killed many raiders and deterred others. Still, a few Germans got into the trenches, but they were immediately fired upon and left. When the 4/5 returned, they found one German soldier stuck in the mud. He had not been able to extricate himself and escape with the others. He was now a prisoner of war. He seemed not unduly sad about it. It was the same mud that the 4/5 and others worked in day and night. These appalling conditions contributed to a large number of trench foot cases. The war diaries did not record that the trench mud should get a decoration for taking a German prisoner.

The 4/5 lost one man killed and 15 wounded, three of whom later died in hospital.

At about half-past eleven that night, everything remained quiet, and a tot of rum all round was being issued.

"Tommy...Tommy. Can you hear me?" The voice came from the German trenches opposite.

The men looked to Captain Stewart, who was still in the trench helping with the wounded and rum. He answered.

"I can hear you, Fritz. What do you want?"

"Have you seen my Hauptmann?"

"Hauptmann, that's a German captain. Is that prisoner an officer?" Stewart asked around.

"No, Sir." Came the response from a Corporal. "He's a Private soldier."

"Fritz." Shouted Stewart.

"Yes, Tommy."

"We haven't seen or got you, Hauptmann."

"Scheisse. Thanks, Tommy. Happy New Year."

"Happy New Year to you, Fritz."

"It'll be a happier New Year if they'll all go fucking home," said a corporal to no one in particular.

"Amen to that corporal. Until they do, Happy New Year, Men." Stewart raised his tot of rum and downed it in one. There was a chorus of Happy New Year's all around as the men downed their drink. Another Christmas and New Year's passes, and the war drags on thought, Rob.

FORTY

January 1917 continued just like previous months. The 4/5 Black Watch moved between their various trench dispositions as before. If they were not in the front-line trenches, they were behind the lines forming working parties or training, lots of training. There was also close order drill and lectures. The inevitable list of casualties got posted. These were light in comparison to recent lists.

It was a relatively easy time for Rob and his pals. January accounted for twenty men killed or wounded. That was only four more than the number lost in the New Year's Day raid. Not bad for a whole month.

On Burn's Night, 25 January 1917, the mud in the trenches changed. There had been a severe frost. It became solid. It turned out to be a bit of a blessing in disguise. Work could not continue in the conditions, except for wiring. That always got done at night.

"It's Burns night," said a voice close to Rob in the trench.

"Burns, my arse. I'm fucking freezing," said Rob.

"Can anybody recite Burns stuff?"

"Aye. I ken the Address to A Haggis." another man volunteered.

"Is that address somewhere in Scotland?" Asked another wag.

"Very funny, Dewar." It was the voice of the Sergeant. "Are you the poet Todd?"

"Yes."

"OK. Let's hear it then."

The man named Todd started the poem. As it is a very long poem, it kept the men interested for a bit. As he finished, he said: "This is when the knife gets plunged into the haggis to open it ready for the meal."

"The pudden wid be cold by the time that ended," observed Dewar drily.

"I'd settle for cold haggis, tatties and neeps right now," said Rob. "Better than yon stuff they call bully beef we get served." The pangs of hunger in the men increased at the thought of a haggis supper.

Now that Rob and his pals could not moan about sweating while digging trenches, they moaned about the cold. The hard frost continued well into February. Rob didn't know whether to thank or curse the ice. "Sweating from heavy labour or freezing from inactivity. What a shite choice," he opined one day to no one in particular. Still, close order drills and training kept the men busy and warm. It also added to the whine.

Captain A J Stewart, OC Rob's company, was decorated with the Croix de Guerre by General Nivelle, Commander of the French Army, on 16 February.

March was also a quiet month, with only 11 men killed or wounded.

April saw Rob almost return to his childhood roots. They expected a long rest. They marched to Houtkerque, where they bivouacked in farms and outbuildings. Rob found himself on a farm in an environment with familiar smells.

"That's a smell I remember well," said Rob to his pals. "The ripe smell of cow, pig and horse shite."

"Smells just like the stinking trenches," said Douglas Watson. "billeted in sheds with the rest of the animals. Lambs to the slaughter."

"Cheery bastard," muttered a voice further along.

"Still, we might get the odd fresh egg," said Rob. It turned out to be a false hope. The long period of hoped-for rest was cut short. The unit needed to furnish men to construct a light railway.

"More fucking humping and digging," moaned Douglas. "We're fucking navvies, not soldiers."

"Navvies dig roads and railways away from the front. Soldiers get shelled and shot. I know which I prefer," answered Rob. "Take your pick... or shovel."

The railway was a prefabricated narrow-gauge French system. The tracks were easier to lay, with the correct number of strong men. They were also easy to repair if damaged by shells. Take the damaged pieces out and replace them with new sections. The engines on these tracks were combustion engines. They did not produce smoke that might give the enemy artillery an easy target.

The railway tracks were as close to the front line as possible, so still within the range of enemy artillery. The work was hard, heavy labour.

"We might get a chance to ride on one of these," said Dennis Watts turning and spitting the dust from his mouth. "Be better than marching everywhere as we do now."

"Just so," said Rob. "It also means we get to the front quicker."

"Bugger. That slipped my mind. Still, we could be going the other way."

"We can only hope."

It was not all work. There was a series of football matches against the previously undefeated 21 Siege Battery, Royal Garrison Artillery football team. The 4/5 lost 4 - 1 in the first match. Rob did not play in this match as he was engaged in digging trenches. It was clear from the action that the Artillerymen had played together many times before. The Black Watch lot was a scratch team.

Infantrymen in the Black Watch remembered that allied artillery had killed some of their comrades. They now had a chance for some retribution. The game had some sporting skills, but there was also a lot of naked aggression, with both teams kicking lumps out of each other.

Dodging bullets and dashing for cover when shells were landing showed Archie Gemmell, the football team captain, that Rob was quick and nimble on his feet. He pressed Rob into playing on the right-wing for the second game.

"I'm no very good at football, Archie."

"I've seen you run when we're doing exercise. I've also seen you dancing about in the trenches ducking shells. We can use somebody like that on our wings. The artillery guys are big but slow."

"I'm not very good at kicking a ball."

"All you have to do, Rob, is kick the ball past the man, run around him and kick it into the middle of the park. One of our guys will do the rest."

"Aye. If you think I can help, I'll do it."

During the first half of the second game, Archie's plan worked. Rob got the ball a few times, kicked it past his lumbering opponent, danced around him, and kicked the football into the middle. One cross resulted in a goal, just like Archie described. The Black Watch led 1-0 at halftime.

At halftime, the Artillery team captain remonstrated with a big defender. The man he was talking to was Big Shuggie. Shuggie was to take care of that wee Jock bastard on the wing that was causing trouble.

It took several minutes after the start of the second half for Shuggie to complete his mission. A high ball was heading towards Rob on the wing. He planned to head it forward and run after it. Unfortunately, as the ball arrived, so did Shuggie. It was an unequal contest. Rob was well and truly 'taken care of'.

Lying dazed on the pitch, Rob did not witness the melee that followed Shuggie's 'tackle' on him. What Rob did see were stars. His head buzzed, and his face was in the mud of the pitch. There was much pushing, shoving, swearing, fist-pumping, and finger-pointing all around. Rob's prone body did not get in the way of a good punch-up. It took several minutes for an RAMC man to take care of Rob properly and help him to the side-lines. The military police from both sides calmed the opposing teams and supporters down before the game continued. Shuggie was called forward by the referee.

"That was a deliberate foul. Don't let me catch you doing that again."

"I won't need to." Shuggie walked towards his team captain with a smirk and winked.

The 4/5 won the second 2 - 0 and the decider a day later 2 - 0. Bragging rights for the Jocks.

From April to June 1917, the unit suffered very few non-football casualties. July would see an end to the easy life.

Between the 1st and 9th of July, the Black Watch was on the canal bank near Ypres. They got shelled repeatedly and occasionally gassed.

"Gas. Gas. Gas." Came the call in the trench, along with the clanking of metal shell casings banged together. Men who had been in the war for more than a couple of weeks did not need a second invitation to don their gas masks. The gas killed relatively few people, but it had a great panic and fear factor.

"Fuck, fuck, fuck," muttered Rob as he fumbled for his respirator. He managed to get it on just in time. He was lucky in that the cloud of gas was moving across his front towards men further along the trench.

Those further along the trench system who did not get their masks on quickly enough got lungs full of gas. The upshot was that injuries were severe, meaning some were medically unfit to continue to fight. Being sent home disabled with significant breathing difficulties for the rest of their lives might not have been worse than staying in the trenches. Some would die relatively young of painful lung disease.

The gassed men were withdrawn to the first aid station and then to the casualty clearing station. There got categorised as either trivial, treatable or terrible.

Their first treatment was a two-minute shower to remove the oily liquid from clothing and skin. Men with blistered hands and legs were considered relatively mild and treatable. They received continuous sodium hypochlorite soaking to the small blisters on the hands and knees. These were the parts of the body exposed by the kilt.

Gas burn left a permanent yellow mark on the skin. It also left a psychological scar on the man. Gas fright was also another symptom of Shell-Shock.

Those in the hospital with chemical burns were actually among the lucky ones. On 31 July, the Battalion would become involved in the action that would result in almost half of the men being killed, wounded or missing.

Tommy Douglas, who had come to France with Rob, was one of those who were not quick enough to get his mask on. He got a lung full of gas and skin burns. He got evacuated to the UK, where he survived a few months before dying of respiratory disease.

FORTY-ONE

Rob was back in action on the 31st of July. He and his comrades were taking part in the third battle of Ypres. Since this was the third battle, it seemed that the first two had achieved very little. This battle was also known as the Battle of Passchendaele. That was the village and nearby ridge, which were the ultimate objective.

General Haig mistakenly believed that the German army was on the point of collapse. It was to be a costly belief for the allies. It became infamous for the amount of mud on the battlefield due to heavy shelling from both sides and almost constant rain for several months.

Men frequently drowned in muddy shell holes. From no-man's-land came the smell of rotting, decomposing flesh of hundreds of Allied and German men that hung in the air like a mist. Even for men used to the smell of death, it was nauseating.

On the day before the action was due to take place, Rob and his comrades were several miles east of the town of Poperinghe. They got an order to move forward for the coming battle. They got ready and started their march at 20:40. No one told them how far they had to march. They commenced in the half-light of dusk.

It was not so much a march as a squelching trudge through deep mud. The battalion was about half strength. The other half were working elsewhere on the front. It was tiring trying to make headway in the dark. They walked through mud and over occasional shaky duckboards. It was a long slog.

They struggled for about seven or eight miles in the dark over this terrain before reaching their starting positions. After that trek, Rob and the rest of the battalion were very tired and hoped there might be time to rest. They were disappointed.

Rob stood with his depleted platoon. There were only about twenty of them waiting for their order to go. The men of A company led off, followed by B then C company men. The lines of soldiers were at 25 yards intervals.

"Here we go again," said a voice in the dark to Rob's right.

"Forward men. Keep your distance." came the voice of Captain Stewart.

"Fucking mud up to my ankles," muttered Rob as he marched off. His wounded shoulder was still stiff and occasionally ached. It did not take long for the carnage to start.

The Germans shelled with heavy guns. Dashing through what was now almost knee-deep mud looking for cover was not a practical option. Men around Rob started to fall. This is it, thought Rob. The bastards will get me today.

Being towards the back of this parade of frightened men, Rob was not surprised to see small groups of wounded men and German prisoners coming back towards him as he squelched forward.

The company eventually got to Oblong Farm. There, Captain Stewart ordered a halt and rest. He could see that the men were as tired as he was from the previous night's march, lack of rest and their long walk forward through deep mud. The weight of the sixty-pound packs on their backs was an added burden that Stewart did not have.

Rob squatted down next to a man called Arnott. Shells and bullets continued to rain down on them from the German artillery and machine guns.

"How are you doing?' asked Rob above the din.

"O.K. for the moment. What about you?"

"Same. It is bloody hard going in all this mud. This fucking pack doesn't help. All the stuff we're ordered to carry and most of it not used. My shoulders are rubbed raw."

"I'm about done in. That march last night and today in mud is hell. My arms are sore, the pack weighs a ton, my kilt is soaked and heavy, and my boots are full of water and mud. I'm more like a packhorse than a fucking soldier."

"Have you any idea where we are or where we're supposed to be going?"

"No idea where we are, but I think we're supposed to be heading for that village over there. I expect it has a name, but I don't know what it is." Arnott did not look up but nodded his head in the general direction of some buildings he had seen earlier.

"What country is this?"

"Belgium... or France. I heard someone say we might be in Belgium. The mud looks the same whatever country we're in?"

"Looks and smells the same."

"OK, men. On we go." Shouted Captain Stewart. "We're going forward in platoon rushes. We're getting killed sitting here, so we might as well give the Bosche a moving target. We're heading for those gun pits over there." The Captain was pointing at the pits, which were some seven hundred yards away, across a mud bath.

"Fuck." said Arnott looking out in the direction Stewart was pointing. "That's a bloody long way over that fucking shite."

The ludicrous nature of this attack was becoming more apparent, even to the ordinary soldier. They were getting shelled by Allied guns. The going was treacherous, and the Germans were still well organised. Still, the 'Ladies from Hell', as the Germans called them, ploughed on as ordered.

They were bogged down now and under intense fire from rifle and machine guns. Captain Stewart sent up three S.O.S. flares. It was a signal for allied artillery to shell that area. They waited, and nothing happened. After waiting most of the morning for help, Stewart had had enough. His position was hopeless, and he decided to get the hell out of there.

"Right, men. We've no chance here we're retiring back to the river. Make your way back, and we'll consolidate there."

"What happened to the chaps over there?" Rob casually enquired of the man now next to him. A couple of platoons of men had gone to silence a machine gun nest in an old farmhouse.

"Gone. The whole bloody lot cut off and slaughtered."

"Fuck. Let's get out of here before we're next for the chop," said Rob. With that, men started struggling through the mud to get back to the river.

What remained of C Company made it back to the riverbank. They got shelled mercilessly for the rest of the day. Worse still, the Allied artillery thought that no Allied troops had made it across to the German side of the river so, they shelled what they thought was the German side. All of the Black Watch companies were on that side of the river. They got blown up and killed by both sides. Everyone knew what was happening. There was nothing Stewart could do. He had no way to communicate with the artillery on the other side of the river. The air was ripe with foul language aimed at the Allied Artillery.

Not only were shells falling on the bedraggled men, but so too was heavy rain. It went on throughout the night. The shell holes that the men were sheltering in soon started to fill with water.

"I'll never complain about swimming in the fucking cold North Sea again," said a shivering Rob who was up to his waist in muddy, cold water. Rob's shivering was not from cold but was a mixture of exhaustion and fear. It was the worst situation that he had faced up to this point in the war, and he felt sure he was going to die, blown to bits, just like Willie Ross some eighteen months earlier. Some of the men around him were so exhausted that they fell asleep in the water-logged shell holes and nearly drowned.

Sometime during the night of 1/2 August 1917, Rob and the exhausted men left alive were ordered back to La Brique. Deep mud and rain made the march seem much longer than it was. What might have been a relatively short walk in good conditions took about eight hours through the rain and mud.

Here, there was at least time to eat some of their field ration packs, drink some water and have a tot of rum. Rob lay down in the wet mud and fell fast asleep. He was not alone. At midday, they were rudely awakened and told to reform the battalion, such as it was. Looking around at the numbers of men expected to remake the Battalion, Rob almost laughed.

"I've seen more people in a queue for a bus," quipped a man Rob did not know. Someone had done a count of what remained of the battalion. Soon, Rob heard the order that B and C company personnel were to form one platoon. The four hundred men of two companies had become less than forty men of one platoon. They then moved into the old German Front System. Sleep was pressing, and the relative quiet made this possible even if it meant lying in mud or holes dug in the trench wall.

Mid-day on the 4th of August, the men moved again. It was a forward move to the river yet again. This time it was to relieve the men of the Rifle Brigade who were holding a front some 400 yards long, slightly in front of where they now were.

More shelling and rain followed. Men fell asleep wherever they stopped. The noise of battle and the falling rain, ignored. It was always a short uneasy sleep broken by the sound of wounded men screaming. They were under heavy and continuous German shelling. Rob could not remember when he was more tired and shattered. His whole body ached, his shoulder wound seemed to play up more often, and his leg muscles screamed in pain from the weight of the pack he was carrying and the added weight of mud in his boots. He thought that death might be a release from the agony.

Eventually, on the 5th of August, the battalion was relieved by the Bucks Regiment. It was not a simple task as the shelling continued, making movement without cover even more dangerous.

As the remnants of the 4/5 Battalion Black Watch trudged back to Reigersburg, they must have looked a sorry sight. There were only 140 men left. They were exhausted, unshaven and caked in mud. Rob was only one of six men from C Company who remained after this abortive attack. He felt as bad as he looked. He did not mind admitting to himself that he had been terrified. Everything about the battle haunted Rob. The terrible weather, the mud, the noise, the chaos and the scattered dead bodies all added to his physical and mental fatigue.

"I'm done in," said James Copland, sitting next to Rob.

"I was done in ages ago," said Rob. "How many are left?"

"I don't know. We started with less than half the battalion, and we look like we've got just a company strength left?"

"That's a lot of telegrams and letter writing for some officer. Have we any of them left?"

"I saw Captain Stewart somewhere. I expect he'll get the job of letter writing."

On the 8th and 9th August, the four hundred men who had been employed elsewhere in the area returned as well as nearly two hundred new conscripts.

FORTY-TWO

The major battles were coming around more frequently now. The brass had discovered that the 'Ladies from Hell' were an excellent fighting unit. They were to be used more often from now and to the end of the war. On 26th September 1917, the Battalion was back in the front line near Zwarte Leen.

The march to the assembly point was horrendous, as it was over marshy ground. Frequent shelling and rain had created more water-filled holes. Some was over duckboards that did not offer the steadiest footing. Rob did not know where they were, but looking at the ground, he might have thought they were back at Passchendaele, a name he had learned after that battle.

The parade that was the hallmark of the British battle plans was ready to advance. Assembly for the attack was in water for the most part.

Rob and his colleagues watched the men of A, B and D companies march forward. As he watched from his trench, he saw the line weave about as they moved off into the distance.

"Right, men. Move up." came the command from the company Commanding Officer. Rob moved forward as ordered to the assembly point.

"Line up on the tape by platoon. Keep your dressing." It was not a parade but a march towards machine guns, and there would be no saluting some brass as they went. They would be dodging lead and lots of it.

Rob looked down at the tape by his feet. Much of it was deep in mud. 'It's like a fucking ceremonial parade," he muttered.

"Quiet Corsar, or you'll be on defaulters parade when we get done here." His platoon Sergeant was not best pleased.

Rob looked at the terrain before him. The order was to move from here to there and set up a reserve position. 'Over there' was the side of a hill given the number 60, not all that far as the crow flew.

'There must have been a wood here at some time,' Rob thought. The landscape had become littered with shattered stumps of trees sticking out of the ground like angry splinters. Slipping and falling against one of those could cause serious injuries or even be fatal.

The bombardment from the Germans during the initial parts of the advance was not heavy. If Rob had thought that this might be easier than previous battles, he was soon proved wrong. As soon as the advanced companies got close to the Bosche lines, all hell broke loose on them.

The ground they crossed had the bones and decomposing body parts of soldiers killed here in previous battles. Left to rot and decompose in no-man's-land, constant shelling from both sides had disinterred and scattered their remains even further.

"Forward." The order was difficult to hear above the din.

Rob moved off and immediately slipped in the mud. He steadied but now marched with his head bowed, looking at his footing. He had no desire to fall into one of those deadly mud holes. Tripping over a disinterred body part was also to be avoided.

When he paused to look up, his comrades were spread-out all-over no-man's-land. Each one was looking to avoid the deep mud holes. He realised that he had been heading in the wrong direction. He tried to see a way forward. He was looking for a way to take him back on course. Plodding slowly on, he eventually made it to the side of hill 60. Some men were still struggling to get there.

"Dig in here." Came the command.

Those that had made the rendezvous unshipped their entrenching tools or shovels and started to dig into the water-logged dirt. As other stragglers made the rendezvous, they did likewise. Now there was a wait for the expected German response.

After about an hour of digging, there was a loud shout. "Dewar, Pringle, Corsar and Whyte. Over here." It came from Sgt Duncan

The four men shuffled along their shallow trench to Lt. Brown and Sgt Duncan.

"We're short of supplies. The resupply has not happened, so you four get back to the supply dump and pick up as much as you can carry. Here's the dump and the list of what we need," said Sgt Duncan handing a piece of paper to Pringle, who was nearest to him. "Get back here as fast as you can and find out why the fuck the resupply is not happening."

"Yes, sergeant," said Pringle. With that, the four made their way out of the trench and scampered down the hill. They started back across the land to their lines dodging holes and stepping on duckboards where they could.

Up ahead, they heard a weird shouting. In a big mud-filled hole, there was a man. He was up to his shoulders in the mud. He was ranting and raving like a lunatic while trying to claw his way to safety.

"He sounds English," said Whyte. "We should try to pull him out.

The four agreed. Rob and Davey Pringle, being the lightest, were to try to grab the man's webbing. John Dewar and Jack Whyte were the tallest and heaviest. They would keep a hold of the other two while they tried to pull the man out. As Rob reached into the mud pool, he heard Jack shout. "What's your name?'

The response from the drowning man was unintelligible. It was gibberish. They found his webbing under the surface of the pool.

"Do you have his belt?" asked Rob.

"Yes," said Davey. "You two get ready and hold us fast. We don't want to join him in there."

Try as they might, they could not shift the man one inch. The suction of the mud was too strong. They were getting tired. There also a possibility that either Rob or Davey would slip and end up in the pool with the unknown man.

"It's no good. He is not budging," said Rob.

"We'll need to get on and collect our supplies," said Jack.

"We can't leave him here like that," said Rob. "That's no way for a man to die."

"What else can we do then?" asked Davey.

"On a farm, we'd put suffering beasts out of their misery."

"Are you suggesting we do that to him?" said Jack in astonishment.

"Yes. We can leave the man here to drown in mud."

All the while, the man was thrashing about and slowly sinking deeper into the mud. It was up to his neck now.

"I'll do it," said Rob, "but we all must agree."

"OK. Let's do it," said Jack.

"Davey, John?"

"I don't like it, but I'd hope somebody would do that for me," said John.

"Agreed," said Davey.

With that, Rob raised his rifle, loaded a round, pushed off the safety catch and raised his rifle to his shoulder. He was looking the drowning man square in the eye. There was a look of recognition in the man's eyes, and he nodded once. Rob fired and hit him clean between the eyes. The man stopped thrashing, and slowly his head started to disappear under the mud.

"Let's go, or we'll be for it when we get back," said Davey. "Say nothing to anybody about this." There was a chorus of Ayes from the other three.

Rob was haunted by what he had done. He knew it was right, but that did not make him feel any better. John had been right when he said that he hoped somebody would do that for him in similar circumstances. All soldiers in Flanders knew that death from bullets, grenades and shells were always a possibility. They reluctantly accepted it as part of the life they were leading. Death by drowning in mud was like a gas attack. It evoked terror, not just fear.

"Fuck," said Jack. "That's the leg of a horse in there." He pointed to the left. In the middle of the muddy shell hole, there was indeed a leg of a horse sticking out.

Their return was not quick enough for the Sergeants liking.

"Have you lot been slacking off? What took you so long?"

"The coordinates you gave us were wrong, Sergeant," said Davey Pringle. "The dump was over here. They moved while we advanced." He pointed to another reference on the map. "We struggled to find our way back through the mud holes. The heavy loads made us sink deeper into the mud."

"OK. You're here now. What's the resupply situation?"

"They're trying to sort it out, Sargent."

"When will that be then?"

"They didn't say. I passed on your message about our situation. Like us, they are trying to struggle through the mud. That's what he said"

It was not an exaggerated account of the return journey. It had been hard going, and the four men were still tired from the seven-mile march the previous night. No one mentioned it. It would have cut no ice. Those fighting in the trenches were equally tired, and they needed supplies. The four 'donkeys' had at least had a quick hot drink as they waited for the rations.

Half-awake and half-asleep in a lull during the battle, Rob noticed his hands were shaking badly. He was wet, muddy and tired, but not cold. It was the effect of the continuous terror, exhaustion and hunger. It was a symptom of what the men called shell-shock. He did not want to seem scared or shocked, but they all knew, particularly those who had been in the many previous battles. There was nothing Rob could do. He'd have to cope with it. Show a good 'stiff upper lip'. That's what the army wanted, so that's what they got. No sooner had he noticed his hands than the Bosche artillery opened up with a very heavy bombardment. He now had a different reason to shake.

"Heads down, lads. Wait for the counter-attack," bellowed the sergeant.

Sure enough, the enemy started to advance on Rob's position. He shouldered his rifle and commenced firing as they came within range. Rob saw a couple of Germans fall after he shot in their direction. He could not tell if it was his shot or the Lewis guns that got them. A couple of Lewis guns had also opened up on the Germans. The Lewis guns did enough damage to repel the counter-attack.

The German bombardment continued until the morning of 28th when the exhausted men of the Black Watch withdrew by bus to billets at Westoutre.

FORTY-THREE

In October 1917, Rob got promoted to Lance Corporal. He could now wear a single L/Cpl stripe on his upper arm. He was second in command of a section within his platoon. His job was to ensure the men under his command were present and properly presented at all times. Any man in his team found in default could mean instant demoting back to private. His pay rose from 1 shilling and 1 penny a day to 1 shilling and 4 pennies a day. Enough for an extra beer, if one could be found.

The month of October for Rob and the Black Watch was quiet by comparison to what had gone before. There were, however, several men injured by gas on 29 and 30 October. Only two men were killed during the month.

The following month, the Germans increased their gas attacks, and the Black Watch suffered many casualties. They racked up 181 casualties described in the diaries as NYD (Gas). Not Yet Diagnosed.

The year ended quietly for the Black Watch. Another Christmas had come and gone, and the war was still not over.

January 1918 was a quiet month, and the men were beginning to think everything was OK. Auld Years night was no celebration for Rob and his comrades. At 01:15 on the morning of the first January 1918, they were lined up and marched from their present base at Senningen, which they had only just reached the previous day. It was a short march to catch a train. The unit was on its way to Irish Farm. The farm was not in Ireland, which would have been good. It was near Ypres, which was not so good. They did not stay long as in no time they were off on their continental travels yet again. Next, they stopped at Houtkerque some sixteen miles south-east of Dunkirk.

It was not a normal New Years' Day for Scotsmen. Drinking usually started at the stroke of midnight and carried on all night in various houses around the towns or villages. It was not unusual for the womenfolk not to see or hear from the men for a day or two. Not that Rob had any experience of this. He was too young and poorly paid to have enough money to get roaring drunk. He had managed a few drinking sessions in local towns in France and Belgium but not enough to get drunk. His father's habit of throwing drunks into the garden played on his mind, even if he was a long way away. Habit was a strange thing.

During January and February, there was the usual steady trickle of killed and wounded.

By March, everyone in the battalion knew that something was about to happen. Rob and the rest of the men in 4/5 could see the build-up of German forces, guns and supplies quite clearly from their own trenches. What they saw was not the usual resupply of German troops. It was much larger. There was a lot of idle chatter among the men as to what was going to happen.

"They'll just keep sending troops until we run out of ammunition to kill them," said George Dyer.

"No. Not even the Bosche are that callous. No. They have some devious plan. They haven't brought that much stuff up to the front for no good reason," opined Len Prescott. "What do you think, Rob?"

"I don't know any more than you, but you can be sure that whatever it is, we're not going to like it."

Thursday 21 March 1918

Rob and his comrades felt extra tension. The rumours of a big imminent German attack had intensified. Not that Rob and his pals needed rumour. They could see the activity on the other side of no-man's-land. There were massive amounts of men and equipment poured into the German lines. Behind them, Rob could see the build-up of artillery. It is not good, he thought to himself. No one needed to tell him that the Germans were up to something. He could see for himself.

It seems that the brass even knew the date of the attack. The Battalion was turned out at 06:00 and told to prepare to move off quickly. They were ready by 07:00. They were still standing waiting ten hours later at 17:00. They were in Moislains, about halfway between St Quentin and Arras. They were suddenly rushed to Longavesnes by bus. They quickly dug defensive trenches at Tincourt Wood, South, South West of the town. They dug throughout the night.

"Fritz is going to be heading our way soon," said Rob to his section as they dug. "Make sure we're ready and protected." Rob and his comrades toiled all night to make the trench ready as they could for the following morning.

These were hastily dug trenches without dugouts for extra protection. All the men could do in the time was to dig a ditch like structure as deep as they could in the time.

22 March 1918

At 06:30, the 1st Cheshires and 1st Cambridgeshire occupied the trenches that the Black Watch had just dug. The Black Watch was ordered back to Longavesnes in support.

The communication to retire to Longavesnes did not get to C Company, so, in the time-honoured tradition of the army, without orders, they did not move. They got stuck in their hastily constructed trenches with the Cheshires. The intensity of the shelling from the German side forced the men to huddle up under the rough parapet. Most of the shells seemed to be heading behind the trenches.

"The lads in support are getting the worst of it," Rob said to Jackie Robinson, his platoon corporal.

"I'm sure that when they do come, they won't forget about us. Keep a good watch."

Suddenly, the company was under fire. The attack was not from the front as expected. There were being fired on from their left and to their rear. They were being outflanked and surrounded. Not knowing where the Boshes were, some of the men fired blindly into the misty night. Rob and the rest of C Company were soon up to their necks in large numbers of German Storm-troops who broke through the hastily constructed defences. They had received no order to retreat, but the dicey situation meant that some men were on the move anyway, orders or not.

Second Lieutenant McNicol shouted to those around him. "Everybody seems to have retired back to Tincourt Wood. We'll do the same." He was merely ordering what he could see some of the men were doing already. Word passed as best it could be to those left, and they fell back, fighting as they went.

Those that heard the order got back to the battalion much later that day, only forty men at this point. Rob was not one of those that got any order. He and several others had not heard any instruction over the din of battle. They stayed where they were.

There were Germans everywhere around Rob and the forgotten men of C Company. Bullets were coming at them from every angle. He looked up and saw a group of Germans rapidly advancing on his position. He was out of ammunition. He grabbed a dead man's ammunition pouches. He saw it was Reg White when he pulled him back.

"Sorry, Reg," he mumbled.

He had little time to act. He had no time to get the bandolier off Reg. He ducked into the trench and pulled Reg's dead body over his. Survival instinct had kicked in. He did not want to get shot, or worse still, bayonetted. He'd done it to others and had no desire to die that way. It terrified him to think of it. He lay in the trench with Reg's body covering him. Reg' was lying face-up on top of Rob. The holes in Reg's head would show any inquisitive Germans that he was dead. Rob was afraid to make any sound lest he gave himself away. He hoped that the Germans would be too busy pushing forward to give a dead body any time. His breathing was slow and shallow as he tried not to panic.

His back was deep in mud. Reg's pack was still on his back. Between the backpack and Reg's back was a small space. It gave Rob just enough room to breathe. He waited and hoped.

Things eventually quietened down around him and the remainder of his comrades. In the mist and dark, the Bosche had passed where they lay hidden.

Rob pushed Reg's body to the side and struggled to extricate himself from the mud.

"Thanks, Reg."

Once free, he slowly raised his head above the parapet of the shallow trench. His eyes darted around to ensure that it was safe to get up. It was, and he saw two more kilted men running back towards what they thought might be safety. Rob grabbed Reg's bandolier and clambered out of the trench. He raced after the fleeing Scotsmen.

As he ran, he tripped on a dead body and swore as he fell into the dirt. He scrambled upright. Looking around, he found his rifle. As he picked it up, he saw lots of dead bodies all around, Bosche as well as Black Watch troops. In his fearful state, he did not identify them. He knew that he knew most, if not all.

Rob caught up to the two men.

"There's a Bosche behind us, Davey. Shoot the bastard." It was one of the fleeing men.

"I'm not a German. I'm Black Watch. Hold your fire."

"Just as well said the second man. I have no ammo left."

"Where are you headed?" asked Rob.

"Away from here."

"Have you any idea where the rest of our men are?"

"Those that aren't dead seemed to be heading this way." The first man pointed in the direction he had been running. "What's your name?"

"Rob Corsar. You?"

"I'm Jerry Ryan, and he's Taff Evans,"

"You're a Lance Jack, so you must know what to do," said Taff.

"No more idea than you two. I've not seen you before. What's your unit?"

"We're both new conscripts. I arrived out here six weeks ago and joined A company. Not much left of it now."

"Rest up for a few minutes, and let's take stock. No point in rushing about until we know where to go. Who was it that was out of ammo?"

"I am," said Taff.

"Right. Let's sit in this hole and take stock of what we have. Then we'll work out where we need to go. OK?"

"You're in charge," said Jerry.

"First, let's pool our ammo and rations. Lay them out on the ground."

The other two unshipped their packs and did as asked.

"We have enough water and some rations. We'll split it and the ammo up evenly between the three of us. OK?"

They did as asked.

"Throw out the rest of the stuff in your packs. It's no use to us in this situation."

"Won't we get in trouble for the loss of equipment when we get back?" asked Jerry.

"I doubt it. I've lost loads of stuff in battle. It's men they want, not wire cutters and the like."

"So, which way do we head, boyo?" It was Taff in his broad Welsh accent.

"Let's work it out. We were facing Fritz, who was in the east when they attacked. If we were in retreat, we'd be heading west. You say you saw some Allied troops heading that way." Rob pointed where the two men had been running when he intercepted them.

"That's right," said Jerry. "They seemed to be going that way."

"That's west or south by my reckoning," said Rob. "We'll head that way."

"I don't know that I can run all that far in this mud," said Jerry.

"We won't run unless we have to. We might run into a bunch of Bosche. We'll move quickly but keep our eyes peeled to avoid the enemy. OK?"

The pair nodded, and they rose to follow Rob in the direction indicated.

23 March 1918

Ducking and diving to avoid the advancing Bosche, Rob and the two strays eventually got back to the Black Watch lines without encountering any Bosche. Many others did not make it. That much was clear from the bodies he had seen. It was late morning when they got back, and confusion reigned. It was so bad that the Brigadier had come forward into the line to assess the problems first hand. He could not communicate with his front-line troops, and he was blind to the situation. The Bosche plan was working.

He ordered the Black Watch to head for St Denis and reform there. The men lined up, ready to march out. Rob thought there might be about half of the men left standing. It included Rob and the few that had initially fallen behind. They had fought their way back and joined just in time for another route march. The air was ripe with foul-mouthed obscenities from tired and bedraggled soldiers.

The Brigadier changed his mind and had the men march to Mount St Quentin. They had no orders to do anything there except wait for further orders. While they were resting at St Quentin for orders, the decision got made for them. The Bosche attacked in force, so they retreated again. A and the remnants of Rob's C Company were to cover the retreat. They were soon up to their ears in Bosche troops again.

No one of those left in C Company noticed A Company moving out. There had been an order to retire. Yet again, C Company did not receive it. Outnumbered and outgunned C Company attached themselves to a new outfit from the 21st Division. Survival was uppermost in their minds. Safety in numbers, they hoped. Retreating and fighting for their lives, they eventually crossed the river Somme and found what remained of the 4/5 Battalion.

24 March 1918

The morning was quiet. The British troops were on the south bank of the Somme with Germans opposite them. The strength of the Battalion was now just 150 men, 13 officers and 1, medical officer. Two officers and 23 men of the homeless Trench Mortar Battalion attached themselves to the 4/5 bringing their total strength to 195 men, or a company strength.

That night was quiet while the men of the Black Watch waited for the Germans to come at them again. They grabbed what little sleep they could. Looking across the river, Rob could see great German activity.

They were bringing up supplies ready to cross the river and continue the fight. There were enormous numbers of men and guns. The carnage was a long way from being over.

Before he fell asleep, Rob looked around at the remains of the Battalion. They were a sorry lot, short of numbers and badly beaten up. They looked as bad as he felt. Lying in mud, he slept. His dreams were awful, and he woke several times shaking.

It did not take long for the German advance to happen. It occurred in the region of Clery-sur-Somme. They took it and passed right through, heading towards the Black Watch.

25 March 1918

This evening, the Officer Commanding the 1st Cambridgeshire Regiment reported that the enemy had also crossed the river and occupied La Maisonette. Now the situation was even worse. They looked like they might be outflanked again and cut off. Germans, in great numbers, were crossing the river everywhere.

Looking out towards the river in the distance, Rob could see the trouble coming their way. They would not have to wait long.

Some 35 men and one officer set up a defensive line with the 1st Cambs. They never got anywhere near the line before the order to withdraw to Herbecourt was given.

Throughout the day, the beleaguered men continued to get shelled intermittently. At 22:50, another order to retreat. This time they were heading to Bois Vert about 100 yards behind the small town of Herbecourt.

The battalion, such as it was, was ordered to stand and hold the ground. It became impossible as the enemy broke through on the right and threatened to cut them off again.

It was clear the situation was chaotic. Survival for the men was now uppermost in their minds. Rob agonised between surrendering and standing up to get shot. Either way, this hell would be over for him. Before he had time to choose, the men got ordered to a new position.

26 March 1918

At about 02:00, the remainder of the Battalion got into their new position. Despite the chaos, a hot meal magically appeared and some fresh socks. It made Rob glad that he had not chosen either of his previous options. It was the first decent food he'd had for days. Things seemed better on a full belly of something described as meat. Rob fell asleep feeling better than he had previously.

At 08:00, the troops in the forward trenches started arriving in the support positions. They had bad news. The enemy was advancing on Herbecourt in large numbers. On receiving this news, Brigade HQ ordered the men to hold. They were to stop any troops from retreating.

"Easy for them back there to say that," said Peter Dunne. "We're to ones who are to shoot any scared men retreating."

"I'll not shoot any of our men trying to stay alive," Rob said, remembering the man he shot in the mud.

No sooner had they digested this news when large numbers of the enemy started advancing towards their position.

"Fuck." A voice from somewhere in the ranks expressed everyone's feelings. "How many of them are there? We've killed hundreds, and they still keep coming."

No one needed to speak. Some were so exhausted they could hardly do anything, let alone think or talk. The allied machine guns were inflicting heavy losses on the enemy, but they just kept coming on in waves. All around, supporting allied troop positions were collapsing, and the men were in extreme danger yet again.

By mid-day, the position was deemed hopeless, and they were to withdraw about one thousand yards to a ridge. It was attempted but failed because the enemy was already in possession of it. There was even more chaos. Soldiers were looking in vain to their officers for guidance.

The Battalion retreated to a point on the Bray - Proyart road. It led to the loss of three more officers and around twenty-five men. Rob was not one of the casualties. Reaching the new position meant that the men got some rest at last. The night was relatively quiet. Rob and the rest of the men slept through sheer exhaustion.

27 March 1918

Rest and sleep ended at 07:00 as the enemy started to advance yet again. The 4/5 fought and stood their ground until the enemy was within one hundred yards of their position. The situation was almost tragically comical because, by now, the once one thousand strong Battalion could only muster 53 men in total.

They retreated south to a point on the Estrees Amiens road. The location was of no interest to Rob.

It could have been on the moon for all he cared. He had been backpedalling and fighting for his life for what seemed like forever. He felt like an animal, pursued by a German hunting party. He'd seen and left dozens of dead and dying comrades all over the ground he had retired over. He felt glad to be alive, but he also felt some shame at not being able to help them. He had survivor guilt. Why had he survived when so many others he knew had not? The Black Watch found units of the Durham Light Infantry and Devonshire. They had guns in a position to help. Despite this, they got an order to retreat to Caix.

"If we retreat any more, we could end up in Montrose," said Rob to the man he did not recognise next to him.

"Montrose. Where's that?" said the man with a strange accent.

"Home for me, North East Scotland."

"In that case, we'll pass my home in Yorkshire."

"Well, best get up and head to wherever we're going."

28 March 1918

The enemy had also crossed the Somme at Morcourt and were advancing from there. It put them behind the 4/5. The order to retreat would have taken them into the advancing Bosche, so it got cancelled. The chaos in the Allied ranks was clear to see. The few officers that were left had no idea about the situation. Rob could hear discussions about where the Bosche were advancing.

"They're advancing in big numbers here," said one pointing to a map.

"No. The Bosche are over here," said another, pointing to a different location

"I heard that you both might be correct," said the third.

While the discussion continued, Rob turned to the rations that he and two others had to share.

It was one iron ration pack. Iron rations consisted of 1lb Preserved Meat, 1lb Biscuit, 5/8oz, Tea and 2ozs Sugar. Not a lot to share between three hungry, tired, pissed off men. The hot meal he'd had a couple of days earlier was beginning to look like a banquet to Rob.

However, at 08:00, it was reinstated. Getting out of positions quickly, the 4/5 made it to Caix. The Battalion count was now seven officers and 43 men. The joke Rob had heard previously about seeing more people in a bus queue was not so funny now.

The desperate men got a new order to march to Cayeux-en-Santerre. They were to occupy and hold a line between the Wiencourt and Marcelcave. Again, when they got there, they found the enemy occupying the position.

After another march, the men received more orders to occupy a line between Wiencourt and Marcelcave. Another order sent by men not acquainted with the situation on the ground. How could less than fifty men defend a line stretching over a mile, especially as the German already held it?

"I wonder if anyone knows what the fucks going on?" asked a man close to Rob.

"Doesn't seem like it. We're scurrying here and there like rabbits, being chased by a pack of German dogs," replied a shattered Rob.

The remainder of the three Battalions of the 118th Infantry Brigade got reorganised. They became one single Battalion of about nine hundred men. The 1st Cambridgeshire and 4/5 Black Watch had enough men to form one company. Two whole Battalions, reduced to company strength. Nothing illustrated their desperate situation better than this and what happened next.

At 14:30, the hastily constructed Battalion got ordered to launch a counterattack on the ridge held by the Germans.

"What do those bastards at headquarters think we are?" said Rob to Archie Gemmill, who was lying next to him in the mud.

"How many fucking men do they think we've got?" replied Archie. "We're one platoon, and they want us to rush a hill held by Germans who have already spanked us several times. Fucking brass." The comment needed no response.

Despite their weakened state, the attack was successful, and they occupied the ridge. The German troops had fewer men than those attacking them. The Black Watch attack took them by surprise. It seems they thought the allies were further back. A small win after days of terrible losses.

However, at 22:00 that night, the exhausted men were ordered to a quarry just outside Aubercourt. To make matters worse, the sunshine during the day had turned to rain.

29 March 1918

At 03:00, the men were ordered to move, yet again, to a position about half a mile to the north. When they arrived, they found it full of Royal Engineers. They slipped back about five hundred yards and dug in yet again. They received orders to counterattack on four occasions, which they did. They were not successful attacks. By this time, the men that remained were on their knees with exhaustion. Many were out of ammunition.

A group of Australians and cavalry arrived to help in the counterattack. However, they were seen and heavily shelled.

Eventually, on the 30th March 1918, the Black Watch were to be relieved. At this point, they had only one officer and about 30 men left. The rest were dead or missing. This hungry, beaten-up, tired and desperate army headed to billets in Longeau via Cachy and Gentelles.

FORTY-FOUR

Germany started Operation Georgett on the 9th of April. The objective was to capture the Channel ports and cut off supplies to the Allied armies. The situation became critical for the British troops. On the 11th of April, Douglas Haig produced a Special order of the day to those same tired, beaten up men in the trenches.

Lt Col Cruickshank, Officer Commanding, had the battalion paraded. He could read out the Special order to the men.

"General Haig has produced a special order of the day. I am going to give you the salient parts." With that, he proceeded to tell the men just how bad the situation was.

"The Bosche has pushed us back over 40 miles. They seem to be trying to capture the Channel Ports. If they do that, then our supplies will be cut. We will be defeated. We cannot allow that to happen. We must stand and fight, or the Bosche will be able to cross the Channel and invade our country."

"The past few days have been hard on you men, but I must ask another huge effort from you. We must stop Fritz at all costs. We will be fighting for the freedom of mankind. I'll read you the last paragraph of the General's order."

'There is no other course open to us but to fight it out. Every position must be held, to the last man: there must be no retirement. With our backs to the wall and believing in the justice of our cause, each one of us must fight on to the end. The safety of our homes and the freedom of mankind alike depend upon the conduct of each one of us at this critical moment'

"Thank you, men. I know that you will not let your country down."

The parade got dismissed. Some of the men returning to their posts got fired up by the speech. Men like Rob, who had more time in the trenches, had a different view.

"What do you think, Rob?" asked Hugh Brand.

"We're in for more shite. It's alright for the General sitting in his office in London. He's not going to be doing the fighting. Fucking toffs. I'd like to see them out here in the mud, eating field rations, sleeping in holes and then getting up to fight for their lives. We'll need to sort them out when this war is over."

"Steady on, Rob. That's revolutionary talk."

"Don't worry, Hugh. I'll do my bit when the time comes. It's the only way I'll survive."

In May, the state of the battalion was apparent to everyone. The men had been re-equipped and formed into two short-handed companies. Two full-strength companies would number nearly five hundred men. Just looking around, Rob could see how short-handed they were.

The 9th Battalion Black Watch was also short-handed. They were absorbed into the 4/5 to produce a near full-strength battalion.

His company were involved in a raid on the enemy trenches at the end of May. The men got caught up on the enemy wire and were forced back by heavy machine-gun fire, but not before they bombed the enemy trenches from their wire. One officer and eight men were slightly wounded.

Rob was on this raid. The objective was to bomb trenches and capture prisoners. Caught up on the wire, Rob managed to lob his two bombs into the dug-out in front of him. He struggled to free himself before falling back without any prisoners.

Between April and June, the battalion took part in extra training. It was to get the men of 9th and 4/5 working together as a single unit.

Towards the end of June, they were in the line again. The Bosche were now on the defensive and used gas as a weapon on the Scots. Reaction times to gas alerts were better now so, relatively few men were affected.

In July 1918, Rob was in the trenches again at Fampoux near Arras. The Germans shelled the trenches with gas, and Rob was affected. He had his respirator on quickly, but some of the gas burned his exposed hands and knees. His exposure was minimal compared to others. Those severely exposed spent weeks in hospital, and some evacuated to the UK for specialist care. Rob had small blisters on his exposed skin. It required a period in a hospital to have the burns bathed and dressed until the blisters went down. He was out of the line for only two weeks. It did at least get him out of some of the hard labour and training that was going on.

Back with his Battalion, Rob was sitting on his cot in the billets in Berles near Arras. They were all waiting for the next order when a voice asked, "Are you, Rob?"

"I am." Rob turned to see the man. "Who are you?" It was a face Rob had seen before. So many had come and gone that he could not place it.

"Arthur. Arthur Herschell. We met on a march some time ago. I've not seen you since. Thought you might have copped it."

"No. Not yet. I'm just back from the hospital."

"Gas?"

"Yes. I've got a few small blisters on my hands and knees. The yellow skin will go with the hole in my back where I had shrapnel removed."

"You're not having much luck, are you?"

"I'm not dead yet. I suppose that's lucky."

"I suppose so. I've lost lots of pals since I came here."

"We all have, and if the brass has their way, we'll lose lots more."

"Aye."

"You're from Montrose, aren't you?"

"I am."

"My older brother has a family there."

"I remember you telling me. Isn't your brother out here somewhere. I thought you told me that."

"He's in the Field Artillery."

"Does he have eye problems?"

"What do you mean?"

"Well, that lot has shelled us as many times as they shelled Fritz."

"Aye, that's about right. Back there, they've only got some map reference to aim. If it's wrong or we got there too quick, then we're in for it. My company lost a few men when our officers rushed forward too quickly. Bad enough getting killed by Fritz, but our guns, is terrible. I wonder if my brothers' battery was one of the lot that shelled us. I'll give him hell when we get out of this."

"You got a family?"

"No, not yet. What about you?

"No. I had a lass that promised herself, but she found another man."

"That's bad. Is he at home?"

"No, he's out there somewhere. She fell in with him when he was home on leave."

"That wouldn't take long. Leave is very short and getting to Scotland takes up much of it."

"One night it seems, and she gets pregnant."

"Fuck. That's terrible."

"Aye. Still, water under the bridge now. She'll have had a bairn by now. He might be dead for all I know."

"Not in our lot then?"

"No, he's with Pontius Pilates Bodyguard."

"What are you going to do when this war is over?"

"If I'm not lying in the ground, I'll get drunk for a week."

"After that?"

"Don't know. No idea what jobs a broken-down soldier is fit for. Don't know what jobs might be available. I'll have to wait and see. What about you?"

"Lots of jobs in Dundee. Don't know what I'll do. I don't want to be like my brother."

"How so?"

"He's a bad-tempered labourer with a wife and seven kids in two rooms."

"Did having a big family make him bad-tempered?"

"No. He came back from the Boer War like that. He'd already seen what we're seeing now. Never really understood why he joined up again."

"Maybe his wife made him"

"Maybe so. Best get some sleep. We'll be on the move again tomorrow, I hear."

"By the time this war's over, I'll have marched over every bloody mile of France and Belgium."

"Night, Rob."

"Night, Arthur."

The rest of the month proved Rob correct. There was the usual march here, march there with the occasional train ride in between.

If it was not bad enough getting shelled by Bosche artillery, his aeroplanes flew over and dropped bombs. Not many killed this way, but it was another way to be afraid and die.

Rob could now add a second wound stripe to his uniform. He could also add a Corporal stripe to his arm. He was only acting corporal. If he behaved, he'd get full corporal. Rob guessed that, because he had served with the battalion for three years, he was getting promotion based on long service and not getting killed.

FORTY-FIVE

On the 1st of August, the Bosche were in retreat. The allies were in pursuit. As they went, they put up a fierce fight before moving back. By now, Rob and his comrades were near Buzancy some hundred miles from where he was last wounded.

During an advance on the retreating Germans, the Black Watch came under heavy fire by artillery and machine guns. Leading his section in the attack on a machine gun position as ordered, Rob got hit by a bullet in the leg. The round did not go all the way through. He dressed the wound with a field dressing, but he could not continue.

Once more, Rob was being helped back to the dressing station, cursing and swearing as he went.

"That won't help the wound, Corporal," said an RAMC man on his right assisting him hobbling back.

"I fucking know, but it makes me feel better."

"OK then."

The MO looked at Rob's wound and extracted the bullet from his leg.

"Would you like to keep the bullet, Corporal?"

"I'd like to shove it up Frtiz..."

"I get the picture."

"This is the third time those bastards have hit me."

"What happened the other times?"

"I've had shrapnel here." Rob pointed to his shoulder. "I got gassed not long ago." Rob showed his knees and hands. "They seemed determined to get me."

"So, I see. Not having much luck, are you?"

"Better luck than those men over there." Rob nodded towards several men on stretchers. It became evident that some would die or lose limbs.

"I suppose so. You'll need to rest up for a week, or so then we can send you back and see if the Bosche can finally get their man."

"That's not funny."

"Sorry. Gallows humour."

"Sorry, Doc."

"OK, Corporal, we'll get you to bed for a couple of days, then start the therapy after that if all goes well."

Getting back to his battalion, Rob was in time to witness increased aerial attacks by German planes. These bombing runs took place day and night. At about this time, Rob became a full Corporal. His promotion meant more money and less chance of losing his stripes for a minor misdemeanour.

On the 8th of August, the King passed through the village of Penin, where the Black Watch were resting. The battalion lined the route and gave three cheers.

Corporal Robert Corsar was unfit to parade for the King, which was just as well.

"It must be safe here, or they wouldn't allow him to come," said Rob to Ernie Finch, who was lying beside him on a cot. Ernie was also recovering from a wound.

"It can't be that safe if we got wounded."

"You don't think the brass would let him anywhere near danger, would you? He's the King. The high up yins don't get anywhere near the fighting. He's the highest of the high up yins."

"That's not very nice of you, Rob. Don't you want to be out there to see him?"

"No, I don't."

"You're not like one of those Russian Bolsheviks we've heard killed their Tsar, are you?"

"No, Ernie, I'm not."

"He's our King. We're fighting for him. You should show more respect."

"I'm not fighting for him, Ernie. I'm fighting to get home safe and away from all this killing and death. I would even prefer to back on the farms digging spuds and neeps in the rain."

"What's a neep?"

"They're turnips, you Sassenach."

"Were you a farmer before this?"

"I was a lot of things Ernie but not a farmer. I was a farm labourer. I also laboured in a shipyard, dug roads, humped logs and rocks and anything else to stop from starving."

"Sounds like a tough hard life."

"It was, but not as terrible as this."

"No. It's rough."

"You go and cheer if you want to, Ernie. I'll go nowhere near him. Anyway, the doc says I have to rest."

Unfortunately, Rob was fit enough for a grand parade on the 12 of August, where the French Croix-De-Guerre got given to twelve men from the Black Watch. Rob was not one of the heroes. His only decoration was a third wound stripe on his arm. More bloody brass to clean, he thought.

There was more time to rest now. Rob's nightmares regularly failed to bring the gentle oblivion of sleep. His sleep became punctuated by images that might fit well into Dante's inferno. These images were often unrelentingly terrifying. Waking, screaming was the body's defence mechanism saving him from a complete loss of mind. For the new conscripts, this was a difficult sight to behold. For longer serving soldiers, this was a well-recognised effect of the war. Shell shock was a complex set of symptoms. Rob's symptoms were not sufficiently severe for him to get removed from service. The army had plenty of men just like him.

All the while, the army was moving forward, and the Bosche got pushed back. The Bosche stiff resistance meant that it was two steps forward, and one step back kind of advance. Reminded Rob of the dancing practice he had with his sister in their back green.

On the 26 of August, the Black Watch travelled on the light railway. It was the one they had helped build earlier in the war.

"What do you think, Dennis? Going back or up to the front?" Rob had remembered Dennis's words when the pair were part of the group building the railway line.

"The engine's pointing up the tracks towards the front line."

"Perhaps if we wait on the platform, we'll catch the next one out of here."

"Nice thought, Rob. I doubt the army would agree to that, or we'd have no troops to fight."

"Aye. Let's get on with it then."

Back in the trenches on the 3rd of September, Rob had just started breakfast after the morning stand-to. He heard aeroplanes approaching.

"They're Allied planes," shouted someone. "They're after that Bosche balloon."

Sure, enough the Allied planes were heading towards the German spotter balloon. The spotter in the basket hanging below the balloon was frantically waving to his winch team below to get him down.

The Black Watch troops were cheering the planes and jeering the Bosche spotter. There were numerous insults and suggestions about what should happen to this spotter, eventually ending in a terrible death.

The German winch team were not quick enough for the spotter who launched himself out of the basket. Despite the shouted hopes that the spotter's parachute would not open, it did. He floated down just as the Allied planes started shooting the balloon that exploded in a ball of flames.

The Black Watch trenches were full of cheers and gave the airmen thumbs up as they flew by.

Rob was in the front line again at 06:45 on the morning of 2nd the of October. A German soldier descended upon them, holding his hands up and gave himself up to Rob. He said that his regiment was withdrawing. He was very young and hungry and did not want to continue to fight. He was taken prisoner and escorted to the battalion HQ for interrogation. In response to information from the prisoner, some troops moved forward to occupy ground left by the retreating Bosche.

There had been other Bosche deserters, but this was the first for Rob. It was a good morale boost for the troops. There was fresh hope that this war might be over by this Christmas.

Over the next few days, the men noticed that German shelling of their position was less frequent. There was still a steady trickle of dead and wounded men.

On the 6th of September, the battalion launched a raid against the enemy in the Hulluch Sector. They reached their objective and waited four hours but encountered no enemy. No one knew where they'd gone.

"More first-rate intelligence," said Les Beveridge. "Maybe if we tell the Bosche where we're going to raid or attack, they'll all go home."

"If only that were true," said Second Lieutenant Brock.

The month continued with small attacks and counterattacks by both sides. More men lost as a result.

FORTY-SIX

On the 2nd of October, C Company were in the front line when a German soldier gave himself up to Rob's section.

"Rob. Bosche soldier coming towards us with his hands up." Shouted Norman Gillman, who was on guard.

"Keep him covered and tell him to come forward."

The man did. When questioned by Rob, he stated that his army was withdrawing. This news heartened the soldiers, but their joy was short-lived. A patrol was sent out to scout the enemy and met heavy resistance. Two men got killed and seven wounded. If Fritz was retiring, he was doing so in anger.

On the 3rd of October, a platoon pushed forward towards a Metal Works. They came under heavy fire, and none of the men returned. There was hope that they had been taken prisoner rather than killed.

Between 11th and 13th October 1918, the Black Watch got the task of repairing roads.

On the 6th of October, C Company got into the factory and found an old piano in good condition. They brought it back to Headquarters. There was entertainment that night.

The enemy continued to retreat, but made sure the allied advance was not smooth. They shelled and machine-gunned the 4/5 as they advanced, inflicting heavy casualties.

On the 21st of October, Rob and the men of 4/5 Black Watch passed a milestone. They left the French town of Mouchin and crossed the border from France into Belgium. They were cheered by happy inhabitants of every town and village they passed through. These were people showing their gratitude for being liberated by the Allies. Rob even got a kiss from a local woman.

"Merci." He muttered as he got pushed on by the men marching behind him. Seeing the joy on the faces of the local people was gratifying. It was the first time that Rob felt his hardship and endeavours in this war might have been worthwhile. By nightfall, the Battalion was three miles inside the Belgium border at L'Ecuille. Morale was high.

It was not the first time Rob had been into Belgium. During the previous years of the war, he and the Allies have advanced and been pushed back over the border several times. They never knew what country they were in, but this time it was different. They were marching through liberated towns and villages, and the waving flags in the crowds changed colour after they crossed the border. Not only that, but this time crowds were cheering them. Previously, Rob had mostly seen scared refugees carrying small quantities of their belongings to safety.

Some of the newer conscripts thought the war was over. That night they were rudely awakened. The town came under heavy bombardment. There was a resigned look on the faces of those who had been in the war for longer. The killing and wounding would go on.

After another night of heavy shelling on the 23rd, the army routine continued. All four companies took part in training exercises.

On the 25th of October, the Battalion was in L'Ecuille celebrating their Commanding Officers birthday. Unknown to Private Arthur Herschell in D Company, some fifty miles further south, near St Quentin, his elder brother Alan died of wounds received the previous day.

On 30 October, C Company were in billets when they were shelled by gas. A quarter of the 200 men were wounded in this attack. Rob was not one of them. Luckily, he was out of the way training when the attack happened.

Being in a different country did nothing for Rob. Why would it? The confusion continued to reign.

On the 6th of November, the Battalion heard that the enemy was retiring. They got the order to move up. They did. Unfortunately, the information about the enemy retreat was again wrong. The Bosche might have been hungry, tired and dispirited, but they were not going down without a fight. The Battalion was ordered back to where they started the day.

The following day they were ordered to move up. This time the information was correct. The Battalion consolidated their new position, and there they stayed, at least for a short time.

Further moves forward were ordered, and on the 11th of November 1918, the unit was in Blicquy between Tournai and Mons.

News reached the Battalion C.O. at 09:00 that hostilities would cease at 11:00 that day. He made it known to the men.

"Men. At eleven hundred hours, an Armistice is to be signed. Hostilities will cease. The war will be over."

When they heard, there was nothing except a murmur among the men. They had already got promises that the next big push would win the war. They did not. They had been promised much in the past, but those were hollow promises. There was some scepticism about this news mixed with hope. Might this carnage be over?

Hostilities might be about to cease in a couple of hours, but shells were still coming at them. Lots of men could die in the remaining two hours of this war. They continued to keep their heads down. It all seemed too good to be true.

At 11:00 hours on the 11th of November, 1918, hostilities ceased. It took a while to reach Rob as the 4/5 were on the road marching towards Huissignies.

They got the news at about 11:30. A great cheer went up among the marching men. There were slaps on backs and handshakes, but the march continued.

Rob felt elated and numb. Glad that there would be no more fighting and dying. He had survived. He also realised that he was suffering from shell shock. It was not on his medical records, but he had all of the signs and symptoms. He often had uncontrollable shaking fits, he twitched as he found to his cost while shaving one day. Others around him could have added to the list, but none did as many had the same. He also had occasional blackouts.

The shelling stopped. Exhausted, disillusioned men had hope of going home at last. That was the talk in the ranks as they marched.

These were men who thought that they had no future. Most had thought they would die at the front, but now they had a future. What might they do with it?

"Does that mean we won the war, Rob?" asked Jamie Ritchie, who was marching beside Rob.

"I guess it does, Jamie. We've not to lay down our guns, so I suppose we did."

"What'll happen to us now? When will we be sent home?"

"I don't know, lad. You know the army. They'll need to decide what to do next. They'll have to have some plan. After that, we'll get our marching orders soon enough, I expect."

"I wonder what England will be like this Christmas?"

"Where are you from, Jamie?"

"Whitby in Yorkshire."

"What's a Sassenach like you doing in a Jock outfit?"

"I was called up and sent here. I didn't have a choice. You've not been a bad group of lads. It's been OK fighting with your lot."

"Do you enjoy fighting then?"

"No. Nobody in their right mind enjoys fighting in a war." Jamie was shaking and not just because he was cold.

"Well, you'll be seeing your folks soon, I expect."

"I'll be glad to be out of this and back on the boats."

"Are you a sailor then?"

"No. I'm a fisherman on the trawlers. That's why I came out here lately. We were held back until there was no choice, I heard."

"I'm from a fishing town in Scotland. I always liked a bit of fish for my tea if we could afford it."

"If you're ever down our way, come and see me in Whitby, and I'll get you one of the best fish suppers in the world."

"If I'm your way, I'll take you up on that."

There were many new conscripts in the ranks of the Battalion. Not so many like Rob, who had been there a long time. Going home was all the talk in the billets.

Rob remembered his only visit home after his back wound. It was not a happy experience. He did want to go home, but he could not think of a compelling reason not to. Unlike many others, he had no girl waiting for him. For the last three years, he got told what to do, and he did it, like a good soldier. Now that he could make his own decisions, he did not know where to start. How soon he could pack his kitbag and head home out of this carnage was the thought uppermost in his mind.

Thoughts of what he might do when he got home did tumble across his mind as he worked. He was not sure what he might be fit to do. His shoulder still ached at times. His other wounds were better, but the gas had left their mark on his exposed skin. He had occasional headaches, and his nightmares had become worse. He awoke screaming more frequently. That too, he thought, would go after he got out of this hell. He also had the odd blackout. He had no idea what caused them. He was sure it would all become better when he got home away from the war.

When Rob spoke to Jamie Ritchie about winning the war, he was partially correct. There was an armistice, and the fighting stopped, but the German army did not lay down their weapons.

Rob reached Huissignies in the early afternoon. It was not the marching orders that Rob had told Jamie to expect. Still, what else could a soldier expect from the army?

The following day the men set to cleaning their new billets. There was training in the afternoon. No celebration, but they did their work with a lighter load.

The following day they prepared for a ceremonial parade. It was not until the 15 of November that they eventually got some recreation.

FORTY-SEVEN

The war was over, but these men were still in the British army, and they had their way of doing things, as the soldiers soon found out. While fighting, their commanders accepted a certain lack of army dress discipline. That changed now that fighting was over.

The ceremonial parade on the 13th was a portend of things to come. Infractions of the dress code that got overlooked previously brought loud bollockings and threats of charges. Kit and billet inspections became equally fraught for the troops.

"I've had enough of this bullshit," said Donald Muir. "I got called up for the duration of the war, and that's over now. I want to go home."

"Yes," said Fred Brumby. "I agree it's time the army sent us home."

"We all want to go home," said Rob. "This is the army. They're only in a hurry if it suits them."

"I don't care," Donald spat out. "I've done my bit, so the better bloody hurry up and get me home, or I'll kick up a stink."

"That won't do you any good, Donald. The army can do what they like with you. They have us all by the throat."

"I didn't want to be in the regular army with all that spit and polish bollocks. I just wanted to do my bit and get home quickly. I think my papers say that I got conscripted for the duration of the war. The war's fucking over, so time to go home."

"We have to attend some lectures tomorrow, so maybe we'll find out then what's going to happen."

"It better be news of when we can go home, or there will be trouble."

The lecture the following day did tell them what was going to happen. There were going to be more lectures, education courses and vocational exercises to help get the men ready to return home.

"Any questions?" said Captain Mathews.

"Sir." Donald stood up.

"Yes, private."

"I have all the skills I need and a job to go back to, so when will I be going home?"

"It's not that simple private. There are hundreds of thousands of men to go back. We don't have the transport to take you all together. The army can't send you all back to the same camp to demobilise you. We have to arrange clothing, money, identification documents and much more. It will take time, but we will get you all back as quickly as possible."

The lecture broke up, and the men returned to their billets.

"They got us out here quick enough," complained Fred. "They had all the organisation to do that. Just put that in reverse, and we could all go home."

The men found out that Rob had been correct. The army had them by the throat and would do what they wanted with disgruntled men. The men had heard rumours that there was mutiny somewhere in France that got put down. Still, the discontent grew. Men who had recently come to the war were among the first to be repatriated. It only increased soldiers' anger. Those left behind heard that the men sent home early had the abilities needed back home to rebuild the country. It did little to appease the impatience in the ranks.

There had been a general election in the UK as soon as the armistice was signed. The coalition government of David Lloyd George won a majority. Reading a paper about the result, Rob quickly realised that the new government was the old government. "Plus, ca change," he muttered to himself as he read. It was a little of the French language that he had picked up. The bureaucrats were still in charge.

It was also the first election where women could vote. Rob liked that. His dad had been agitating for that for years. Over his youth, Rob had been exposed to and taken on his father's socialist ideals. He would even have been a pacifist if he'd known what was in store for him in this war. Rob regretted not understanding his father's angry words that he'd soon be dancing to a different tune. He realised he could not have gone back. He had made a legal declaration, and he would keep his word.

He remembered talking to Lizzie about her getting the vote. IT brought back some dark, painful memories. It did not help that since that betrayal, he had heard a few similar stories from other men in his battalion. He tried to put these thoughts out of his mind while concentrating on cleaning his webbing and boots for the next parade.

In April 1919, all of the men that could leave the 4/5 battalion had got home. The few that remained became re-enlisted regulars.

Rob was one of those who left France in early April 1919. Before he headed home, his first call was to the Medical Officer. He was medically examined and given a Form Z22.

"I've checked your medical record, Corporal. You've had a rough time of it," said Captain Reynolds.

"I suppose so, Sir."

"I'm going to give you the once over, so will you take your clothes off and sit here. You can leave your underpants on."

The doctor worked around Rob, checking his chest, pulse, eyes, ears, blood pressure and wounds.

"That's a bit of a hole in your back. How does it feel?"

"It still aches a bit, and it feels kind of tight when I exercise."

"Yes. Your skin got stitched tight to close the wound, but it seems OK. The marks on your hands and knees were chemical burns from gas, I see."

"Yes, Sir. I got my mask on. I could not cover my hands and knees with my kilt."

"Not an unusual set of scars for Scottish regiments who wear the kilt. I see that you have complained of having some blackouts. Is that correct?"

"That's right, Sir. I occasionally fall without warning. I've not tripped up, just fallen."

"Yes. It's recorded here as exhaustion. I'm not so sure. I've seen a few similar cases of men, like you, who have spent a long time in this war. I think you might have epilepsy."

"Sorry. Epilepsy. What's that?"

"It's a nervous disorder of the brain."

"What caused it?"

"We don't know. There are some theories, but none proved. It might have happened because you were close to the blast of shells. I suppose you were?"

"Aye, I was. So, what did that do to me?"

"We think that frequent explosions damage a small part of the brain. Perhaps only a nerve or two. It forces the brain to reroute some of its messages to the rest of your body. When it has difficulty finding a path, that's when you blackout. At least that's the theory at the moment."

"So, this war has given me brain damage, has it?"

"In a way, I think it has. Your symptoms are consistent with epilepsy, and they are attributable to your service in the army."

"Another bloody war wound."

"Just so. I see the three wound stripes on the sleeve of your uniform. You won't get another for this, but my report will enable you to get help when you go home."

"Is there a cure for epilepsy, and will my nightmare go away, doctor?"

"There is a treatment for epilepsy but no cure that I know. As for the nightmares, many men in this army have them. The shock of explosions gave you epilepsy, but the dreams and nightmares come from what you have seen. We have no idea how long these might last. I'm sorry to tell you that we don't have the answer."

Rob dressed and walked back to his billet, cursing under his breath. "Brain damage, shell shock, gassed, holes in my back and leg, fucking epileptic all for a couple of bob a day." It was at this point that something triggered Rob's memory. He remembered the football game where that big guy bashed his head and knocked him out. He wondered if that might have something to do with his epilepsy. Maybe he should mention it, but he forgot about it almost immediately.

He seemed to be stuck with occasional blackouts, headaches and shaking, but these were not something he considered might be permanent. Away from the war, he thought all that would disappear along with the nightmares.

Before he left to go home, Rob went to the battalion orderly room. Here he was given an Army Form Z44 (Plain Clothes Form) and a Certificate of Employment showing what he did before he joined, and what his time in the army had taught him. He was now a corporal and had some man-management experience. Man, management in the army at war was relatively easy. You order men to do something, and they do it or get shot for disobedience. They're soldiers who expect to take orders. Those ordering men about try to gain the respect of their men. However, when bullets are flying about your ears, men need orders.

A Dispersal Certificate recorded his personal and military information. It also gave the state of his equipment. If he lost any of it after this point, it would get taken from his outstanding pay.

Rob got the train to the docks at Boulogne and boarded a ship for Southampton. It was a long slow journey. He did fall asleep on the boat but woke shouting from a nightmare about the British soldier he shot in the mud at Passchendaele. He saw the look of hopelessness and terror on the man's face, his pleading eyes and his gratitude for what was about to happen. Rob knew he'd done the correct thing. It did not make living with it any easier.

During his waking hours, Rob's sense of guilt for what he did that day weighed more heavily on him than any load he'd carried during the war. He rationalised he had given the man a swift end rather than a slow lingering drowning in mud. He'd had no compunction about killing the enemy, but this man was on Rob's side.

Rob had presumed that he would not live to see the war ended. The episode with Lizzie only added to his thoughts that he had nothing to look forward to except death. The world had changed while he was away. More importantly, so had he.

He looked into a mirror and hardly recognised the face staring back. It was thin and ashen, resembling a man much older than one approaching his twenty-second birthday. His back ached, and his scarred hands and knees looked unsightly. He had a slight stoop as if he was carrying something heavy on his back. In truth, he carried the heavy load in his head. He could not unsee what he'd seen. He could not erase it like the chalk letters on his school slate years ago. His blackouts only added to his sense of worthlessness.

After a night's rest at the nearby camp, Rob took the train from Southampton to Reading. Here he changed trains and headed for Edinburgh another long slow journey. Adding to his black nightmare thoughts was a picture of the five men and two officers that had made the outward journey with him. They were all gone now except Joe Murray. He thought Joe was still alive but missing some body parts. Having seen the piles of amputated limbs while in the hospital, he wondered if Joe's were among those. The thought sent a shiver down his spine and added to his sense of horror.

There was another change of train in Edinburgh. The train crossed the Forth Bridge into Dunfermline. It went on to Cowdenbeath and Kinross. Rob got demobbed at Dispersal Centre 1A at Kinross in Fife.

The processes at the demobilisation were centre was far from smooth. There had been tales of men having to sleep on blankets on concrete floors because of a lack of cots or beds. There was also a lack of food and money to pay the soldiers what they were due. It cut no ice with men returning from war that the logistics for the demobilisation of millions of men were impossible. They had endured difficulties in France and Belgium. The army had been quick enough to enlist or conscript men. Demobbing them should be equally swift.

At the centre, he had another medical. Epilepsy was noted on his medical record, as was the fact that it was attributable to his war service. Unknown to Rob at this time, this record would turn out to be most helpful in years to come.

He also received numerous forms, including a fortnight's ration book and a civilian proof of identity. The paperwork he now carried was not quite as heavy as his army pack, but it was not for want of trying. Rob had listened to what these were all for and why he needed to have them. It seemed life in civvy street was very complicated now. He thumbed through the various forms. He tried to remember what they were. In the army, all choices were made for him. He got told what to do, where to go, what to wear and what to carry. He even got his food and drink given to him. He had become institutionalised. Like all regular soldiers, he was comfortable with the routine, even if it meant change. Change in a wartime army was almost routine.

The boundaries of change were limited to the requirements of the immediate battlefield situation. He was now free of that but did not know what to do with his freedom.

He had the choice of a suit of clothing or money in lieu. Rob remembered that he had told Arthur Herschell he would get drunk for a week when he returned. He chose the fifty-two shillings and sixpence rather than the suit. After all, he was unlikely to be working in an office, so why would a labourer need a suit?

Rob's idea to get drunk for a week also took a severe knock. Prime Minister Lloyd George, a teetotaller, had made drinking a more difficult task than it had been before the war. He had reduced the specific gravity of the beer, making it weaker. His new rules on a whole range of brewing issues raised the average price of a pint to five pence. It was almost twice what it cost at the start of the war. He had also severely limited the opening hours of pubs. Returning soldiers and working men were not best pleased.

They knew what difficult was. Difficult was squelching about in mud towards murderous machine-gun fire. Administering a war was easier on the army than organising soldiers for demob.

Rob was finally demobbed from the army on 25 April 1919. On that date, 43392 Corporal Corsar R.S. of the 4/5 Battalion Black Watch, who had three wound stripes and epilepsy, became plain Mr Robert Corsar, civilian.

He left there to go home to Montrose, still in his uniform, steel helmet and greatcoat. He also received a cash payment of £2 to be charged against his account; a service gratuity of £1 for each year of service and a calculated war gratuity, said to be to compensate him for the loss of the ancient privilege of looting.

FORTY-EIGHT

The fighting might have ceased, but Robs war was without end. Rob's physical injuries were evident, but he could operate successfully in the army, or so his Medical Officer said. There was unseen trauma in his brain. Its consequences and his poor mental state was a much more difficult question. Soldiers medical records were often annotated as NYDN. It was shorthand for Not Yet Diagnosed, Nervous. Colloquially this was known as Shell Shock. In 1918, Shell Shock was a catch-all phrase for a very complex medical condition. Some coped quite well, but many did not. Rob was to fall into the latter group. Three wound stripes on his sleeve stood as a testament to the visible damage on his body. The impairment in his brain was not evident. There was no wound stripe on his sleeve to signify it.

Arriving home in Montrose, his mother greeted him in her usual fashion. The lodger had returned from his day's work. His father was more caring, as were his siblings. All could see that the young, fit and healthy lad who had left in 1915 had been replaced by this worn out broken man. Rob was still not quite twenty-two years old but had the careworn look of a much older man.

His sisters were very worried about him. He was not the fresh-faced brother that had gone to war.

"Are you alright, Rob?" asked Mary. "You don't look well."

"I'm no bad, Mary, but I'm awful tired."

"Is that wound we saw you with healed now?" asked Emmy. "You look a bit bent."

"It sometimes hurts a bit, but it's not that bad."

"I'll make you a cup of tea," said the young Jess.

"Put your stuff in the back room," said his mother.

While he was out of the room, there was a short general conversation about how poorly Rob looked. His younger siblings asked questions, but Rob gave few answers. Rob had no wish to relate and therefore relive his wartime experiences. He was tired, and not just from the long train journeys. Despite being among the family, Rob also felt strangely alone. It might be his family, and he was glad to be back, but he felt an outsider. In the trenches, it was not very difficult to talk to men who had experienced what you had. None of those around him had any idea what he had experienced, and he had no wish to elaborate. He wanted to forget all of that.

After his meagre meal and cup of tea, Rob wanted to go to bed. He was to sleep in the same bed as Frank. Frank was nearing his fifteenth birthday. The bed was no deluxe multi sprung divan, but it felt that way to Rob as he lay down. Compared to mud, dirt, concrete and army cots, this was deluxe to Rob. He fell asleep almost immediately and did not wake when young Frank entered the bed.

What happened later that night would severely impact the Corsar household for a long time afterwards. Rob woke shouting and thrashing, smacking Frank on his back. Frank recoiled from the blow. Seeing Rob thrashing and shouting made him afraid. He jumped out of bed, and as he was about to rush to his parents, he met his Dad coming towards him.

"What's going on?" asked an ashen Sandy Corsar.

"It's Rob. He's gone berserk shouting and thrashing about."

Sandy entered the bedroom to see that Rob had quietened down and was awake. "What's up, lad?' asked Sandy.

"I had a nightmare. Did I shout? Did I hurt Frank?"

"Yes, Rob. We heard you all over the house. You're not hurt, are you, Frank?"

"No, dad." Frank was with his back to the wall.

"I'm sorry, Frank." At that point, Rob fell back and started to convulse on the bed. He was talking as he twitched.

"He's having a fit."

"What's that?" inquired Frank.

"It's a disorder of the brain. I've occasionally seen it in animals."

"Is it catching?"

"No, lad. I imagine something in the war did this to Rob."

Rob stopped shaking after about a minute. He lay for a short while as he came around and reoriented himself with his surroundings. He sat up.

"Did I blackout?"

"You had a fit, lad," said his Dad. "Has that happened before?"

"Yes. A few times. The army says I might have something called epilepsy due to my service. What happened?"

"You fell back and started twitching all over," said Frank, who pressed himself against the wall away from Rob.

"What did the army say, son?"

"They only saw it after the war ended, and I only did it once or twice. That's what was put it on my discharge medical."

"Is that all they wrote?"

"No. They put my wounds on my form."

"What about the nightmare? Is that something you've done before?"

"Aye. Quite a lot of us had bad dreams and woke shouting. I expect it'll pass after I've been home for a while."

"Well, get some sleep, you two. See you in the morning. Night."

"Night, Dad," came the response from Frank and Rob.

In bed, Rob turned to Frank. "Sorry, Frank."

"OK, Rob. Night."

The rest of the night passed off quietly.

Unfortunately, the nightmares and shouting episodes continued. Frank had a position as an apprentice shipwright in Montrose docks. He was up early and worked hard all day. Frank was tired when he came home and needed his sleep. He was becoming more agitated by his brother's condition. Not only that, but Rob was not always sympathetic. He could be downright rude to Frank and the rest of the household. At other times he was the amiable lad who had left for the war. No one in the family knew which Rob they would encounter. As a result, they often avoided him.

Rob tried to get work, but as soon as the Employment Exchange saw his epilepsy diagnosis, they were reluctant to put him forward for anything. There were few jobs available. Those that were available entailed dangerous labouring. Rob got consigned to a life living off the state. He did not like it but rationalised the situation in his mind.

"I fought for the crown and country. I got precious little in return, except wounds and head damage. They'll need to give me some payback for all I went through." Rob was talking to Frank one evening.

"Was it bad, Rob?"

"Aye, lad, it was."

"Can you tell me?"

"No, lad. I don't want to talk about it. It brings back those horrible nightmares that I have. I'm sorry if they upset you."

"You will get better, won't you?"

"I don't know. I hope so."

Just after Frank's fifteenth birthday at the end of August 1919, Sandy pulled Rob aside one day and spoke to him.

"These nightmares and your fits are upsetting the family."

"I can't help it. The bloody war made me this way." Rob was angry and defensive.

"Calm down, lad. I understand that. I've heard about shell shock. We've no idea what you went through out there, but it's affecting us now. We need to think about what to do."

"There's nothing to do. I can't get work because I could fall over in a fit. I can't forget the things I've seen. They come to me in my dreams. I'm a casualty of that bloody war."

"That you are, boy. Some things can be done. I've spoken with a few people in the Labour party who know about these things. They suggest seeing a doctor at Sunnyside who has some experience in these matters. Would you be willing to go and see him if I can arrange it?"

"Go to the asylum? A place for lunatics. Do you think I'm mad?"

"No, lad. Not mad, just disturbed by your experiences. There's a chance that this doctor could help you cope better with the nightmares. They also know about epilepsy at the hospital. Perhaps they can help with that."

"It would cost money we don't have."

"I can get some help from the Labour Party. They have funds to help soldiers returning from the war. They can help you cope with civilian life. They've helped a couple of chaps who lost legs get wheelchairs. I've spoken to the treasurer, and he's agreed to help."

"I don't know, Dad. Me going to the asylum doesn't seem right."

"It might be right for you and your condition. If it helps, then it will be worth it. You can't go on like this forever, Rob. It's upsetting for the whole family. Frank's not getting the sleep he needs to do his job. Your mum might not show it, but she's worried you might do something that will get you hurt. We all need you to do something about this."

"If that's the lie of the land, then I guess I'll just have to grin and bear it." He said it with a sort of insolent resignation.

"Right. I'll get on to the Party and set it up."

FORTY-NINE

Sandy set up the meeting at Sunnyside. Doctor Clarke had asked if Rob would mind his father being present for some of the consultation. The reason was that he wanted to know what Rob was doing while he was having a seizure.

"Rob, I've asked that your father be present because, during a seizure, you do not know what is happening. He can tell me things that you cannot."

"Aye. That's fine by me, doctor."

"Your father needs to get back to work, so can we deal with the seizures first? We'll get to the other issues afterwards."

"Fine," said Rob.

"Rob, do you have any warning that you are going to have a seizure?"

"What sort of warning do you mean?"

"Is there a distinctive smell or taste just before it happens?"

"I've never really noticed. I've not had a lot of fits so far, so I'm not sure if there are any smells or tastes. Is that something that happens with epilepsy and something I should look out for?"

"It can happen in some cases, but not all. If you do notice something like a taste or smell just before your seizures, it will give you a chance to get yourself into a safe place. Sandy, can I ask you what happens while Rob has his seizures. You've seen him while he fits, haven't you?"

"I've seen two."

"What happens?"

"He falls on the floor and fits."

"Is that all?"

"What do you mean?'

"Does he just fall and fit, or does he talk, bite his tongue or anything else?"

"He talks while he's fitting. It's not like a proper conversation, more a bit of a rant. Not shouting like he does during his nightmares."

"I didn't know that," said Rob.

"I didn't think it was important or relevant."

"It's very relevant, Sandy. It helps me with my diagnosis. Is there anything else you'd like to add? Does he bite his tongue, for instance?"

"No. I've not seen him bite his tongue. He talks."

"That's fine. If you want to get back to work, Rob and I will continue with my examination. Thanks for your help."

"Thanks, Dad."

"See you later, lad." With that, Sandy Corsar left the room and headed for his work.

"Now, Rob, can you strip off your clothes down to your underpants, please, so I can look at your war wounds?"

He ran his hands over the wound in Rob's back. He assessed where the wound was in relation to his neck and head using his fingers as a guide.

"This indentation in your back seems to be about the size of a small palm. It stretches up towards your neck but not as far as your head. Do you get any headaches from it?"

"I get headaches, but I didn't put them down to the wound."

"What did you think caused them?"

"I don't know. Drink. I got quite drunk for a bit after I came home."

"Are you still drinking now?"

"Not much. I've not got enough money. The bru doesn't pay that much, and my mum needs what I get to feed me."

"I'm going to put you on some medicine for your epilepsy. Don't drink when you're taking it as it can cause side effects, and it won't work so well."

He turned his attention to the chemical scars on Rob's hands and legs.

"These scars were caused, by gas I believe. Do you know what gas it was?"

"Mustard gas, I think. I'm not sure. I spent a few days bathing with some medicine until the blisters went down. I don't know what that was either."

After the physical examination of Rob's wounds, the doctor made copious notes as Rob got dressed. Rob made himself comfortable in an easy chair. The doctor looked up and continued.

"Your father mentioned your shouting nightmares. It was also in the note I got from him. I've had some experience of men who have come back from war with what you are experiencing. There's some literature on the treatment of the condition. Craiglockhart hospital in Edinburgh has had some success with cases like yours. They call it talking therapy. We'll need to talk about your feelings and nightmares. I think it would be best if you spent a few days as a resident of Sunnyside. Would you agree to that?"

"This is an asylum for the insane. Do you think I'm insane? Will talking cure my bad dreams?"

"No, Rob. You have a difficult mental issue brought on by your experiences in the war. I believe that I can help you manage those terrors better. It would be good for you and your family if we make that happen. I can also start you on medication that might help your epilepsy. That's all I'm suggesting. It is a quiet, safe place. You might benefit from just being here. How about it? It's your decision."

"It would just be temporary till I get my head straight?"

"Yes, it would be temporary. The brain and the mind are complex organs that we do not fully understand. We might not be able to get your head straight, but we may make it a bit less lopsided."

"Can I have time to think about it?"

"Yes. Talk to your family and friends. See what they advise."

"I've no friends left alive. The few that I had died in the war. The people I made friends with at the end of the war came from all over. None from this part of the world."

"That's sad, but not unusual. I have one other patient in a similar situation. Let me know what you decide."

Rob stood up, shook the doctor's hand, thanked him and left. On the way home, he thought about the prospect of going into an asylum. The stigma attached was daunting. On the other hand, life at home was hard. His family were upset. Young Frank was afraid of him.

He could see the fear in some of the other youngsters. He felt very isolated even in his large family. Maybe it would be best if he tried the asylum. It might help him and give the family a rest from his fits and bad temper. He remembered Arthur Herschell telling him how bad his brother was when he returned from the Boer war. Am I just like him, thought Rob?

That night, Rob talked to his dad and mum about what had happened. They spoke for only a short time. When he asked what they thought about the doctor's advice, each said it was Rob's decision. It did not help Rob.

That night in bed, he talked to Frank. It was clear Frank was scared of Rob and what he might do. Fear of the unknown. It was this short conversation with his younger brother that helped Rob decide. He would accept Dr Clarke's invitation and let him know the following day.

FIFTY

When he went to Sunnyside in June 1920, Rob got one of the small side wards on his own. He was a fee-paying patient so, he had privacy for the time being. Rob and his family thought it might be a short stay, and he would leave in a better medical condition than when he arrived.

It proved not to be the case. The medical treatment for epilepsy had some effects. There was no known cure. Talking therapy started straight away but made little headway.

Epilepsy got treated using bromide. The side effects of bromide included impairment of memory, blunting of intellectual ability. It also produced an apathetic state in Rob. His natural aversion to talking about his war experiences meant talking therapy made little progress.

"This Bromide stuff. Is that the same stuff the army put in the tea to curb sexual desires, doctor?"

"I don't know if the army put it in the tea or not, but yes, it is one of its effects. We are going to try this first and see how well it works. I also suggest we start talking therapy sessions."

"What are they?"

"They are what they imply. We spend some time talking about your experiences in the war."

"I'm not sure I want to do that," Rob answered quickly.

"I know how you feel. I have had this response from others, but it is the best way that we know to get to the seat of your nightmares. I assume you would like to try and stop them if you can?"

"Will it work?"

"There is no guarantee Rob. It works for some, but it is the best we know at the moment."

"Aye. OK."

Dr Clarke tried hard to get Rob to view his shell shock as another war wound. It did not take the doctor long to change his epilepsy medication. He was finding it increasingly troublesome to get Rob to talk about his nightmares. Rob had become apathetic. He seemed to have lost his ability to engage with the doctor to talk about his mental problem. The bromide dulled his senses, and he had difficulty concentrating. The whole point of this form of therapy was to get the patient to talk through his feelings and fears. Only then could they be addressed. His lack of engagement made this impossible.

"Rob. I have decided that the bromide medicine is not right for you, so I am changing it to phenobarbitone. It is quite a new treatment used by some of the leading specialist epilepsy centres in London and the Chalfont Epilepsy Colony."

"OK, doctor." His tone told the doctor that his patient could not care less.

After several weeks of the new treatment, Rob said he felt better and wanted to go home. He was a voluntary patient. Dr Clarke could not stop him from being discharged. He advised against early release, but Rob was adamant.

For a short while after his discharge, Rob was better. He still had nightmares, but they were less frequent, or so he thought. He was still taking his epilepsy medication, but that did not stop him from having seizures. It only reduced the frequency. Slowly his demeanour and personality deteriorated again. Frank was quite outspoken about what was happening while his mother and father voiced their concerns more gently.

One day Rob was standing in the Labour Exchange queue waiting for the routine message that there was nothing for him when he felt a tap on his shoulder.

"It's you, Rob, is it no?

Rob turned to see Jimmy Reid standing behind him.

"Hello, Jimmy."

"How's it going, Rob?"

"Not so bad, Jimmy. How's yersel?"

"Same, Rob. Had any luck with a job yet?"

"No. You?"

"No. All the jobs had gone by the time I got back."

"I didn't see you leave. When did you come back?"

"Late March when I got back. You?"

"April."

"Land fit for heroes, my arse. No jobs. My wife's skivvying just so we can eat and pay our rent. My Bru doesn't go far. What about you?"

"Much the same, Jimmy."

"You're up next, Rob. Best not keep the clerk waiting."

"See you, Jimmy."

By early spring of 1922, Rob decided to go back to Sunnyside. His epilepsy was a bit better, but his nightmares were not. Frank had made that clear to Rob on several occasions. He felt uncomfortable at home. Doctor Clarke arranged his readmission. He had anticipated that this might be the outcome when Rob discharged himself.

Rob had to rely on local authority funding for his admission as the Labour Party had withdrawn their financial support. Rob was now in a large ward with eleven other male patients. These patients were a mixture of ages and conditions. Two had epilepsy. Some had delusions, hallucinations, schizophrenia, paranoia and even a combination of mental diseases. These were the lunatic patients that the locals feared. If the relatives of these men were still alive, they never visited. There was a general public assumption that lunacy was somehow contagious. Many, otherwise decent people, thought that it could be catching.

His depression and mood swings slowly decreased when he returned to the hospital. At the end of the war, Rob had thought that his blackouts and nightmares would cease once he was back home. He was now beginning to understand that his epilepsy was manageable but incurable. Dr Clarke also indicated that what Rob had seen during the war could not be wiped from his memory. He assured Rob that with ongoing therapy, and help from the hospital, the memories could also be manageable in time.

"How long a time?"

"I don't know, Rob. Treatment is different for every individual. Not everybody was as young as you when they went to war. Nor did they see the same things you did. We have to treat you, the individual. Every individual is different. It will take as long as it takes."

"Oh, so you have no idea, then?"

"No, Rob. We will go as fast as we can. I wish I had a magic wand to make all your trouble disappear. Unfortunately, I am just a doctor doing the best that I can for you."

"Will I be able to go home soon?"

"I think that is very likely. Your treatment aims to get you fit enough to re-join your family and society. We will let you home as soon as we possibly can. Even so, remember, we are always here should you feel the need to come back for further help. Let us start a session now."

Rob was still in Sunnyside in May 1922, when his sister Annie married David Fraser. He did not attend the wedding just in case he had a seizure in the church. Annie said she was disappointed but was also glad. She did not want to see him have a fit in the church. More than once, she had seen Rob having one of his screaming nightmares. It frightened her. Also, he had been in the lunatic asylum mixing with lunatics, and she had no idea if he might have caught some mental disease. She did not know what epilepsy was, what caused it, or whether it was contagious. She had made no effort to find out. In truth, she was often scared of Rob when he was in one of his fits or nightmares.

Life in the asylum was not dissimilar to life in the army. The general view of treatment for mental illness was bland food, fresh air and activity. It had persisted since Victorian times. Living in a ward with eleven other patients was like being in a billet. Like the army, the hospital expected him to make his bed, clean and polish the ward floor and exercise. If he was not having treatment, he needed to work elsewhere on the estate.

Because of his farming background, he worked in the gardens or on a small farm. He helped produce some of the food that the patients ate. Rob enjoyed his time in the garden and on the farm. In the summer months, gardens were full of ripe fruit and vegetables. While gathering the crops of peas, strawberries, gooseberries, raspberries and apples, he could sample the goods. It reminded him of his youth when he was happy.

When he was a youngster, his father often spoke of how hard their lives were. Rob, the child, had no idea of what hard meant in this context, as he had nothing to compare. Everything that happened in his little life was just ordinary. Everyone around him was in the same situation. Again, he had no comparators.

There were times when he was sad and other times when he was happy. He was not pleased when he had to go into the fields to work in the rain or cold. He was not elated if he was hungry and had no food to eat. He was happy not working and spending time in the open air wandering the hills and woods on his own.

Hand-me-down clothes, infrequent baths and overcrowded beds were commonplace. Looking back, Rob remembered the time he had to himself and smiled as he sat on a bench at the edge of the hospital gardens eating some peas from the pod. He remembered spring as the snowdrops appeared, birds starting to build nests, lambs and buds on the trees. He remembered the squidgy feel of the frogspawn as he scooped it into a jar. Not a particularly good feeling, but better than the mud in the trenches.

He remembered the colours of the autumn as the trees and heather slowly died. There were times when the colours were so intense that it looked like the hills were on fire. In the winter, he liked the white snow-capped slopes and the chance to slide down them on a homemade sledge.

Sitting on his bench, he remembered these things fondly. Looking back, he could see why his father said that their lives were harsh, but he did not remember feeling that at the time. Given what he had been through, Rob felt nostalgic for his childhood.

Looking down into the basket on his lap, he said, "These peas aren't going to pick themselves. Best get on and do some work."

"What?" said a nurse walking by.

"Sorry, Jim. Just talking to myself."

"Where better to do that than in here, Rob."

"Just so, Jim. Just so."

Rob liked the outdoors activities of the hospital. He did not even mind the rain. The mud in the gardens was nowhere near as bad as the trenches, and he could always pack up and go inside if it got too bad. There was birdsong in place of exploding shells and men crying in agony. He could not forget what he had seen, heard and done. Outside in the gardens, he could forget for a short time those terrible things. Asleep at night was a different proposition.

There were female patients in the asylum, but cohabitation was discouraged. Male patients tended to do heavier work on the land while females worked in the kitchens or laundry. There was no segregation in the large dining hall at mealtimes, but the staff kept a watchful eye. His history with Lizzie gave him a very jaundiced view of women, which he had no desire to repeat, especially with women who had mental illnesses. The occasional dances in the hospital hall brought back painful memories. He had enlisted to go to the ball for free. He had met Lizzie, and her subsequent betrayal still upset him. He was not naive enough to think that he would not have gone to war had he not joined up. He was a low skilled labourer and would have been the first to be conscripted. Still, he wondered if he might have met a different lassie if he had not gone to the ball. Perhaps that part of his life might have been better. Maybe he would now have a wife and children.

"Best not think like that, Rob," he mumbled to himself. "How could I have supported them with my epilepsy denying me employment. They'd be worse off. Maybe it was all for the best that I didn't meet anyone else?"

The following year Dr Clarke encouraged Rob to apply for a pension from the government. He could not work because of epilepsy, so he had a disability.

"I'm not disabled. I still have all my limbs."

"Yes, Rob, but you have epilepsy. That is stopping you from getting a job. That's a disability by the Government definition. You should apply."

"When I'm here, I work outside in the gardens. That's OK."

"Yes, you do. But that is part of your treatment, and it's done in a safe place. There's a theory that working reduces epilepsy attacks, but nothing proved. Factories, docks or railways are not safe places to work. There's machinery to worry about. An employer won't want you losing fingers or an arm in one of their machines."

"Oh, I see."

"If you apply for a pension, what's the worst that can happen?"

"I don't know."

"They might say no. There's nothing else that they can do. It's worth a try."

"OK. I'll do it."

1923 was a year of conflicting issues for Rob. His younger brother, Frank, had difficulty finding work.

"I'm going to join the Black Watch." Frank was speaking to Rob after another unsuccessful day trying to find work.

"You're an indentured shipwright, Frank. You've got qualifications. Surely there's a job for you somewhere."

"Since the end of the war, shipyards are closing down because the country doesn't need more ships. Because I'm qualified, I command higher pay, and nobody will pay my wages. Things are tough, even for qualified people like me."

"Are you sure about the army? You could be sent somewhere like me."

"We're not at war, Rob. I think it's safe to join, and at least I'll get paid and not have to stand in the Bru queue."

"You might not have to stand in the Labour Exchange queue, but life in the army is full of queuing."

"Well, I'm going. I've told Dad, and he's not happy, but I'm off anyway. " In January of that year, he travelled to Perth and joined the Black Watch. This dredged up painful memories for Rob of his own war experiences and set his treatment back.

In early June, Sandy Corsar contracted tonsillitis. Like all poor families, he could not afford doctors or medicine. His condition worsened without the medical help he needed, and the tonsils became septic. The sepsis took over his whole body travelling to Sandy's heart. Rob was at home when his Dad's heart finally gave out. He watched his father die in his bed. Rob had seen many men die, but this was his father, and this was personal. Two days later, Sandy got buried in Sleepyhillock Cemetery in Montrose. Rob had a seizure at the burial. His family were more devastated.

The loss of his fathers' income to the household and Dr Clarkes' instigation had pushed Rob into applying for a disability pension. Making an application was not the same as getting a disability pension. The bureaucracy was significant. After filling out the appropriate forms, he had to wait for an initial appointment. It would decide whether he was a relevant candidate to assess

The process took twenty months before Rob got his pension. The army had listed his epilepsy as being due to his service in the war. It was a recognised physical condition.

During his third admission, Dr Clarke discovered two more issues that Rob had hidden. Rob told him the story of his relationship with Lizzie Ross and how she had treated him. A soldier coming home from war to find his girlfriend expecting another man's child was hardly new. Dr Clarke understood Rob's anger at what happened. He had come home physically wounded, only to suffer a greater wound to his emotions. Rob was young and immature, so the effects on his self-esteem were understandable.

What came as a shock to Dr Clarke was Rob's eventual confession to his shooting of the Allied soldier drowning in mud during the Battle of Passchendaele. The description of the event split the doctor's conscience in two. On the one hand, killing a comrade in cold blood, so to speak, sickened him. Giving a comrade a swift death, as opposed to a slow drowning in mud, he could see as a kindness.

He asked Rob to explain the difference between killing an enemy or a comrade in cold blood. He struggled. The enemy would kill him if he could. This man might well have done the same for Rob if he were in that situation. He knew he'd done the right thing, but he could not get it out of his mind and his nightmares. He could still describe in intimate detail everything about the event. He had not forgotten one single aspect. The terror on the man's face when they came across him. The inane gibberish of a man who had lost his mind. His eyes when he realised what was about to happen. The man's seeming nod of assent gives Rob permission to end his terror and misery.

Listening to Rob's description of the event and his feelings, Dr Clarke suddenly felt compassion. There was an immature youth, faced with a horrible decision. He took a terrible burden upon himself. This young man's treatment would take considerably longer than it might otherwise have. The depth of his guilt was profound.

One night, Rob fell out of his hospital bed shouting and screaming for help. That day, he had an appointment with Dr Weeks.

"I heard you fell out of bed last night screaming for help, Rob. Was it a dream?"

"It was."

"Do you remember it, and can you tell me what it was?"

"If I have to."

"You don't have to tell me, Rob, but it might help me with your therapy. Will you tell me?"

"Fine. I was back in the war. I was up to my waist in a mud pool. Coming towards me were thousands of giant rats and giant lice. They were going to eat me alive. Beside me was a rope tied to the stump of a tree. It was in easy reach, but I was frozen. I could not move my arms or hands, so I could not grasp the rope and pull myself to safety. As the beasties got closer, I could see their hungry eyes and mouths, and I got frantic. My brain kept telling me to pick up the rope and pull, but my body would not respond. Just as they were about to eat me, I found myself on the floor of the ward shaking and sweating."

"So, your brain was telling you that you could save yourself, but your body refused to obey. Is that it?"

"That's right. I've had similar dreams before when I could not move in a dangerous situation. I never find out if I survive in the dreams. What does it mean?"

"Dreaming of being in a helpless situation often denotes feelings of inadequacy. Your condition means that you cannot lead what you perceive as a normal life. The desire to have what others have, such as a job, a house, a wife and a family, is strong. The rope is your pathway to that life, but the mud is the manifestations of your medical conditions stopping you from taking that path. It is not an easy thing to treat. Your medical condition is permanent, so we will need to try to find ways to help you come to terms with that."

"What do I need to do?"

"I don't know, Rob. I'll have a chat with some of my colleagues and see if we can come up with a plan to help you."

In 1925 the family morale improved. Rob's sister Mary married Robert Shearer in January. In February, Rob was awarded his disability pension and got assessed as Class 4 for pension purposes. The maximum award was forty shillings a week which was well below average earnings for a labourer. Not much, but better than nothing. In October, Rob's sister Emmy married Alexander Key in Montrose. Young Jessie was a witness, but Rob did not attend either because of the event at his father's funeral two years earlier.

At 19:00 on Friday 4th January 1935, Rob's brother Frank married Gertrude Herschell in the Church of St Mary and St Peter in Montrose. Gertie, as she was known, was the niece of Arthur Herschell. He was the man who served in the trenches with Rob in the 4/5 Battalion of the Black Watch. Neither attended the wedding. Rob was in the hospital, slowly growing weaker. Arthur was alive, but his whereabouts were unknown. There were only the bride, groom and two witnesses at the ceremony. Gertie's brother, Jim and Rob's youngest sister Mable.

Ironically, Frank left the following day so that he could take up his new job as an attendant in the Rosslynlee Lunatic Asylum south of Edinburgh.

FIFTY-ONE

While living outside the hospital, Rob was required to find work. After another fruitless visit to the Labour Exchange, he was shuffling down Montrose High Street, going nowhere slowly.

"Rob. Rob Corsar. It's you, isn't it?"

Rob turned to look at the female voice calling his name. She seemed to have come out of a shop. He was not sure he recognised the face.

"Sorry, I...

"Rose Kirk, Rose Mitchel as was."

"Sorry, Rose. I'm not very good with some things."

"That's fine, Rob. I heard you had a rough time in the war."

"We all did, Rose. How about you? Rose, Kirk, must mean that you're married."

"I am. I married Jamie Kirk a year ago."

"Congratulations Rose." Rob nodded towards Rose's distended abdomen. "You look like you're ready to start a family."

"Yes. We expect it to come in about six weeks or so."

"I don't suppose you're still working at the farm then?"

"No. We all got to let go as soon as the men came back from the war. I work at the jam factory. It's not such heavy work, and it's inside out of the rain and wind. Not like the farm."

"What do you do, Rob?"

"No one will take me on, Rose. I have fits."

"What do you mean, fits?"

"I have blackouts. It's called epilepsy."

"Did you catch it in the war?"

"I supposed I did. It had something to do with being close to explosions. It caused damage in my head."

"I'm sorry to hear that, Rob. When you came back on that leave, I remember, you had a wound at the top of your back. Was that the cause?"

"No one seems to know."

"What are they doing for you?"

"I'm having treatment up at Sunnyside for it and other things."

"I'm sorry, Rob." The mention of Sunnyside shocked Rose. Like most people, she was suspicious of people from the Asylum.

"Not your fault, Rose. I remember you were kind to me on the farm that day and before."

"I was so sorry for what she did to you, Rob. Still, she got her comeuppance."

"Her comeuppance, how so?"

"Soon after you left to go back, the family got the news that their son was dead. Lizzie lost the baby. Old man McArdle asked her to leave his house. She wouldn't be marrying his son, and she wouldn't be giving him a grandchild. They did not want anymore."

"That's hard."

"I thought you might be happy about Stuart McArdle being dead."

346

"I'm not happy, but I'm not sad either. There was a time when I might have killed him, but not now."

"Why not now then?"

"No. I've seen enough of all that. Did her folks take her back?"

"She tried, but her mother would not have her. Her dad might have let her in, but her mother was having none of it. She stayed with us for a few days, then left. My mum and dad were a bit soft and let her stay in the spare room."

"Left? Where for?"

"She said she was going to the city. She didn't say which one, and I didn't ask. I was glad she was gone. I didn't like what she did, and I didn't want her staying in our house. She just upped and left without much of a goodbye. She changed a lot after she lost the bairn."

"How so?"

"She became very moody, bad-tempered. She didn't treat the rest of us lassies well. She had got airs above her station when she lived in the big house. She thought she was better than the rest of us."

"I suppose she thought things would turn out well when she got pregnant by the farmer's son. It seems from what you say it all went rotten after McArdle's death."

"That's a fact, Rob. I'm off to meet Jamie now. 'Bye Rob. Take care of yourself."

"Bye, Rose. You take care of yourself and the bairn when it comes."

Rose moved off in the opposite direction that Rob was travelling. He thought for a short time about what she had said about Lizzie. Much troubled water under the bridge. I've enough to worry about without thinking of her and what she did.

Surgery for epileptic seizures was a well-known intervention. It had been in use since the nineteenth century. The doctors discussed it with Rob. It had an uncertain outcome, so he dismissed it.

Rob also didn't undergo lumbar punctures in a process known as Pneumoencephalography, or PEG. The process involved removing cerebrospinal fluid from around the brain and replacing it with air.

"Will this PEG help you cure my epilepsy, doctor?"

"It's known to produce variable results, Rob," said Dr Adam Hardy. "It's not the most pleasant treatment, but it can sometimes be helpful if you agree to have it. The decision is up to you?"

"What happens to me during the operation?"

They explained the procedure in detail to Rob.

"You will be strapped to an open-backed chair. We will inject a small needle into your spinal column about here." The doctor indicated the spot on the back of Rob's neck. "Then, we will drain the cerebrospinal fluid from your head. We will fill that space with air. It will enable us to get a clear X-ray picture of what to treat."

"You're going to empty my head of fluid and put air in its place?"

"That's essentially correct. We will not damage your brain in any way. It will remain firmly fixed in your head."

"Then what?"

"We will rotate the chair into different positions to try to get a good x-ray of your brain tissue."

"I'm not sure I like the sound of that. Does it hurt?"

"Yes, it does, and some patients get headaches and vomit."

"Anything else?"

"It can be fatal in very few patients."

"So, the Bosche could not kill me, but you might?"

"It's unlikely, but that might happen, yes."

"You don't make it sound the most inviting treatment. It sounds terrible. It's my choice, is it?"

"Yes, it is."

"In that case, I think I'll not bother. Having epilepsy sounds better than that."

For the rest of his life, Rob alternated between voluntary in-patient treatment at Sunnyside and life in the community. His visits to his home became shorter, and stay in the hospital longer. His general health gradually deteriorated. He was wasting away.

His nightmares never really left him. He still woke up screaming, but it was less frequent. His epilepsy was a barrier to getting a job. The mention of epilepsy made people recoil as if it were an infectious disease. The reaction of ordinary people to epilepsy and other mental conditions might have been understandable. They did not understand it and were afraid. People knew that Rob lived in the Asylum on occasion, so he was a lunatic in their eyes. Rob never got used to the fear that he generated in people in the community, so, used Sunnyside as a haven.

EPILOGUE

In the nineteenth century, the life of farm servants and their families in rural areas was a harsh subsistence existence. Sandy Corsar was lucky in that each contract he acquired came with a farm cottage, even if one did have a burn running through it. Many were not so fortunate. Their families had to live with relatives or end up in Poor Houses. Child labour was not specific to rural areas.

The brutality of the Scottish education system continued into the twentieth century and was still in use when I went to school in the 1940s and 50s.

In December 1914, the 1/5 (Angus) Battalion of the Black Watch left Scotland with about 1,200 men. By the time Rob joined them in December 1915, their war diaries indicate they were about half strength. The 1/4 (Dundee) Battalion was in a similar situation. They merged to form the 4/5 battalion. Both Battalions had lost about half their men despite not being heavily involved in battles during that year. In January 1916, the army's losses and lack of volunteers required the introduction of conscription.

In the nineteenth century, the British army fought more than two hundred battles. The tactics they employed were still in use during the early part of the Great War. Men were lined up in rows and walked towards the enemy. War diaries record the laying of tape ready for an attack. It was a common practice to keep military dressing during an advance.

Over the four-year course of the war, the diaries show that they had lost the equivalent of four times a battalion strength. It was just one battalion among hundreds in the Allied Armies. History shows that around 600 men from both sides died each day during the Great War.

They had left thousands of men in military cemeteries all over France and Belgium. Many more were now at home, disabled, disfigured broken men. At the same time, they had turned good farmland into a landscape fit only for nightmares. It was a land strewn with body parts of men, animals and the detritus of war, some of which would continue to kill adults and children for the rest of the century. Even after the Second World War, French farmers continued to unearth some of the unexploded munitions of the Great War. Around 850 people living near Ypres have been killed or wounded since 1918. All over Flanders fields, the story is the same.

After the war, in officers messes all over the army were men with gallantry medals who had only seen the front through binoculars. The nearest they had got to shells was to watch them loaded onto lorries. That's not to say that many senior officers did not see action at the front and deserve their medals. Not all of those who had medals did see front line action. Men, like Robert Corsar, and Arthur Herschell, who were wounded, swam in mud and kept their senior officers safe, got very little for their trouble. Their hardship, physical and mental wretchedness earned two or three standard medals given to everyone. Men who served only a few days got the same medals as those who fought in Gallipoli, on Hill 60 and the mud of Passchendaele. Scant recognition of their sacrifice.

That soldier's proximity to the repeated blast of shells can cause epilepsy is well known. After the Great War, treatment for epilepsy was rudimentary and occasionally barbaric by today's standards. Even today, epilepsy and mental disease garner suspicion and ridicule. Centres for mental conditions and epilepsy got built as far away from towns as possible in the 19th century.

During what became known as the Battle of Britain in July 1940, a WW1 soldier died of his war wounds in Sunnyside Mental Hospital, Montrose. Rob was only forty-three years old. His cause of death is 'Cerebral Disease with Epilepsy and Cardiac Failure. Cerebral Disease and Epilepsy brought on by his proximity to multiple explosions, conditions that he did not have in 1914 when he joined up.

Rob's life expired in July 1940. He eventually died as a consequence of German army activity. His military history vanished two months later. The German air force bombed The National Archives in September 1940.

Rob's Sunnyside medical records are in the Archives of Ninewells Hospital in Dundee. They fall under the hundred-year rule and will not be available until 2040.

There was no military funeral or burial for Rob. No gravestone tended by the War Graves Commission.

He was just another civilian death among the thousands dying each day in this Second Great War. Rob was buried in Sleepyhillock Cemetery, Montrose. He rests in the same plot as his father.

The grave is on a slight slope and has an uninterrupted view across the Montrose basin and the Angus countryside.

At about the time of Rob's death in 1940, the Black Watch was part of the 51st Highland Division fighting in France, yet again. In the Black Watch at this time was Lance Corporal Edward Herschell. He was the nephew of Arthur Herschell, who had fought with Rob in 1916. He was the older brother of Rob's sister-in-law Gertie who had married Frank, Rob's younger brother.

The Black Watch, the Seaforths, the Camerons and the Gordons, plus a few English soldiers attached to the division, were tasked by Churchill to fight to the last man. They were to hold the line so that Churchill could show the French that he was willing to sacrifice British troops in defence of their country. They were to fight to the last man. By the time of his order, the beaches of Dunkirk had been cleared.

Asking soldiers to fight to the last man in a seemingly hopeless situation showed that Haig, in 1918, and Churchill, in 1940, had much in common. Like Highland Regiments before, these latest men carried out their orders as best they could. They fought Rommel's tanks with a few anti-tank weapons, rifles, grenades and grit. Finally, out of ammunition, supplies and no hope of rescue, their General ordered surrender to stop the slaughter. Some of the men refused, saying they could fight on. In the end, they obeyed their

Commanding Officer's orders. On 12 June 1940, what remained of the 51st Highland Division surrendered at St Valerie-en-Caux. They were rounded up and marched to POW camps. Like Rob before him, Eddie Herschell marched across France and Belgium. He then went through the Netherlands, Germany and finally Torun in North-East Poland. A march of about one thousand miles in the heat of summer. As prisoners of war, their food and water rations were inferior to those in the WW1 trenches. Like Rob, Eddie survived his war against Germany. By the time he got home, Rob had died.

Churchill's order to the 51st reminds me of Lt Col James Wolfe writing in 1751 when he said of Scottish soldiers:

They are hardy, intrepid, accustomed to a rough country, and make no great mischief if they fall.

There is very little remembrance of the sacrifice at St Valerie. Col Wolfe was correct.

AUTHORS NOTES

Robert Corsar was my uncle. He died four years before I was born. My father talked very little about his family. I have almost no knowledge of the life that Rob lived. I stumbled across his life when doing some family research for my wife. There is a wealth of official information available.

Rob was the third of ten children born to my grandparents. The frequent recording of births gave me locations for each. In this way, I was able to track his nomadic youth.

Information about the life of Farm Servants is well documented in many publications on social history, as are school activities of the time. I used the description of infant schooling from some books and my own experiences. School for me, in the 1940s and 50s, had changed little from the turn of the century.

The locations of Rob's unit come from their war diaries, held in the National Archives. The curators of the Black Watch Museum in Perth were very helpful. They were able to confirm the company he got allocated on enlistment. Whether he remained with the same company is not known.

I also uncovered various government bulletins that gave the names and dates of wounded soldiers. It gave me approximate dates of Rob's wounds. I knew that Rob had a hole in his back and scarring from gas on his hands and legs. It was one of the stories told by my father. He never mentioned a third wound or the sequence of these events.

There is a great deal of information about WW1 battlefield medical facilities and treatments. I have sprinkled the story with facts from the diaries and medical reports.

As a retired director of an Epilepsy Charity, I had access to historical data on the treatment of the condition. The Charity I worked with was the Chalfont Epilepsy Colony. It is the one mentioned in this story. Today, the blast effects of shells on the human brain are well recognised. Some of the young men coming back from the war in the Middle East suffer the same brain damage as Rob.

Treatment of epilepsy after World War 1 was rudimentary, even a little brutal. Rob will have experienced some of these.

I have refrained from using the Montrose dialect in this story for two reasons. Firstly, I do not understand it. I had to have my mother interpret during our summer holidays there in the 1950s. Second, it would be impenetrable to all, perhaps even those who live in Montrose today.

My treatment of my grandmother may seem harsh. I never met the woman, but my older sister did.

Granny Corsar's hospitality to her family comes from her experiences. During my father's one-week summer holiday in the late 40s and early 50s, he would visit his mother. He recounted that he would walk into her house. She would look up from what she was doing and say, "It's yersel then." No nice to see you. No, have a cup of tea and minimal conversation for as long as my father could stand it. It happened every year until she died. There is only one photograph in existence showing Granny Corsar. She was a hard, dour unforgiving woman. Given her hard, harsh married life as an itinerant Farm Servant's wife and mother to ten children, I'm not going to judge. I suspect she did what she thought was best.

This book is a fictitious life woven around historical records and research. It is my homage to my uncle and the many like him all over the United Kingdom. They had a harsh childhood, a dreadful war and lived with the consequences of that war. Politicians, and those that don't know what they endured, call them the Glorious Dead.

THE GLORIOUS DEAD

The Cenotaph in London was unveiled On 11 November 1920. On it is the inscription 'The Glorious Dead'. I despair when I see those words. They are offensive because they are untrue. There is nothing glorious in dying for your country. There's nothing heroic in being blown to bits or cooked alive in a burning ship, aircraft or tank. What's gallant about drowning in mud for your country. There is no triumph in being hung up on barbed wire like a scarecrow. How is living with the disability of amputated limbs and facial disfigurement wonderful? Where's the honour in living in stinking oozing trenches full of rats and lice. What's noble about being unable to get your clothes dry and your body clean. There is nothing glorious in any of it. Those are words used to assuage those who would have others do their dirty work. War is a dirty bloody business to be done by ordinary men and women. Money, influence and status can keep those that have it away from the filthy, dangerous toil of war.

Printed in Great Britain
by Amazon